NO GREATER LOVE

BOOKS BY FRANK G. SLAUGHTER

No Greater Love
Doctors at Risk
Doctor's Daughters
Gospel Fever
The Passionate Rebel
Devil's Gamble
Plague Ship
Stonewall Brigade
Women in White
Convention, M.D.
Code Five
Countdown
Surgeon's Choice
The Sins of Herod
Doctors' Wives
God's Warrior
Surgeon, U.S.A.
Constantine
The Purple Quest
A Savage Place
Upon This Rock
Tomorrow's Miracle
David: Warrior and King
The Curse of Jezebel
Epidemic!
Pilgrims in Paradise
The Land and the Promise
Lorena
The Crown and the Cross

The Thorn of Arimathea
Daybreak
The Mapmaker
Sword and Scalpel
The Scarlet Cord
Flight from Natchez
The Healer
Apalachee Gold
The Song of Ruth
Storm Haven
The Galileans
East Side General
Fort Everglades
The Road to Bithynia
The Stubborn Heart
Immortal Magyar
Divine Mistress
Sangaree
Medicine for Moderns
The Golden Isle
The New Science of Surgery
In a Dark Garden
A Touch of Glory
Battle Surgeon
Air Surgeon
Spencer Brade, M.D.
That None Should Die
The Warrior

UNDER THE NAME C. V. TERRY

Buccaneer Surgeon
The Deadly Lady of Madagascar

Darien Venture
The Golden Ones

NO GREATER LOVE

Frank G. Slaughter

DOUBLEDAY & COMPANY, INC.
GARDEN CITY, NEW YORK
1985

Except for historical personages or events, easily recognizable as such, the characters and events making up this novel are entirely the products of the author's imagination. It is an accident if the name of any living person is mentioned.

Library of Congress Cataloging in Publication Data
Slaughter, Frank G. (Frank Gill), 1908–
 No greater love.
 I. Title.
PS3537.L38N6   1985   813'.52
ISBN 0-385-18872-2
Library of Congress Card Catalog Number 84-10340

NO
GREATER
LOVE

Chapter One

Dr. Ted Bronson stepped through the self-closing door of the air-conditioned baggage claim section into the warmth of an early June evening. Dropping his suitcase to the sidewalk, he looked past the taxi and airport bus lane to the reserved section of the parking lot. Six feet two, with the lithe grace of the college athlete he'd been, Ted Bronson was the epitome of a successful young surgeon. His pale green slacks and camel's-hair sports coat were a bit rumpled, however, from the cramped seat of the stretch Boeing 737 that had just brought him in the short space of three hours from Pittsburgh, Pennsylvania, to Miami, Florida.

Spotting what he was seeking, a sleek Mercedes 380-SL sports coupe with a lovely red-haired young woman at the wheel, he picked up his bag again. Dodging through the busy departing traffic with the same skill that had earned him an *H* as a tailback at Harvard—before he'd gone on to gain his M.D. there—he crossed to the parking lot.

"Hello, darling!" He leaned down to kiss Dr. Elizabeth MacGowan before opening the car door on the right side and dropping his bag behind the bucket seat. "Been waiting long?"

"Maybe ten minutes. It was sweet of you to call me from the Atlanta airport and tell me you'd be late."

"It's a sin for anyone as beautiful as you are to be a doctor," he said, giving her a quick, appraising glance from the long, shapely legs past the athletic but still distinctly feminine body to the rich Irish color in her cheeks and hair.

"What else would you want me to be?" She gave him a quick, warm smile as she backed the sleek little car out of the slot marked "Reserved for Miami Police." "A *femme du monde?*"

"My God, no! Say the word, though, and I'll make you a wife and mother in short order."

"By now I should know how potent you are. But how can you be certain you're also fertile?"

"Heredity. I have six brothers and sisters."

"Ha!" she said in mock triumph. "You just confessed to the ambition of turning me into a brood sow."

"I still say a woman who's as beautiful at seven in the morning as she is dressed for dinner at seven in the evening is missing her real calling in not having at least two toddlers around. Besides, there are still such things as nannies."

"And they're expensive."

"So what? Between us we make more than half as much as the President of the United States and we're just really getting started with our earning capacities."

"How was the seminar?" Liz MacGowan changed the subject abruptly.

"Fantastic! Who would have thought dear old once-grimy Pittsburgh could ever become the transplant center for the East—maybe even outstripping Stanford in California one of these days."

"It produced the man who's going to make Miami the transplant center for the South, didn't it? That should be proof enough."

At thirty-three, Ted Bronson was already near the top in the most glamorous field of surgery—that of organ transplant. Trained as a surgeon at renowned Massachusetts General

Hospital, he had finished an additional fellowship in organ transplant at Pittsburgh before coming to Biscayne General, teaching hospital for the Medical School of Biscayne University.

Fresh from an OB-GYN residency at Duke, Elizabeth Mac-Gowan had arrived at about the same time. The romantic chemistry between them had been instant and passionate with only one point of tension: an associate professor in the Medical School—as was Ted—Liz had turned down his proposals of marriage again and again. Usually she gave the argument that her career was not yet satisfactorily enough established to take on the extra responsibilities of marriage and children, and the controversy had occasionally become so intense as to threaten their relationship—though never for very long.

"In the last six months the Pitt. transplant team has achieved a success rate of almost ninety percent with cadaver kidneys," said Ted. "My best record to date is not much more than fifty percent."

"That's still better than the national average."

"Maybe. But by using cyclosporin, plus smaller doses of steroids than usual postop, I hope soon to be chasing their coattails at Pitt."

"Cyclosporin?" Liz MacGowan frowned as she guided the Mercedes out of the airport parking area and headed for the East-West Expressway. "I thought that was one of the new antibiotics announced in each new issue of the JAMA." The acronym identified the prestigious journal of the American Medical Association.

"Cyclosporin was just another drug discovery—and not such a successful one at that—until somebody noticed that it attacked lymphocytes in the body and put two and two together," he explained.

"Two and two being the obvious conclusion that, if cyclosporin attacked the lymphocytes of malignant disease, it could also attack the ones that are the primary cause of rejection in organ transplant?"

"Bingo! You're as smart as you're beautiful."

"That's because I've been closely associated with you for most of the past two years," she retorted. "A guy with a two-track mind."

"Namely?"

"First, getting yourself into my bed. Second, making it permanent."

"The way I've missed you since last Thursday night when I left for Pittsburgh convinces me that the second is even more important than ever." He changed the subject. "What's the latest scandal with the faculty?"

"Nothing new—besides the usual liaisons and breakups."

"So long as we're not among the latter, I won't argue about anyone's right to go to hell in his own way."

"Do you want to stop by the Terrace and change before we go to Coconut Grove?" she asked.

Once a luxurious bayfront hotel, Biscayne Terrace had been turned into ultrasmart condominiums when land overlooking Biscayne Bay was preempted for the now massive University Medical Center. A new bulkhead guarded the extremely valuable land dredged from the bottom of the Bay, protecting it from the hurricanes that sometimes swept this extreme southern end of the Florida peninsula. The Terrace, located across from the hospital, afforded extremely convenient living quarters for the upper-level members of the faculty who could afford the expensive condominiums, which both Liz and Ted, as rising department heads in the school, owned.

"I figured the plane would be late so I took a shower and changed before I left for the airport this afternoon," Ted told her. "If it suits you, we can go directly to Coconut Grove."

"By the way, I haven't wished you a happy birthday," said Liz. "Remind me to give you a kiss later."

"The kind of kiss I'm expecting from you for my birthday can come a whole lot later."

"Don't push your luck. You told me this dinner with Michael Corazon's family has been an annual affair, but I don't remember your mentioning it last year. What prospective bedfellow did you take then?"

"I was away at a meeting of the Organ Transplant Society last year; that's why you haven't met the Corazons yet. Since my parents died, they're the nearest thing to a family I have. Michael and I decided while we were in college that, since we both had the same birthday and are such good friends, we would always try to celebrate our birthdays together—preferably with Mama Maria and the rest of the family."

"Sounds like sort of a last man's club."

"I used to spend every Christmas holiday at the Corazon estate in Coconut Grove," he explained. "Believe me, it was a welcome change from those Boston winters and, besides, you've never experienced real Cuban cooking until you taste Maria Corazon's."

Liz's eyebrows lifted. "They're reported to be one of the wealthiest families of Cuban émigrés in Florida—but she still cooks?"

"She loves it. Papa Juan left Cuba in the fifties when Fulgencio Batista was dictator. He managed to get his money out, too, and had the good sense to buy a lot of land in Coconut Grove and the Homestead area south of Miami, as well as orange groves farther up the coast around Vero Beach. By the time Papa Juan died, Pedro and Manuel were old enough to take over the estate. Pedro manages the groves around Vero and Manuel the vegetable farms in the Homestead area. Michael had the choice of becoming either a priest or a lawyer, that's customary in old Spanish families, but he chose the law and public service."

"From what I've read, he's done very well," Liz commented.

"He's a real dynamo; you're going to like him. Mike came home from Harvard Law and spent a couple of years as a clerk to a district federal judge. When he ran for the legislature, he naturally carried the Cuban vote—"

"By that time one of the largest blocks in Dade County."

Ted nodded. "Mike could have become a state senator after his first term as a freshman legislator in Tallahassee, but even in college he was a realistic idealist like you. With the cocaine and drug traffic in Miami what it is, becoming a federal prosecuting attorney was the natural thing for him to do and one of these days he'll either be in the U.S. Senate or become a federal judge."

"Is Michael the youngest son?"

"No. There's a much later son named Arturo. You'll meet him tonight."

"Do I gather that I'll have to pass muster with the Corazons, if I ever decide to let you make an honest woman of me?"

"Nobody in his or her right mind could fail to appreciate your sterling qualities," he assured her.

"Thank you; you may have earned yourself an extra birthday present with the compliment."

II

"It's a tropical fairyland!" Liz exclaimed a few minutes later, when she drove through the open gate in a high stuccoed wall.

Like many other estates in this oldest luxury section of Miami, the wall shut the luxurious waterfront home away from the street. From outside only the tops of palms rustling in the breeze from the Bay, now that darkness was falling, had been visible above the wall. Inside, however, bathed in an almost magical brilliance by lights set here and there among the trees and the flower beds, the whole effect was that of the tropical fairyland she had labeled it at first sight.

Clumps of jacaranda with its blue blossoms were interspersed between dark green mango trees heavy with ripening yellow fruit. Orange trees still boasted huge Temple oranges even this late in the season, reminding the viewer of the golden apples of Greek mythology. Flower beds were set everywhere between the trees, giving a breathtaking view of riotous color, each lovelier than its predecessor.

"Someone obviously loves this place," Liz commented as she guided the car along the curving driveway toward the house, which was still largely hidden by the foliage. "Is it your friend Michael?"

"Keeping up the estate is Arturo's job," Ted told her. "The flower beds, in particular, are his pride and joy."

"He must stay busy."

"It's a labor of love with him."

The driveway ended in a circle before the long, low house of Spanish-style stucco and, as she drew the car to a stop, Liz could see even more flower beds banked around the house, surrounding it with a riot of color.

Ted opened the door and got out, coming around to help her out and giving her a kiss that quite took her mind off the garden.

"My! If you had more than one birthday a year, I doubt that I could cope with it."

Holding Liz by the arm lest the high heels of her fragile sandals sink in the gravel and trip her, Ted guided her to the door and pressed the bell. It was opened almost immediately to reveal the smiling face of a young man in a white suit, blue shirt and red tie. Liz caught her breath involuntarily at the sight of him for, even though she had never seen him before, his features were as familiar as the illustrations in a medical text on congenital anomalies.

The young man's head was small in proportion to the somewhat plump body and flattened just enough, when viewed from front to back, to be outside the limits of strictly normal. His eyes were blue and warmly bright but the inner folds of the lids at the base of a slightly flattened nasal bridge gave them an almost oriental look. In short, the entire grouping of his features fitted perfectly a medical picture with which Liz was quite familiar, that of Down's Syndrome—a kindlier name than Mongolism, by which it had first been known because of the oriental cast to the eyes.

"Dr. Ted!" The young man embraced Ted Bronson warmly, his childlike happiness at seeing the surgeon shining in his eyes. Ted returned the embrace without embarrassment, then reached out for Liz's hand. "Liz, this is Arturo Corazon," he said. "Arturo, meet Dr. Elizabeth MacGowan."

"Welcome to our house, Doctor." The slight hesitancy in Arturo Corazon's speech was also a characteristic of Down's Syndrome and the same happiness shone in his eyes that had been there when he had greeted Ted. When she took his hand, Liz couldn't help noticing the shortness of his fingers and the widened space between his thumb and forefinger, further evidences of the congenital abnormality from which he suffered.

"Thank you," she said, smiling, for his warmth was infectious, as was so often the case with Down's Syndrome sufferers she knew.

The house itself was magnificent in the classic Mediterranean style that characterized so many buildings in Florida's earlier period. A short entry hall gave way to a high-ceilinged living room, one side of which was partially formed by four sliding glass doors that gave access to a tiled and illuminated swimming pool. Beyond it, the broad expanse of Biscayne Bay and the lights of the residential section of Key Biscayne just south of Miami Beach were visible far across the water, a scene of subtropical beauty that was breathtaking.

As Liz and Ted followed Arturo Corazon into the living

room, several people who had been sitting at one side facing the glass doors rose to meet them. Michael Corazon she recognized at once from newspaper photos. Taller than most Cubans, he was, she judged, probably in his middle thirties, about the same age as Ted but with the high-planed face of a Spanish aristocrat and a touch of gray already in his shock of dark hair.

"Liz, this is Michael." Ted made the introduction and the two shook hands while Arturo stood by beaming happily upon them.

"Ted raves about you every time I see him, Dr. MacGowan —which isn't very often," said Corazon.

"Please call me Liz," she said. "Your home is beautiful and the garden—"

"You can thank Arturo for that. He's a genius at growing things." Michael Corazon offered her his arm in a courtly, Old World gesture. "Let me present to you my mother and Estrellita Mendoza, my fiancée."

"You're as lovely as Ted told me you are." In her seventies, Maria Corazon was erect and slender, her iron-gray hair showing no hint of the artificial blue tint favored by so many older women. "Please call me Mama, dear—everybody does."

"And this is my fiancée, Estrellita Mendoza." Michael Corazon reached out a hand for the dark-haired girl who had followed Maria across the room to meet the newcomers.

"We have a mutual friend in Dr. Paul Fraser, Dr. MacGowan," said Estrellita. "He brought me into the world."

Fraser was Professor of Obstetrics and Gynecology as well as Chief of Service, of which Liz was a vital part at Biscayne General.

"Paul has been very kind to me," said Liz. "He let me have my own section of the hospital before I'd been there a whole year."

"Where Liz is already the authority on amniocentesis," said Ted.

"Congratulations!" said Maria Corazon. "We were just having *piña coladas* before dinner, Dr. MacGowan. We Cubans think they're practically mother's milk but you don't have to drink them if you don't like them."

"I love *piña coladas*. And please do call me Liz."

"It was so warm today that we opened the doors to the Bay," Michael told her. "If it's too cool for you in that short-sleeved dress, Liz, I'll be glad to close them."

"I'm quite comfortable," Liz assured him as the group moved across the room toward the sofa and chairs. "I spent six months in Alaska just before I came to Miami; it will take another year or two to bake the cold out of my bones."

"What were you doing in Alaska—if it's not being nosy to ask?" Estrellita Mendoza inquired.

"My subspecialty is studying genetically related conditions," Liz explained.

"Do you mean the chromosomes and genes I've been watching on TV and reading about in the news magazines—but not understanding?" the Cuban girl asked.

"They *are* a bit difficult," Liz admitted. "I had a government grant to study the effect of in-breeding in some of the Eskimo groups who don't come in contact much with what we call civilization."

"Don't tell me you had to live in an igloo," said Michael.

"I would probably have been warmer if I had." Liz laughed. "The Great White Father in Washington decided that prefab houses are the most appropriate living quarters for the Eskimos but the walls were far less effective in keeping out the cold than a foot of packed snow in an igloo would have been."

A smiling Arturo appeared with a tray, upon which were tall glasses containing *piña coladas*.

"Thank you, Arturo." Liz accepted one and was rewarded with a beaming smile.

"Ted told me you spent your residency at Duke, Doctor—I

mean Liz," said Estrellita. "I earned my law degree at the University of North Carolina in Chapel Hill."

"We may have been practically neighbors, then," said Liz. "That section of North Carolina was rated by one of the news magazines recently as one of the ten best places to live in the country."

"Pittsburgh was another," Ted chimed in, "even with the lousy climate."

"Miami was lovely when we first came here," said Maria Corazon, a little wistfully. "But that was before drug selling and crime became Dade County's largest industry."

"I'm going to change that," said Michael firmly.

"I shouldn't think one man could do much alone," Liz commented.

"You don't know this one." Estrellita Mendoza put her arm around Michael's waist. "A new federal grand jury will be convened tomorrow morning. Michael is going to drop a bombshell that will make all the front pages in the country."

"Are you going to try to sever the Colombian connection, Mike?" Ted asked. It was common knowledge that more cocaine and marijuana came into South Florida from Colombia and adjacent areas in Central America than through any other port.

"State and federal law-enforcement agencies have been working on this project for months but from a somewhat different angle," the lawyer explained. "The Florida coastline has so many secluded harbors where small boats can land cocaine and marijuana after unloading ships at sea, that it's almost impossible to keep the stuff from coming in. This time we're going after the moneymen who profit most from the dope traffic. One of the biggest banks in Miami has been laundering the take from cocaine sales directly to Swiss bank accounts, so we're going to hit the narcotic tycoons where it will really hurt—in their pocketbooks."

"With the outflow of cash to Switzerland and other countries closed, the pushers and the drug kings will probably start killing each other off in order to get part of the loot," Estrellita added. "That's where the state attorney's office will come in."

"Are you with it?" Liz asked.

"In a small way."

"Don't let her fool you," said Michael Corazon proudly. "She's the smartest assistant state attorney in Florida."

"You two sound like an unbeatable combination," Ted commented.

"In the old days when Papa and I first came here from Cuba, Miami was a friendly city and everybody in Coconut Grove knew each other." Maria Corazon rose to her feet when a bell sounded from another part of the house. "Dinner is ready. Shall we go in?"

III

The food was everything Ted had promised Liz it would be. And the obvious pleasure of the Corazon family and Michael's fiancée in being together made Liz feel more at home than she could remember feeling since she'd come to Miami. The *arroz con pollo* was delicious, as was the sliced avocado and fresh peach salad, the tiny biscuits and the slice of key lime pie topped off with whipped cream, and then steaming black coffee served on the brightly lit patio around the pool.

"This procedure Ted said you're an authority in, Liz?" Michael Corazon asked during a lull in the conversation. "What exactly is it?"

"Amniocentesis is a medical procedure used in obstetrics to obtain information about the fetus," Liz explained.

"Do you mean telling whether it's going to be a boy or girl?"

"That, too, but we can also tell a lot about possible hereditary conditions and abnormalities of fetal development."

"It all sounds like magic to me," Maria admitted.

"Actually, the procedure is quite simple," said Liz. "You see, for the nine months while the baby is developing inside its mother's uterus, it lies inside a sac called the amnion that contains quite a bit of fluid."

"What we used to call the 'bag of waters'?" Maria asked.

"That's the popular name; actually the fluid contains a number of chemicals as well as some cells from the skin and other tissues of the fetus. By inserting a long needle through the mother's lower abdomen into the amniotic sac, we can draw out a small amount of the fluid and culture the cells it contains. In a few weeks, they will develop to where we can study the chromosomes and genes in the body cells of the fetus and determine not only its sex but the presence or absence of a number of inherited defects."

"I remember now seeing a TV program on 'NOVA' about that." Estrellita shivered. "I'm needle shy and it gave me the willies but it was really fascinating."

"I'm glad doctors didn't know about such things when I was having babies; I would have been scared to death knowing all the bad things that could happen." Maria turned to Arturo. "Why don't you show Dr. MacGowan some of your paintings, Brother?"

"Would you like that?" Arturo asked Liz eagerly.

"I'd love to see them."

"Brother has his studio in what used to be the garage," Michael explained. "We're really proud of his work."

And well they might be, Liz decided when the younger son took her out to the wing containing the studio. His paintings could be classified, she decided, as "primitives" in the manner of Grandma Moses, but they had a personality all their own, too, indicating a distinctly unusual talent. Most were of shrubs and flowers in the garden around the house but some were landscapes of the Bay with ships of various sorts, some moving and some at anchor. A few contained images of people, and Liz easily distinguished Maria Corazon along with Michael and two other men.

"How long have you been painting?" Liz asked.

"Since I was ten years old. Will you let me paint your picture sometime?"

"Of course. I'd love for you to paint me."

"Estrellita let me paint her picture; it's over there on the wall."

The painting was small but expertly done, catching the dark beauty of Michael's fiancée, yet presenting the characteristic touch of Arturo's brush.

"You must be kept busy taking care of the garden and painting, too, Arturo."

"I like to stay busy." He changed the subject abruptly again as seemed to be his habit. "Are you going to marry Dr. Ted?"

"Someday. Why?"

"I like to see people I love happy and Dr. Ted is like one of my brothers."

"How old are you, Arturo?"

"I'll be twenty-five my next birthday. Will you come to my birthday party? Dr. Ted always comes."

"Then I'll come, too," she promised. "Maybe we'd better go back to the living room now. Dr. Ted and I will have to leave soon. He's been away from the hospital for the past four days, so he'll need to see his patients tomorrow morning, and I have to operate about ten o'clock."

"It must be wonderful to be able to make sick people well."

As Liz was turning toward the door leading into the house, she was surprised to see a .22-caliber rifle hanging on a bracket on the wall.

"Do you hunt, too?" she asked.

"Only bad snakes that get in the garden," Arturo told her. "Sometimes moccasins swim down the canal from the Everglades and get in the flower beds. If I find one, I get the rifle and shoot him."

IV

Liz MacGowan was putting on fresh lipstick in the powder room off the foyer of the Corazon home before leaving when there was a knock on the door.

"May I come in, Dr. MacGowan?" Estrellita called through the panel.

"Certainly." Liz turned from the mirror as the younger girl opened the door. "I was just coming out."

"Stay a moment, please; I want to talk to you." Stepping inside, Estrellita closed the door. "I'm worried about something and I hope you can give me the answer."

"I certainly will, if I can."

"It's about Brother—Arturo."

Liz sensed what might be troubling Estrellita but waited for her to continue.

"What did you think of his paintings?" Estrellita asked.

"They're lovely, especially the one of you. He obviously loves you very much but that's not what's troubling you, is it?"

"No. You realized, of course, that he's different from most people."

Liz nodded. "Arturo was born with Down's Syndrome; it's called that after the man who first described it. Most Down's Syndrome children are far more mentally retarded than he seems to be, though. Do you have any idea what his IQ level is?"

"Michael says it's somewhere around seventy or eighty. When he first went to school, some of the other children made fun of him because he's different."

"That's not unusual."

"He had trouble reading and still does, so the family took him out of public school and sent him to a special one in Coral Gables for retarded children."

"His outlook on life appears to be very happy," said Liz. "Actually, I suspect he's a much better person than many people with normal intelligence who have emotional difficulties."

"Is Down's Syndrome hereditary?" Estrellita blurted out the question, confirming Liz's suspicion that this was the reason she had come into the powder room.

"It's congenital but not ordinarily considered hereditary."

"Could—could you explain the difference?"

"When the first fetal cell is formed by the union of the father's sperm and the mother's ovum, a change sometimes occurs in one chromosome of the new cell. From then on every cell in the body of the embryo will show the same changed chromosome and it will develop, as Arturo did, into the picture we used to give the horrible name of 'Mongolism' because of the changed shape of the eyes and the round face along with the other characteristics. When you marry Michael, the only thing that would increase the likelihood of your baby being like Arturo," she added, "is if you wait until after thirty-five to become pregnant."

v

Leaving Coconut Grove just before ten, Ted drove the Mercedes while Liz stretched out in the adjoining bucket seat. As he guided the car past the Coconut Grove bayfront park and onto South Bay Shore Drive, Liz spoke for the first time since they'd left the Corazon estate.

"You're a conniving bastard," she said, but without any rancor in her tone.

"What do you mean?" He feigned innocence.

"Don't deny that you took me out here tonight because you wanted me to see Arturo."

"I won't deny it, but Arturo is worth knowing in his own right."

"I agree, that's why I'm not sore. Do you happen to know how old Maria Corazon was when Arturo was born?"

"About thirty-eight, or maybe a few months older. Why?"

"Don't pretend you don't know that for every year after the mother reaches thirty-five, the chances of a pregnancy turning out to be a Down's Syndrome increase rapidly."

"So?"

"I'm only thirty-two, so the odds at my age aren't very high."

"You've been on the pill for a year that I know of," he reminded her. "Women on the pill often have difficulty getting pregnant after they stop taking it and some even go for several years. By that time you'd be thirty-five or even older."

"Not with a stud like you for a husband."

"Thanks for the compliment." He gave her thigh a quick squeeze. "But I still think you need to be reminded that the years are passing us by—not that you show the effects very much."

"You're being very gallant tonight," she told him. "Could you perhaps have an ulterior motive?"

"Me? Of course not," he said as he guided the car across the short bridge spanning the Miami River and into the busy traffic of downtown Miami. "You know I'm always gallant and charming."

Where Biscayne Boulevard skirted Bayfront Park, they followed the traffic pattern northward until the tower of Biscayne General Hospital, with the brightly lit helicopter pad atop it, loomed against the sky east of the boulevard. As Ted turned off on a broad but less traveled thoroughfare that gave access to the hospital complex on the bayfront and Biscayne Terrace across from it, an ambulance, sirens screaming and warning lights blinking, sped past them and turned into the hospital emergency entrance.

"Looks like the ER"—hospital jargon for Emergency Room—"is going to be busy tonight," Ted observed.

"Hope it's not a ruptured tubal pregnancy, I'm on call for GYN."

"I'll join you in that prayer. Are you operating in the morning?"

"A vaginal hysterectomy at ten," she said as he guided the car up the ramp leading to the hospital parking garage that also served those living in Biscayne Terrace. "What about you?"

"I'll be working all day in the hospital records room."

"Behind on your paperwork again? The clerks are always complaining that doctors neglect to finish their charts."

"Show me a hospital where the same thing isn't true. This time, though, I'll be looking for patients whose kidney transplants were rejected. Any of them lucky enough to survive by means of dialysis after rejection are prime candidates for new transplants, using the cyclosporin and steroid technique they've been using in Pittsburgh. If I can offer enough of them a chance to free themselves from dialysis, I'll be inaugurating a whole new area in organ transplants at Biscayne General."

"Do you really think you can give many patients whose bodies rejected a previous transplant a new lease on life?" she asked as he parked the car in a slot designated by her name painted on the wall of the parking garage.

"I'm positive. Heretofore, the record of success with nonsibling donors was only about fifty percent in even the best clinics, but the last hundred cases or so done in Pittsburgh with the new technique produced close to a ninety percent success rate. The difference could mean not being tethered to a dialysis machine and bring life again to a lot of people who are only half living now. Even if half of the rejectees opt for another try, my surgical team is going to be the busiest one at Biscayne General."

"It's a wonderful dream. I hope you wake up to find that it's true."

"Why don't I run my suitcase up to my apartment while you're starting the coffeepot for a nightcap of Irish coffee," he said as they were getting into the elevator. "I can be down in a few minutes."

"Sounds okay to me. See you."

She had changed, Ted saw when she opened the door for him some ten minutes later. In a lovely silk robe he'd given her for Christmas and with her hair freshly brushed and lying loose on her shoulders, she was about the most beautiful thing he had ever seen. When he took her in his arms, their long kiss left them both a little breathless.

"Coffee's ready," she said when he released her. "I bought a bottle of Irish whiskey this afternoon on the way to the airport so we could celebrate your birthday."

"Right now I've got a better idea of how a birthday should be celebrated." Lifting her in his arms, he started, without opposition, toward the bedroom.

Chapter Two

At seven the next morning, Ted was frying bacon in the kitchen of Liz's condominium and watching the morning news on the small TV set there. She came out of the bathroom wearing a terry-cloth robe and a large towel piled high on her head to form a turban and help dry her hair.

"You swept me off my feet last night before I could give you the present I bought for you." She handed him a small box with a bow of red ribbon larger than the container. "Afterward, I'm afraid I forgot about it."

He opened the box to reveal a pair of gold cuff links with an odd-shaped emblem stamped into the metal in rough form.

"They're pieces of eight," she explained. "Salvaged from the bottom of the sea in the Florida channel off Key West where some Spanish galleon loaded with gold went down during a storm in the sixteenth century—according to the clerk who sold them to me."

"Probably came from the Philippines originally." Ted held up one of the cuff links to study the insignia more closely. "The Spanish sailed galleons from the Far East to ports on the west side of Panama, what was then called the Spanish Main. Then they hauled the gold across the Isthmus by mule train and loaded it on ships that crossed the Atlantic to Spain by way of the Florida Straits and the Gulf Stream. One Christmas during medical school when I was visiting the Corazons, Mike and I went scuba diving but we didn't find any treasure."

"I remembered your telling me about it. That's why I bought them."

"They're terrific! I'll wear them with white tie and tails at our wedding. How soon will you be ready for breakfast?"

"Fifteen minutes," she said, heading for the bedroom. "That coffee smells deli—"

She broke off speaking in the middle of the word when the scene on the TV set changed to one they both recognized immediately. It was the street in Coconut Grove in front of the gate to the Corazon estate, through which they'd driven less than twelve hours before.

"We interrupt this program"—the young announcer ordinarily assigned the chore of reading the early morning news and weather report was fairly stuttering with excitement—"to bring you news of a tragedy whose effects are still being felt at this very moment. Less than fifteen minutes ago, when he drove out through the gates of the family's Coconut Grove estate, Special Federal Prosecutor Michael Corazon was shot down by a burst of gunfire from a car that was obviously waiting for him across the street. A Rescue Squad ambulance is taking Mr. Corazon to the hospital at this moment, so we're not able to tell you the extent of his injuries. But since he is said to have been driving a jeep at the time, his body would have had little if any protection from the sides of the vehicle. It is feared that Mr. Corazon's injuries are exten—".

The pager Ted Bronson carried attached to his belt sounded a high-pitched squealing note, followed immediately by the voice of the paging operator. "Dr. Bronson! Dr. Theodore Bronson! Please call 355-7677 immediately."

Recognizing the number of the Corazon home, Ted took two long steps across the kitchen and lifted the receiver from the wall phone by the window, punching the number buttons rapidly.

"This is Dr. Bron—" he said when the line opened.

"Dr. Ted, the bad men shot Michael." Arturo was sobbing, making his words hardly distinguishable.

"I saw the TV broadcast, Brother. Where did the Rescue Squad take him?"

"I told them to go to Biscayne General, Ted, and call you." The voice of Maria Corazon took over on an extension. "I was cutting flowers near the gate and saw it happen. They shot him down with an automatic rifle, Ted. Will you take charge?"

"Of course. You and Arturo come on to the hospital and notify the rest of your family. I'll talk to you after I've examined Mike."

"Thank God you're there. We're depending on you to save him."

"Save Michael, Dr. Ted," Arturo stopped sobbing long enough to say before Ted hung up the phone.

"The motive for the attempted killing of Special Prosecutor Corazon"—the voice of the TV announcer was steady now—"is believed to be the fact that he was scheduled to bring bills of indictment this morning against several high-placed banking figures in Miami to a new federal grand jury especially selected to investigate the lucrative drug traffic."

"I'm on my way to the Emergency Room, Liz." Picking up his jacket and tie, Ted started across the living room to the hall. "Call the ER and tell them Mike is my patient and I'm on my way."

As Ted emerged from the entrance to Biscayne Terrace, he heard the whine of an ambulance. And as he hurried across the broad thoroughfare to the hospital, the vehicle careened into the ambulance entrance to the hospital and was braked to a stop beside the loading platform. The wheels had barely stopped moving when the technician who was driving opened the door and moved quickly to the back to open the doors to the ambulance itself and allow the wheeled stretcher inside to be removed.

"He's in bad shape, Dr. Bronson." The technician sitting beside Michael Corazon recognized Ted. "Four or five bullets right through his trunk. I started an IV as soon as we got him in the ambulance but his blood pressure has been falling steadily."

"I'll hold the IV flask," said Ted as the two men were removing the stretcher from the ambulance and carrying it to the loading platform. "What was the last BP reading?"

"Eighty over forty but hard to get."

The figure didn't augur well for Corazon's life. And when Ted felt the pulse in the injured man's wrist, while the stretcher was being wheeled up the ramp and into the Biscayne General Emergency Room, he found it thready and almost too fast to count.

The Emergency Room resident, a sandy-haired young Doctor named Edward Thomas whom Ted had helped train, met them at the entrance to the ER.

"I heard the TV broadcast in the cafeteria, Dr. Bronson," he said, "and came on the run in case they brought him here."

"The family called and asked me to take charge," Ted told him. "Start some type O blood flowing as soon as possible, Ed. While you're getting it, a flask of Fluosol would help, too."

"We keep it ready all the time." Dr. Thomas moved to a large refrigerator. "Shall I substitute it for the glucose and saline he's getting already or start another IV?"

"You'll get it in faster through the needle that's already in." Ted was helping the Emergency Room nurse supervisor cut away Michael Corazon's clothing so he could examine his lower chest and abdomen. Moments later, a laboratory technician appeared with a tray for taking blood and deftly placed a tourniquet around Corazon's other arm.

"His BP must be pretty low," she commented as she stroked the skin of the arm below the tourniquet, seeking to feel the veins in the depression in front of the elbow. "I can hardly see a vein."

"As soon as you draw the blood for chemistry, start a cross match for transfusion," Ted directed her. "Meanwhile, we'll be combating shock as best we can with O-type blood and Fluosol."

A remarkable chemical that could carry oxygen, the function normally performed by the hemoglobin and the red cells of the bloodstream, Fluosol had saved many lives since its introduction into the United States from Japan a few years earlier. O-type blood came from universal donors and could therefore be given to anyone with reasonable safety. It was always stored in the hospital as a lifesaving measure.

While the technician was drawing blood, Dr. Thomas substituted a flask of Fluosol for the glucose and saline injection started by the Rescue Squad technicians. Opening the control clamp on the IV tubing, he let the fluid flow in as rapidly as possible to combat shock. Meanwhile, the ER nursing supervisor had wrapped a blood-pressure cuff around the injured man's arm to replace the one the ambulance technicians had been using.

"Pressure's coming up," she reported moments later.

"I see four wounds of entry, all above the navel; we can look for the wounds of exit when we move him onto the X-ray table." While he examined Michael Corazon's upper abdomen and lower chest, Ted was picturing in his mind's eye the anatomy of the wounded man's abdominal cavity, estimating what organs were injured and what course the bullets had probably taken. What he saw did not augur well for the life of his friend.

"I'm in a fairly large vein, Dr. Bronson," the laboratory

technician reported as she drew blood into an empty syringe for the emergency test. "Do you want to put in a Swan-Ganz catheter electrode?"

Ted had to make a quick decision and an important one. If there appeared to be any danger of his friend's heart stopping from shock, a catheter with a wire inside its wall could be slid up the large vein of the arm into the chest and down into the right side of the heart. There it would touch the wall of the right ventricle, allowing electrical impulses to be used as an internal pacemaker to keep the heart going until its own function could be restored. The procedure would take time, however, so he elected against it for the moment.

"I'll put one through a trocar into the subclavian vein if we need it," he told the technician. "His pressure's rising and none of the bullets seem to have passed near the heart."

"Ninety over fifty," the nurse with the blood-pressure instrument reported. "His pulse is steadying a little, too."

"Let's get him onto a hospital gurney and over to X ray, then." Skilled hands moved the injured man's body to the heavy gurney that could also function as an emergency operating table if necessary. Meanwhile, Ted quickly examined Corazon's left side and back, looking for signs that the bullets entering his body might also have left it. He found only two wounds of exit on the left side, which meant that two of the missiles were still inside the body.

II

After Ted left her apartment, Liz dressed quickly and, stopping only for a cup of coffee, crossed the boulevard to the hospital and came in through the Emergency Room entrance. She didn't expect Ted to need her services, knowing he was quite capable of handling any surgical emergency, but hoped to give support to Maria and Arturo. They had not yet arrived she was told by the gray-haired ER nursing supervisor who looked up from the desk where she had been making an entry in the daily log.

"Do you know anything about Mr. Corazon's condition, Mrs. Burke?" she asked.

"Dr. Bronson just took him to X ray, Dr. MacGowan. He was in deep shock when the ambulance brought him here but his condition improved rapidly with IV Fluosol. I heard Dr. Bronson say four bullets had entered Mr. Corazon's upper abdomen and lower chest but two of them apparently passed completely through. He's trying to locate the others with the X ray while they're getting an operating room ready upstairs."

"Dr. Bronson and I had dinner with the Corazons last night. It's hard to believe something like this could happen in a civilized community."

"The lobby is full of reporters and TV cameras waiting for Dr. Bronson to come out of X ray," said the graying ER supervisor. "If you want to star on TV, just step through the doors to the lobby and tell them you had dinner with the Corazon family last night."

"Not a chance."

"I was supervisor on Obstetrics when Arturo Corazon was born," the nurse added. "Did you meet him last night?"

"Yes. He's very sweet and very talented, too. He showed me some of his paintings."

"Dr. MacGowan—2401," the voice of the hospital paging operator came from the loudspeaker in the ceiling of the large white-tiled room. "Dr. Elizabeth MacGowan—2401."

Picking up the telephone on the nurse's desk, Liz dialed the number for Dr. Paul Fraser, head of Liz's own department in the busy metropolis that was a great hospital and medical school.

"This is Dr. MacGowan, Peggy," she told the department secretary who answered. "Did you want me?"

"Dr. Fraser came in just a few minutes ago and would like to see you in his office as soon as you can make it."

"Be there in two minutes."

III

Michael Corazon groaned and opened his eyes as Ted Bronson was helping the technician turn him on the X-ray table in order to take a lateral view of his lower chest and upper abdomen. The anterior-posterior views already taken would show the horizontal plane location of the bullets in the wounded man's body, but lateral views were also needed to determine their position in the vertical plane. By studying the two views after the films were developed, the surgeon and the X-ray specialist could locate the bullets remaining in the body with considerable accuracy.

"Sorry, Mike." Ted steadied Corazon's shoulder. "How do you feel?"

"My right side hurts like hell and my belly only a little less," Corazon mumbled. "I remember hearing shots and feeling something slam into my midsection before I fell out of the jeep."

"What slammed into your midsection were bullets," Ted told him. "Somebody was waiting across the highway from your driveway with a machine gun. Did you happen to recognize the man who shot you?"

"Not the one with the weapon, but I did get a glimpse of the one that was driving—enough to know it was Sam Gianno. That makes him an accessory, if I live to testify."

"You'll survive, but I'm going to have to operate. Mama and Arturo insisted that you be my patient."

"Couldn't be in better hands. Can you start by giving me something for pain?"

"Call Mrs. Barnes in the Emergency Room, please," Ted told the X-ray technician who was taking the films. "Ask her to send over fifty milligrams of Demerol and four-tenths of a milligram of atropine."

A second technician appeared in the door of the room as the first one departed to order the medication. "The first films will be developed in about a minute, Dr. Bronson," she said. "Dr. Davis will look at them with you." Luke Davis was chief of the hospital's section on Roentgenology.

"Ted?" Michael Corazon's voice was still very weak. "There should be a lot of reporters—"

"I hear the lobby is full of them but—"

"Talk to them before you operate—"

"But—"

"And tell them I recognized that Sam Gianno was driving the car."

"Are you sure?"

"Enough to put the heat on him. If we lock Gianno away until I can go back to work, it will put a crimp into the branch of the Jersey Mafia family he represents in the Miami drug trade."

"The OR crew will be down soon to take you upstairs and get you ready for surgery," Ted told Corazon as he turned to leave the room. "I'm going to look at the X rays now."

In the viewing room of the X-ray department, its walls lined with ground-glass screens, Dr. Luke Davis was watching a technician place a series of freshly developed films on the viewing screens along one wall.

"Heard about the shooting on the radio as I was putting my car in the parking garage, Ted," said David. "How's Michael Corazon?"

"Coming out of shock but still rocky. As soon as I look at these films and talk to the media, I'm going to explore his abdomen."

"Another inch upward and one of the slugs would have

robbed you of any chance to operate." Using the pipe he was smoking, Davis pointed to the first in the series of X rays. "Judging by that nick in the lower edge of a rib, one bullet just grazed the bone enough to slow it down. You can see the slug under the skin of his back but, if it had struck the upper edge of the rib and been deflected upward a little, it could have blasted the base right out of his heart."

"What about the liver?"

"The bullet that touched the lower edge of a rib was deflected downward enough to plow into the top of the liver, too. With just a little difference in angle, it could have hit the aorta, the inferior vena cava, or both of them, and he would never have reached the hospital alive."

"Thank God for small favors, at least."

"There's some gas in the abdomen that looks like it might be outside the gut so you'll probably find intestinal perforations."

"That would be par for the course. What else?"

"I don't like that grouping of lead fragments in the area of the upper pole of the right kidney." Davis pointed with his pipe stem to another area, somewhat lower than the spot where they could see a single bullet. "From the looks of things, one slug struck the body of the second or third lumbar vertebra and literally exploded."

"Along with the kidney?"

"Probably. Here's the lateral view of that area. Hmm." Davis stroked his heavy black beard as the technician continued placing films on the row of viewing screens. "From the location of the lead fragments my guess is that you'll find the right kidney pretty well destroyed but you could be sure only with an IV pyelogram."

"There's no time for that," said the surgeon. "I'll explore that area first when I start the operation."

IV

Outside the door to the X-ray department, Ted found two men he'd never seen before waiting. One was short and stocky, the other tall.

"Nick Patterson, Special Agent of the FBI with the Narcotics Task Force in Miami, Dr. Bronson," said the tall man. "This is Steve Pagano, Chief Narcotics Enforcement Officer for the Treasury Department in Florida. How's Mike Corazon?"

"Coming out of shock but he was shot up badly. I hope you caught the assassins."

"Not yet," said the Narc squad chief grimly, "but we will."

"Did Mr. Corazon say anything about recognizing either of the men in the car?" Patterson asked.

"He thinks Sam Gianno was driving—"

"Thinks isn't definite enough," said Patterson firmly.

"I agree," said Ted. "Besides, would a Mafia chieftain like Sam Gianno actually take part in a hit?"

"Gianno doesn't rank very high yet in the Mafia pecking order; the Miami operation is sort of a testing ground for him," said Pagano. "In order to prove himself eligible to be promoted to something like the rank of Godfather, Second Class, in the Mafia hierarchy, he'd at least have to be present at a successful hit, even though he didn't handle the actual weapons."

"Just being there still makes him an accessory, doesn't it?"

"You can be sure we'll arrest him on suspicion of being an accessory to attempted murder," said Patterson, "but he'll be out on bail before you finish your surgery, Dr. Bronson— unless Mike swears out a warrant before you start the anesthetic, placing Gianno at the scene of the hit."

"He's in no shape to do that now and won't be for some days," Ted told them. "Mike wants me to hold a press conference and identify Gianno as the driver of the hit car but I can't wait that long to operate. You two will have to handle the media until I finish."

"We'll hold them off," Nick Patterson assured him. "Tell Mike we're all pulling for him."

"Praying might be more appropriate," Ted told them grimly as he left for the operating-room floor."

Chapter Three

"Go right in, please, Dr. MacGowan," Dr. Paul Fraser's secretary told Liz when she came into the waiting room of the department head's office. "He's expecting you."

Approaching seventy, Paul Fraser was tall, craggy-faced and vigorous. He was talking on the telephone when Liz came into the office and waved her to a seat in a comfortable chair beside the desk. Like many of the doctors' offices in the suite that occupied one floor of the Biscayne Hospital Tower, a wide picture window faced Biscayne Bay. Through it, the Hotel Row of Miami Beach was visible across the sparkling surface of the Bay, and nearer by, the corner of the window gave a slanting view of a portion of downtown Miami, with rows of shining white cruise ships docked at the bayfront.

Dr. Paul Fraser hung up his phone and looked across his desk at Liz MacGowan with a warm smile. "You look wonderful," he said. "How's Ted?"

"Right now he's getting ready to operate on Michael Corazon."

"I saw the broadcast about the attempted assassination on TV this morning at breakfast. Will Ted be able to save him?"

"If anybody can. We had dinner at the Corazon estate last night to celebrate Ted's birthday. It's hard to believe all this could have happened less than twelve hours later."

"It's a lovely spot, one of the few Coconut Grove plantations that still remain," said Fraser. "The Corazons and the Mendozas were among the Spanish aristocracy in Cuba, before Fulgencio Batista came into power. Did you meet Arturo?"

"He met us at the door and after dinner he showed me his paintings."

"I delivered him here at the old Jackson Memorial Hospital soon after Maria and Juan came to Miami. If you saw Arturo's paintings, you know that, like an occasional Down's Syndrome, he's very talented, besides being one of the happiest and most generous people I've ever known."

"He certainly seems to be all of that."

"I had a call last night that will interest you," Fraser told her. "It was from an old friend, Sheik Yossuf Almani, the Ambassador from Telfa to the United Nations."

Liz frowned. "I'm afraid I've never heard of the country— or him."

"Neither have most people except those concerned with importing oil. Telfa is one of the Arab emirates and has been ruled for centuries by the Elzama family. The present ruler, Hassim Elzama III, is an absolute monarch, as were his father and grandfather before him. Actually, though, Telfa has little to distinguish it except a lot of sand, two or three medium-sized cities and the fact that it sits directly over what appears to be an inexhaustible pool of crude oil."

"From what I remember about the geography of that area from high school, that doesn't make Telfa exactly unusual, does it?"

"Maybe not, but it's still different from most of the Arab emirates in at least one way. The greater part of the oil royalties from Telfa's wells go for the benefit of its people instead of fat relatives who spend most of their time gambling in Monte Carlo or living it up in Paris."

"That speaks well for the country—and its ruler."

"Telfa also has the highest per capita income of any of the Arab emirates. Hassim Elzama was educated in America and his schools and hospitals are right up-to-date."

"He sounds like a rarity, an enlightened Arabic ruler."

"Unfortunately, he's dying of leukemia."

"Tough luck!"

"Worse than that. He has no heir—unless the fetus carried by Princess Zorah, his youngest and most recent wife, is a male."

"How does that concern us?" Liz asked.

"That's exactly why I asked you to stop by before you go to the OR," Paul Fraser told her. "When I was a young associate professor at Georgetown before coming to Miami, my wife and I lived in the same neighborhood with Sheik Yossuf Al-mani. He had just graduated from M.I.T. and was studying at the Johns Hopkins School of Advanced International Studies. I delivered his two children and we've been friends ever since. Later, Yossuf moved up to become Telfa's Ambassador to the UN and spokesman for his country along with most of the other Arab emirates. Sorry to bore you with ancient history, Liz, but you need to know it before deciding to accept the patient I'm going to offer you."

"If it's a female, I'd take her on your recommendation anyway."

"Yossuf Almani has been requested by Emir Hassim Elzama to undertake a rather delicate matter, one that needs to be kept at least as secret as international affairs concerning royalty can ever be. Hassim is forty-five years old and has already fathered six daughters by two wives, but according to Telfa law, succession to the position of Emir is restricted to the male line."

"Naturally," said Liz, with a touch of sarcasm.

"If Hassim dies without producing a male heir," Fraser continued, "political control of Telfa will be up for grabs in what might be a civil war between the two leading families and a left-leaning dissident political faction fostered by Moscow. With the money the Russians would be willing to spend in order to own a strategically located bit of land with a thriving port on the Arabic peninsula, the dissidents might even gain control on the pretense of changing the country into a democracy."

"A horrendous possibility—for the Emir I'm sure."

"And for the United States. Hoping to produce a male heir, Hassim took a very beautiful young woman from a good family in Telfa as his common-law wife last year. At this point, she's literally a concubine, but if she produces a son, he would make her Queen—and her family will suddenly become important in the politics of Telfa."

"A nice involved situation," Liz commented.

"According to what Yossuf Almani told me on the telephone last night, Princess Zorah is now about five months pregnant and Hassim is naturally anxious to know whether the baby is a boy or a girl. Yossuf Almani had read—I suspect in some of your published articles—about the progress that's been made through amniocentesis and biopsy of the chorion here at Biscayne General in the diagnosis of gender, as well as hereditary diseases, in unborn children. He called to ask me to undertake the job of determining the gender of the child now developing in Princess Zorah's uterus."

"Sounds like something out of a modern-day version of *The Arabian Nights.*"

"It really is. I tried to call you late yesterday afternoon when I finished talking to Yossuf Almani in New York but you were out."

"I met Ted at the airport; he was just back from a meeting of the transplant surgeons in Pittsburgh. We went directly from the airport to dinner at the Corazon estate."

"Yossuf doesn't need a final answer until this afternoon and I didn't want to interfere with a social engagement by calling you on the beeper last night," Fraser told her. "But I did take

the liberty of telling him that you are more skilled in amniocentesis than anybody in the country. And I promised to ask
you this morning to undertake the job of determining whether
or not Princess Zorah is bearing a boy or a girl."

"How far along did you say she is?" Liz asked.

"Yossuf didn't know for sure but he thought somewhere
around twenty weeks."

"Twenty weeks pretty well rules out doing a chorionic biopsy without some possibility of interfering with the pregnancy or endangering the child," said Liz. "Especially if they
expect me to carry out the procedure in—what did you say
was the name of the Arabian state?"

"I made it quite clear to Yossuf Almani that you wouldn't
risk performing what would have to be a pretty delicate procedure with the facilities available in Telfa. He assured me that
the Emir understands and that, if you take the case, Princess
Zorah will be flown to Miami in the Emir's personal plane."

"When can she come here?"

"As soon as Yossuf can call Emir Hassim on the transatlan-
tic phone. You could perform the amniocentesis within two or
three days after her arrival, couldn't you?"

"Yes, but suppose the baby turns out to be a girl like the
other six? What will happen then?"

"I asked Yossuf that question too—out of curiosity," said
Fraser. "He says that, before he dies, Hassim would set the
mother up with a trust fund large enough to support her and
the child but without any chance of their becoming what
might be considered royalty."

"In other words, he wouldn't make her Queen."

"Not a chance. I imagine he'd simply find another healthy
young woman, get her pregnant, if possible, considering that
he's being treated for leukemia, and probably send her to you,
too, as soon as she's far enough along for the fetal gender to
be determined. Shall I call Yossuf Almani in New York and

tell him to notify Emir Hassim that you will accept the mother and unborn infant as patients?"

"Of course, if that's what you want me to do."

"The final decision has to be yours, Liz, but you're easily the best-qualified doctor anywhere for this particular job. We'll try to keep the media from getting too excited about the whole thing but it's bound to be a storybook case to them."

"Princess or no princess, she'll be just another patient to me," said Liz firmly.

11

In Operating Room 1, high up in the Biscayne General Hospital Tower, Ted Bronson looked with dismay at what remained of Michael Corazon's right kidney—and found the chances of preserving it for future function hopeless. After striking the body of a lumbar vertebra, the largest and frontmost portion of the bony units that made up the vertebral column itself, the lead fragments of the assassin's bullet had literally exploded the soft tissue making up the right kidney, much as it had itself exploded after striking bone. As a result, what had once been a normally functioning kidney, capable of removing all of the body's waste products not detoxified by the liver, had been reduced to a bloody pulp.

Sponging away the accumulation of blood and damaged tissue in the space of Michael Corazon's right flank where the kidney had lain nestled beneath the liver, Ted looked up at Dr. Donald Taylor, chief of the Department of Urology, whom he'd asked to assist him.

"What do you think, Don?" he asked.

"No doubt about the fact that the right kidney is *kaput*," said the urologist.

"Should I explore the left one to see whether one of the bullets struck it, too?"

Taylor shrugged. "We can do that after you stop the hemorrhage by removing the right one. Or, better still, unless there's a lot of blood in the urine from the left one, an IV pyelogram will tell you what shape it's in, so there's no need to add a second incision and increase the degree of shock."

"My sentiments exactly," Ted Bronson agreed and turned to the instrument nurse. "Pedicle clamp, please."

Using the heavy instrument the nurse handed him, Ted clamped the main artery and vein to what had once been a kidney, controlling the main source of hemorrhage. Next he cut away the thoroughly mangled tissue and tied off the vessels, using heavy silk.

"That silk ligature will let you locate the renal artery and vein easily if you have to transplant later," Dr. Taylor observed as he was completing that part of the procedure.

"Pray God the left kidney will still function and we won't have to transplant. I'm going to open the abdominal cavity and look for perforations."

"Any idea how much longer you'll be?" the anesthesiologist, Dr. Peter Craig, asked.

"Quite a while." Ted turned to the operating-room supervisor, who was acting as the circulating nurse. "Dr. MacGowan isn't operating until ten. Will you ask her to come to the gallery? She knows the family and can give them a message."

Before Ted had completed an extension of the incision across the muscles of the upper abdomen, Liz appeared in the gallery. A glass-enclosed area including one wall of the small room that projected about ten feet above the floor of the large, white-tiled operating room, the gallery was designed to allow viewers to watch closely the events being played out on the center stage below without endangering the strict aseptic conditions being maintained in the operating room itself.

"Dr. MacGowan." Ted chose to be professional when he

spoke to Liz by way of the intercom that enabled a surgeon to describe findings to watchers—usually medical students and house staff—in the gallery. "Will you find Mr. Corazon's relatives and tell them his condition is relatively good?"

"They're in the Critical Care waiting room," Liz said by way of the gallery intercom. "Any details?"

"Only that we had to remove the right kidney but, judging from his excellent condition, that was the worst injury. Tell them I'll be another hour or so and, if Pedro and Manuel Corazon have arrived, send them down to the blood bank to be matched."

"Right." Liz left the gallery but neither she nor Ted could have suspected at the moment to just what degree Ted was wrong in his optimistic prognosis.

III

Maria and Arturo Corazon looked up eagerly when Liz came into the waiting area outside the Critical Care section. "Any news?" Maria asked.

"I just came from the operating room," said Liz. "Ted asked me to tell you that Michael is doing very well. One bullet struck the spine—"

"Is he paralyzed?" the older-looking of the two dark-skinned Cubans whom Liz did not recognize asked.

"The spinal cord wasn't injured but one bullet struck a vertebra and was fragmented. It damaged the right kidney so badly that Dr. Bronson had to remove it."

"This is my oldest son, Manuel, Dr. MacGowan," said Maria Corazon, "and our second son, Pedro."

"I'm sorry to have to meet you under these circumstances," Liz told the two Corazon brothers. "Dr. Bronson wants you to go down to the blood bank in the basement of the hospital so your blood can be matched with Michael's in case further transfusions are needed."

"What about me?" Arturo was obviously hurt.

"You, too, of course," Liz told him. "Right now would be a good time for all of you to go, while you wait for Dr. Bronson to finish the surgery."

"Thank God Ted was available," said Maria.

"He'll save Michael if anyone can," Liz promised.

IV

Working swiftly, once he was certain that the blood supply to the badly damaged right kidney had been securely controlled, Ted Bronson extended the incision far enough across Michael Corazon's abdominal muscles to allow examination of the organs contained inside the abdominal cavity. When he opened the thin membrane called the peritoneum lining the cavity, some cloudy fluid spurted out and with it a small piece of what appeared to be bacon.

"There's part of his breakfast," Don Taylor observed, "so you can be sure that at least one bullet perforated the stomach."

"I don't detect a fecal odor, so maybe the Lord was good to him and none of them punctured the colon." Ted reached for the sterile, plastic suction tip lying beside the instrument table and inserted it into the abdomen. A large amount of the cloudy fluid they had already noted began to accumulate in the bottle attached to the suction machine but it didn't contain very much blood.

With the blunt end of a forcep, Dr. Taylor indicated a small but distinctly perceptible perforation in the dark surface of the peritoneum covering the liver. "That looks like where the bullet that nicked the underside of one rib must have gone completely through the liver."

"It's probably the one we saw under the skin of his back on the X ray."

"Probably, but there doesn't seem to be any bleeding from it."

"We can be thankful for something." Proceeding carefully, Ted examined the entire digestive tract, beginning with the stomach and ending in the left side of the abdomen with the descending colon. He found several penetrations of the small intestine in addition to two in the stomach but these were closed easily with a few sutures.

"I guess we'd better take a look at the underside of the liver, considering how close the right kidney lies beneath it," he said when all the openings in the digestive tract had been closed.

Covering his gloved hands with a sterile towel like a muff, he moved to a position in front of several lighted view boxes on which the X-ray films taken downstairs had been placed. "I can see a few fragments of the bullet that got the kidney," he said. "They appear to be on or in the underside of the liver."

"I can see some oozing of blood from that area," said Dr. Taylor.

"We'd better examine it." Ted came back to the operating table and dropped the towel that had covered his hands. "If the bullet that nicked the rib had broken up instead of going straight through the liver, it could have blasted into the liver parenchyma and there would have been hell to pay."

When Ted lifted the lower edge of the liver with a moist gauze pad he saw immediately where the ooze of blood had been coming from. A ragged tear was visible in the dark underside of the organ and from it a steady flow of bright red blood could be seen.

"There's your criminal," said the urologist, "but it appears to involve only a small area on the underside of the liver."

"I agree," said Ted, as he removed a small ragged piece of lead from the bleeding area and dropped it into a basin.

"Absorbable packing should control the ooze, and we won't have to worry about the trauma of removing the pack later, as we had to do in the old days."

Packing a long strip of the absorbable material against the bleeding area where some lead fragments had grazed the soft undersurface of the liver, Ted prepared to close the incision. "I'm glad we won't have to probe into the main lobe of the liver for that bullet that went through, but remind me to remove it when I finish closing the incision."

"Why bother?" Dr. Taylor asked. "It's not hurting anything."

"Maybe the police can find a use for it. They always do in the assassination attempts I see on TV."

"Then do it by all means," said Taylor. "We don't want to go against protocol."

The Corazon family was in the Critical Care waiting room when Ted came down from the OR suite. "Mike came through the surgery in good shape," he told them. "Most of the damage was done by one bullet that struck a vertebra and exploded. The right kidney was beyond repair so I had to remove it."

"What about the left one?" the older brother asked.

"There was no blood in the urine so I'm quite sure it's okay," Ted answered. "The only thing we need to be concerned about now is the liver. The right kidney lies just beneath it and a small area was raked by several bullet fragments. I managed to control the bleeding with a pack, though, so it shouldn't cause any trouble. Another bullet struck a rib and was deflected through the liver but bullet wounds in solid organs generally don't cause much hemorrhage."

But there, as it turned out, Ted was wrong.

Chapter Four

Liz MacGowan's hysterectomy that morning took longer than she had expected. Glancing at the clock on the corridor wall when she came out of the doctors' dressing room after a shower and change to street clothes, she saw that it was already noon and decided to have lunch in the cafeteria before going to her own office to tackle the afternoon parade of patients. Dr. Paul Fraser was ahead of her in the cafeteria line but waited after paying his bill until she came through.

"Sitting with anyone, Liz?" he asked.

"You—I hope," she said with a smile.

"Let's go to the doctors' dining room; the din out here is enough to drive you to drink."

"It's the hospital social hour." Liz followed the older surgeon to the smaller room reserved for staff and visiting doctors. "Actually, this is the main starting point for the grapevine that sees all and knows all—sometimes before it actually happens."

"I had a call from Yossuf Almani just before noon," Fraser told her as they placed their trays on an empty table. "He's going to call Telfa this afternoon and make arrangements for Princess Zorah to be flown to Miami, hopefully tomorrow."

"The Emir doesn't appear to have much patience."

"If I were dying from leukemia and wanted to know

whether I had an heir before I died, I suppose I wouldn't be patient either," said Fraser. "I reserved a suite for the Princess on the VIP floor and Yossuf is flying down from New York to meet the Emir's plane when it lands. He'll bring her directly to the hospital."

"Did Sheik Almani have any more information about how far along the Princess' pregnancy is?"

"Nothing but the rough figure I gave you of about twenty weeks." Fraser gave Liz a quick look of appraisal. "Worried about the risk of amniocentesis that late?"

"A little," Liz admitted. "At sixteen weeks the risk is probably not much more than the normal liability of any pregnancy to end in a spontaneous abortion. Four more weeks shouldn't increase the chances of starting premature labor very much, if any."

"Or having to deliver by Caesarean a premature baby whose chances for survival are pretty slim," Fraser observed.

"Did you have to bring that up?"

"Anyway, I hope you won't have to stay late tomorrow afternoon waiting for the plane from Telfa to land."

Ted Bronson and FBI Chief Nick Patterson, both carrying trays, came into the doctors' dining room just then. When Ted saw Liz with Paul Fraser, he led the way through the now crowded room to their table, where two seats were still empty.

"Mind if we join you?" Ted inquired.

"Not at all," said Fraser, before Liz could answer.

"Paul, this is Nick Patterson, head of the special FBI team that's helping to clear up the drug traffic in Miami," said Ted. "Dr. Fraser is Professor of Obstetrics and Gynecology here, Nick."

"You're a welcome sight, Mr. Patterson." Fraser shook hands with the FBI chief after he'd deposited his tray on the table. "Do you know Dr. MacGowan?"

"Hello!" said Liz and turned to Ted. "How's Mike?"

"He came through the operation in good shape, considering that I had to remove the right kidney and pack a wound where the bullet that blasted it raked the liver. I took out another one that penetrated the liver and lodged under the skin of Mike's back. The police have it."

"What are Corazon's chances?" Fraser asked. "A lot of people are depending on him to change things around here."

"Michael's recovery will depend on how well his liver recovers from the shock and damage done by two of the four bullets that hit him. I didn't think it was wise to do too much exploring."

"*Nolle nocere*—do no harm—is still the first law of medicine and, I believe, part of the Hippocratic Oath," Fraser agreed.

"Have you talked to the family?" Liz asked Ted.

"Yes. All three brothers' blood matched Mike's and the blood bank took a unit from each of them in case it's needed. They were all pretty exhausted and Mike won't be conscious for several hours, so I sent them home to get some rest."

"How was Arturo?" she asked.

"He's harder hit by all this than anyone else, even Maria. Arturo idolizes Mike."

"I heard on the radio as I was coming down to the cafeteria that Sam Gianno was arrested on a charge of attempted murder," Dr. Fraser told the FBI chief. "I'm glad you acted quickly."

"I'm afraid it was a waste of time to arrest him, though," said Patterson a little wryly. "Since the attempt on Mr. Corazon's life occurred in Dade County, the Metro Police made the arrest. That meant the hearing was before a Dade County judge."

"What bail was set?" Fraser asked.

"A half million, but Gianno's lawyer brought it to the courtroom in a briefcase. He was free within an hour."

"What about the evidence Mike was going to present to the federal grand jury this morning?" Liz asked.

The FBI man shrugged. "It was presented by Mr. Corazon's assistant but not in the way he would have done it. The jury asked for more specific evidence against the two banks but that will only give them more time to hide the laundering transactions on their books or ship the money out of the country. Unfortunately, too, they aren't national banks so we can't get any help from the Federal Comptroller's Office in Atlanta and Washington."

"Mike is the key," Ted agreed. "That's why Sam Gianno was willing to take the chance of assassinating him before the evidence went to the grand jury."

"So where do you stand now?" Fraser asked Patterson.

"On hold, but we still have a few tricks up our sleeve—if we can get Gianno into the hands of federal authorities."

"Doesn't the attempt to assassinate an assistant U.S. district attorney put it into that category?" Liz asked.

"We think it does," said Patterson. "If we can get a federal judge to agree, we'll move in spite of Gianno's making bail in a county court. The trouble is that even when Michael Corazon is well enough to swear to the affidavit, Gianno's lawyers are sure to bring up the fact that he's been under the influence of heavy medication ever since the ambulance got to the scene."

"If J. Edgar Hoover were still running the FBI," said Dr. Fraser, "I'll bet he'd find a way to bring Gianno under federal jurisdiction—or make one."

"I wasn't with the Bureau then but from what I've heard you're probably right, Doctor," Patterson agreed.

"What's keeping you from using the same strategy today?" Ted asked.

"Congress!" Patterson's tone was suddenly bitter. "Ever since Watergate, senators and representatives have been so busy hogging the spotlights before TV cameras because they know they can make headlines by attacking practically any investigative agency of the government—particularly the FBI and the CIA—that we have to operate most of the time now in the glare of publicity. Before you even make a move like collaring the Sam Giannos of the country with federal warrants, you have to be one hundred percent sure you've got all the law on your side. And even then lawyers for the mob are making fortunes by tying up our investigations with technicalities designed to let their clients go free."

"I doubt if Michael Corazon would be in Critical Care fighting for his life now if so much publicity hadn't been centered on the Drug Enforcement Task Force," Liz commented as she picked up her tray. "Excuse me, please, gentlemen. In a few minutes, my office waiting room will start to fill with patients and I've got a few letters to dictate before I start seeing them."

"And I've got a date with the clinical record computer terminals hunting for the charts of kidney transplant patients whose grafts failed to take," said Ted Bronson.

II

From the Critical Care Center, Ted went to his office, planning to spend the rest of the afternoon and most of the evening in the hospital record room. He had already alerted the director of the record room by telephone to start a computer search for the histories of patients with kidney transplants that had been rejected.

"Dr. Letterman would like to see you as soon as you're free, Dr. Bronson," his secretary told him when he came into the office.

"Did he say what about?"

"Your request for hospital records, I believe."

Ted frowned. "Why would that require a consultation with the chief of staff?"

"I don't know, I'm sure, Doctor."

"I'll go up to see Dr. Letterman right away and do the mail later," Ted told her as he headed for the elevator.

As the special staff elevator whisked him up to the administrative offices atop the hospital tower, Ted pondered the question of why his request for old records could possibly concern the famous surgeon who was the hospital's chief of staff, a largely administrative post in as large a teaching hospital as Biscayne General. As far as Ted knew, though, everything had been going well with the Organ Transplant Service, created for the express purpose of luring him to Miami from Pittsburgh with a promise of virtual *carte blanche* in directing the activities of the department.

"Dr. Letterman's on long distance, Dr. Bronson," the secretary in the luxuriously furnished waiting room outside the chief of staff's office told Ted. "Just go in. He shouldn't be much longer."

Henry Letterman waved Ted to a comfortable chair beside the desk while he continued to talk. When he hung up the phone, he swung around in his chair to face the younger surgeon.

"Glad you're back, Ted," he said in greeting. "Was the seminar worthwhile?"

"More than that. What I learned in Pittsburgh last weekend is going to revolutionize transplant surgery at Biscayne General."

"That's good news. Why don't you report on it at the Surgical CPC on Friday?"

Clinical Pathological Conferences were held frequently for the hospital, medical school staff and students. And since analyzing case histories where complications and death had ensued was an excellent way of teaching all phases of medicine, the conference room was always crowded.

"I'll be glad to. Was that why you asked me to come up, Henry?"

"Not quite. Mrs. Ponder in Records called me just before lunch about your request for the charts of all our kidney transplants that were rejected. Mind telling me what you propose to do with them?"

"I'm going to write letters to the patients whose transplants failed, suggesting that they return to the hospital for check-ups. I can then bring them up to date on recent progress in the field and suggest that they have another transplant."

"Are those to be free examinations?" Letterman asked.

"I hadn't thought about cost. Is that why you object to my doing it?"

"I haven't said I objected, Ted."

"If we can offer new hope to our failures, it would certainly be a good public relations move for the hospital," Ted said pointedly.

"I quite agree. I also think the reexamination should be free, even though the comptroller will no doubt set up a howl because of the expense. By the way, who's going to sign those letters you'll be sending out?"

"I'm afraid I hadn't thought much about that either." Ted was beginning to see why the chief of staff had called him to his office. "I'm only the surgeon of record on the transplants that have been done in the two years since I came to Miami, so perhaps the surgeon of record in each case done before I came should sign the letters to his patients. In fact, he could even do the second transplant if he likes and I'll be glad to assist."

"You're being very magnanimous," Letterman conceded. "Have you talked to any of the other surgeons about this plan?"

"There hasn't been time but I'll be very happy to discuss the whole program at the Friday CPC if you like."

"I'm not sure that would be wise," said Letterman. "Doctors can be pretty touchy where failures in treatment are concerned. Besides, your letters could remind some patients that they'd spent a lot of money in hospital costs and professional fees without benefit. And that could conceivably lead to repercussions in the form of suits for malpractice."

"Thanks for keeping me from putting my foot in my mouth," Ted said sheepishly. "But I still don't see denying patients whose tissues rejected transplants the right to a whole new li—"

"The question of denial is not even pertinent," Letterman interposed. "What does concern me very much is your own future here."

"I'm afraid I don't understand—"

"You're one of the brightest young surgeons who ever joined the faculty of this medical school, Ted. So far you've gotten along fine with the rest of the staff, even though your knowledge and skill as a surgeon obviously exceed that of most of those on the faculty. I'd hate to see you stir up a lot of antagonism this early in your career just because some of the older men became jealous of your ability."

The answer to the problem suddenly took form in Ted's brain. "Why don't you sign the letters as chief of staff representing the entire faculty in the hospital?"

"That could be the answer," Letterman conceded. "But the idea was yours and you should receive the credit."

"Forget about that; it's the welfare of the patients I'm concerned about. Building up my own self-image isn't important compared to helping people get off dialysis."

"Why not go all the way, then?" Letterman suggested. "As soon as you find out how many possible candidates for retransplant are still alive among our old patients, I'll call a press conference and announce the whole plan as a project of Biscayne General and the medical school. That way, you'll not only appeal to our own failures but gain other possible candidates as well."

"I'm with you all the way there."

"There's one more thing I wanted to ask you about," Letterman told him. "I understand that a press conference on Michael Corazon's condition has been scheduled for five o'clock this afternoon. Isn't it a little early to make any kind of a definite prognosis?"

"I didn't want to hold it but Nick Patterson, the FBI team chief, asked for it. He's anxious to put all the heat he can on the man who tried to kill Mike Corazon this morning."

"Does Corazon know who it was?"

"Before we took him up to the operating room, he identified the driver of the car as Sam Gianno—"

"Making himself a target."

"That's the general idea—plus maybe forcing Gianno's hand."

"I don't think much of the idea," Letterman said flatly. "Even the unlikely possibility of an attempt to kill Corazon while he's in the hospital is bound to put personnel here at risk."

"Patterson has Mike under guard in the Critical Care section now."

"Are you to be the spokesman for the hospital at the press conference?"

"That's for you and Administration to decide," Ted told him. "I only took charge of the case this morning because the family called me right after the shooting and asked me to take care of Mike."

"They couldn't have made a better choice; Don Taylor told me about the operation at lunch."

"Thanks for keeping me from going off half-cocked on this retransplant idea and making a lot of people mad." Ted got to his feet. "If you and the chancellor decide against the press conference let me know."

"If we try to keep something like this from the media, there'll be hell to pay," said Letterman. "I'll clear it with Administration so you might as well go ahead and plan what you're going to say."

III

On the way to the record room, Ted stopped at Critical Care to check on Michael Corazon but found no reason for alarm. The patient's blood pressure was stabilized and the heartbeat displayed on the small monitor at the head of his bed, as well as on the larger central bank of monitors at the nursing station outside, was steady and strong. The nurse assigned to Corazon's cubicle in the one-to-one ratio that made the concept of Critical Care so effective in handling seriously ill patients gave him a wry smile.

"The patient's doing fine, Dr. Bronson," she said. "I'm the one who's got the heebie-jeebies."

"Why?"

"How would you like to have two FBI men looking over your shoulder with suspicion at everything you do for a patient?"

"What makes you think they're suspicious?"

"They are, all right! I was connecting the Q-Six-H dose of ampicillin to the IV a little while ago and one of them wouldn't let me start it until he'd checked the label on the little bag of ampicillin against the postop order sheet."

Ted smiled. "In a novel I read recently, a man was killed when a nurse connected the main oxygen supply valve on the wall at the head of his bed to the IV tubing, pumping his circulatory system full of oxygen. Maybe the guard who checked on you had read the book."

In the record room, a large area on the second floor adjoining the medical school library, Ted found the head clerk seated at the keyboard of the computer terminal for the department. She looked up when he came into the room and smiled, a little uncertainly.

"I hope you aren't mad at me because I checked with Dr. Letterman about sending out your letter, Dr. Bronson," she said.

"Actually, I'm grateful," he told her. "You probably saved me from making a lot of staff doctors mad."

"I've seen it happen. That's why I called Dr. Letterman."

"Everything's all right now. He's going to sign them himself."

"I know; he just dictated a draft of the letter that will be going out to every kidney transplant patient in our records."

"Good. Have you found many rejectees yet with the computer?"

"About a dozen so far, but some of them may have died. If we get no answer to a letter we can still find the patients by checking dialysis records with the national computer records in Washington."

"That's being a real medical detective. I wouldn't have thought of going at it that way."

"We do things like that all the time," she told him. "The government pays for a lot of patients on dialysis and you can bet that a computer in Washington has a record of every one."

"Could you pull the hospital charts for a few of the rejects and drop them by my office before you leave early today?" Ted asked. "I have to stay in the hospital until Mr. Corazon is out of danger and I can be familiarizing myself with some of these cases in the meantime."

"I'll leave them on your desk when I go home," she promised. "If this new postop treatment is as successful as Dr. Letterman was telling me you think it is, a lot of people are going to be given a reprieve from death or dialysis, the next thing to it."

Chapter Five

Liz MacGowan was writing a progress note on the chart of the last patient she'd seen that afternoon—a pregnant young mother who had allowed her weight and blood pressure to climb above a safe level, creating the possibility of a dangerous toxemia—when the phone on her desk rang.

"Dr. Fraser is here with a gentleman and would like to see you, Dr. MacGowan," said her secretary.

"I'll come out to meet them."

By the time she crossed the office to open the door, Paul Fraser and an impressive-looking man with the dark skin and hawk-nosed visage of an Arab aristocrat were standing on the other side of it.

"Sheik Almani just arrived from New York, Liz, and I brought him up right away," said Fraser. "Yossuf," he added, turning to the Arab, "this is Dr. Elizabeth MacGowan."

"I'm glad to know you, sir." Liz held out her hand. "By what title shall I call you?"

"My official designation is that of Ambassador to the United Nations from Telfa, Dr. MacGowan." The dark man smiled as they shook hands. "However, I much prefer to be called Sheik Almani."

"I'll have to leave Yossuf in your hands, Liz," said Fraser. "I'm supposed to be at a staff conference right now."

"Please come in and have a seat," said Liz.

"Thank you, Doctor." The Arab was pleasant enough and spoke English with hardly a trace of an accent. Liz found herself wondering why she was somehow repelled by him at their first meeting and decided it must be because he was almost too prepossessing and sure of himself—in spite of the small nation he represented—to be completely believable.

"I understand that you've been in the United States for quite some time," she said.

"Intermittently for twenty-five years; I even picked up a Boston accent during four years at Harvard," said Almani. "It comes in handy in my position as visiting professor at the Johns Hopkins Graduate School of International Studies in Washington. I won't take up your time with small talk," he added briskly. "I believe Dr. Fraser has already told you that Emir Hassim wishes to have Princess Zorah studied here in order to determine the sex of the infant she is carrying."

"Yes," said Liz. "I must admit that I've never treated royalty before—"

"Perhaps I should explain something, Dr. MacGowan." Sheik Almani smiled, showing even white teeth. "Especially since Dr. Fraser warned me that you're rather active in promoting the women's movement for equal rights."

The tone of his voice changed subtly toward the end of the speech and Liz could feel her hackles start to rise. Nevertheless she kept rigid control of her own voice when she said, "I do support passage of the ERA—the Equal Rights Amendment. But I can assure you that will have nothing whatsoever to do with my treating the Queen—"

"Forgive me, Doctor," said Almani, "but 'Queen' is not the term. In Telfa, women chosen by the Emir as consorts retain that title until they bear a male child. Only then are they allowed to assume the title of Queen."

"What happens if they happen to give birth to a girl?" Liz

made no attempt to keep the hint of sarcasm out of her voice. "Are they then cast into the outer darkness?"

Almani smiled somewhat tolerantly. "Please be assured that they retain all the rights a young woman chosen by the Emir should have. They live in the royal household with the status of princesses and their female children are brought up to be quite emancipated. In fact, many of them attend American colleges when they are old enough to acquire more education."

"What if they bear him no children at all?"

"They still have the title and status of a princess and are highly honored. You see, Telfa is not quite as hidebound by tradition and ignorance as you might expect from some of our customs that have come down through the centuries. Sitting as we do atop what is generally regarded as the largest single deposit of crude petroleum in the world, even the common people of Telfa are much better off than in most of the other Arab states. In fact, even the poorest enjoy a higher income than many Americans at what your government calls the poverty level."

"Then the average citizen does profit from the nation's prosperity?"

"Immensely. We have the highest educational level in the Middle East, the highest per capita income and the highest degree of what you might call political freedom."

"Isn't the Emir still an absolute monarch?"

"Not in the sense you've been taught to understand the term," said Almani. "Rather, we boast with some pride of having been ruled for centuries by the most benevolent monarchy in the whole Arab world in the form of the family from which Emir Hassim comes. If a general election were held today in Telfa, I can assure you that all of the votes would go to the Emir except for those of a small group of radicals subsidized by the Soviet Union."

"I'll take your word for it," Liz assured him with a smile.

"Just what does the Emir want me to do when his current—shall we say 'consort'—arrives at Biscayne General?"

"Princess Zorah is being flown to Miami in one of the royal aircraft, with stops for refueling at Dakar, on the west coast of Africa, and Recife, on the eastern coast of Brazil. The estimated time of arrival at Miami International Airport is tomorrow morning about ten o'clock. The Princess will be brought directly to the hospital by limousine from the airport."

"What about the American press?" Liz asked. "A story like this might be called 'mother's milk' for them."

"The press has already been notified that Princess Zorah is visiting the United States in order to keep abreast of modern developments in hospital construction. As it happens, we are in the process of building a new hospital in Telfa and the Princess has a great deal of interest in it."

"Ingenious," Liz admitted. "I gather that I'm supposed to go along with that as the official reason for her visit?"

"To whatever extent is necessary without compromising your own principles," said Almani smoothly. "Princess Zorah will be seen by you in your capacity as an obstetrician. If you decide that it is safe to use amniocentesis to determine the sex of the child she carries, the necessary procedures will be carried out by you at your discretion. If the Princess likes you, a royal invitation will be issued shortly before she comes to term for you to visit Telfa and be present at the royal birth."

"Depending, of course, on whether or not I discover that the royal infant is male?"

"Of course."

"What if I determine that it is not?"

"Then your job is completed and Princess Zorah will return to Telfa and join the other mothers of royal offspring there. I'm hoping you will find otherwise, however, and that you will enjoy a visit to Telfa." The Ambassador got to his feet. "I'm sure you would find the trip quite interesting and rewarding in many ways."

"We have the same hope." Liz, too, rose and held out her hand to the royal Ambassador. "You can understand, I'm sure, that, to use an American phrase, I have to play this hand the way it's dealt to me."

"Of course," the Arab said with a smile. "I've been in the United States long enough to know that a good poker player has no other alternative."

II

Ted had finished the afternoon press conference and was back in his office shortly after five-thirty. His secretary had already left for the day and the door was open, so he had no difficulty seeing Liz MacGowan when she came into the outer office-waiting room. She was carrying a folded newspaper and held it up for him to see the front page. "You made the news," she said. "I thought you might like to see it."

The banner headline above two photos said:

ATTEMPT TO ASSASSINATE MICHAEL CORAZON FAILS
BISCAYNE SURGEON SAVES PROSECUTOR'S LIFE

The story beneath the headline and the photos recounted the dramatic attempt to kill Michael Corazon that morning and also included an account of Gianno's arrest and the bail of a half-million dollars which had been produced immediately, freeing him.

"Did you ever see Sam Gianno in person?" Liz asked.

"No. Did you?"

"Yes—when I delivered his son last year."

Ted gave her a startled look. "Come again?"

"Dr. Fraser was scheduled to deliver Mrs. Gianno but he was out of town when she went into labor. The baby was a boy and quite large. On top of that it was a breech presentation and I had to use forceps on the after-coming head. Fortunately, though, everything turned out all right."

"The Giannos were lucky that you were doing the delivery," Ted told her. "I've heard Paul say more than once that you're the most skilled operator he's ever seen use obstetric forceps."

"The family was grateful. They even wanted to pay me a bonus of ten thousand dollars but I persuaded them to give the hospital a new incubator for the Neonatal ICU instead. I did meet most of the family, though. They're typical Sicilianos and very charming."

"So's a cobra—until it's ready to strike."

"Do you think Mike Corazon can make the charge stick if Gianno is brought to trial on a charge of an assassination attempt?"

"If Mike lives, he might; he can be pretty convincing. Right now, though, I'm more interested in keeping him alive."

"Is that why you're staying in the hospital tonight?"

He frowned. "What are you? A psychic?"

Liz laughed, a rich sound Ted had come to love. "I saw Maria Corazon just now and she told me you were staying here. She was worried about putting you out but I told her you would stay anyway, whether she asked or not."

"Sounds like you know me pretty well."

"Shouldn't I? After what we've been to each other for the past year and a half?"

"And will be for life. Don't forget that."

"I don't know." She smiled teasingly. "The way things are working out, I may get an offer I can't afford to reject."

"Of marriage?"

"No. As chief of service in a new Arabian hospital."

"You never said anything about this before."

"That's because I only learned about it this afternoon." He

listened while she recounted her conversation that morning with Dr. Paul Fraser and later on with Almani.

"That's quite an honor," he said when she finished the account.

"And a responsibility." Her tone was sober. "Even in normal pregnancies, about three percent of women who have amniocentesis, for one reason or another, lose the baby later."

"Doesn't roughly the same number abort, without amniocentesis?"

"Yes."

"Then the procedure can hardly be blamed, if it happens with the Queen."

"She's not a queen—and won't be, unless she bears a son. Since you're going to be tied up here tonight, I think I'll go over to the university library and read up on Telfa."

"When's the mother due to arrive?"

"Some time tomorrow morning. The plane was due to refuel on the West Coast of Africa and again at Recife, Brazil."

"With that schedule, they shouldn't have any trouble," Ted agreed.

But there, as it happened, both of them were wrong.

III

In the doctors' quarters off of the Emergency Room, where the resident staff on duty could snatch a few hours of sleep—if they were lucky—Ted Bronson woke as usual at six-thirty the next morning. He had worked until almost midnight on the stack of kidney transplant charts delivered by the record-room clerk that afternoon. When he took the elevator to the first floor, where the Critical Care section was located, the nursing staff was changing shifts and the area was bustling with white-uniformed women, as well as a number of young men in white, wearing nameplates with the designation RN— proof that more and more men were choosing nursing as a well-paid and rewarding occupation.

In the Critical Care section, Ted found Michael Corazon asleep. The vital signs recorded during the night were good, however, and he did not awaken the injured man. Since it was only a little after seven o'clock he decided to go to his apartment in Biscayne Terrace where he could shave, shower and change before coming back to start the duties of the day. When he stepped outside the hospital itself, however, he could hardly distinguish the huge, sprawling apartment house across the street, so heavy was the fog that had developed during the night—a not unusual happening on the shores of Biscayne Bay in springtime. Even the traffic light at the corner where he crossed the boulevard shone with an almost ghostly glow and he felt a distinct sense of relief when he reached the other side.

He was putting on a clean shirt, after a quick shave and shower, when the phone rang.

"Yossuf Almani just called me from the airport." Liz's voice was tense. "The plane from Telfa tried to land in the fog but crashed on the runway. The pilot and co-pilot were killed."

"What about Princess Zorah?"

"She's alive, according to Almani, but badly injured; an ambulance is bringing her to Biscayne General. Can you meet me in the Emergency Room and help evaluate her condition —other than the pregnancy?"

"Of course. Where are you now?"

"In the ER. We're expecting the ambulance at any moment."

"I'll be there in five minutes. Is Ed Thomas on duty?"

"Yes."

"He'll know what to do about the Princess' general condition until I get there and you can certainly take care of the pregnancy and the baby better than either of us could. If she's badly injured you might even have to do a Caesarean section."

"I doubt that the fetus would survive at twenty weeks gestation," Liz demurred.

"We'll decide that when you see her. I'll be there right away."

An ambulance, sirens screaming and lights blinking, pulled into the loading platform of the Emergency Room as Ted was crossing the street in the early morning traffic. When he reached the ramp leading to the Emergency Room, he saw a tall, striking-looking dark-skinned man get out of a limousine that had pulled in behind it and move toward the platform.

Inside, Mrs. Burke, the nursing supervisor in the Emergency Room, was directing the Rescue Squad technicians as they wheeled the stretcher bearing the injured woman into one of several brightly lighted cubicles. Liz moved across the room to meet Ted, while the technicians and nurses, under the skillful direction of the Emergency Room resident, Dr. Thomas, were transferring the injured woman to a hospital gurney. Her head, Ted noted, was swathed with a heavy pressure bandage and, as he moved toward the gurney, he saw the resident pick up a flashlight and study the patient's pupillary reflex, an accurate indicator of conditions inside the skulls of patients suffering severe head injuries.

"Her pupils are fixed," Thomas reported. "The left is larger than the right."

"She hasn't moved since we took her out of the plane," one of the Rescue Squad paramedics volunteered. "I had to put the pressure dressing on to control bleeding from a deep scalp wound."

"How about the pulse and respiration?" Ted asked.

"The pulse was bounding but strong when we picked her up," the technician reported. "The blood pressure was a hundred and fifty over eighty a few minutes ago, but her respiratory rate has been slowing gradually ever since we left the airport."

The injured woman had been in the Emergency Room less than five minutes but in that brief period three very important observations had been made and Ted Bronson didn't need to be told their significance. One, the scalp wound was severe enough to require a pressure dressing to control hemorrhage. Two, fixed and dilated pupils had been noted, a picture that could very well indicate a severe brain injury, since blood pouring from an artery damaged by a skull fracture and rigidly contained by the bony case in which the brain lay could dangerously compress the soft but vital brain tissue. Most important of all, the decrease in the injured woman's respiratory rate almost certainly indicated a rising intracranial pressure from hemorrhage which could cause death quickly from pressure on vital centers—unless drastic measures were taken immediately to release the pressure.

"Get the neurology resident down here," Ted told the Emergency Room house officer. "The head injury is the most important problem for the moment."

Liz had been listening with her stethoscope over the prominent mound that was the frail-looking, injured woman's abdomen. When she lifted her head and removed the ear pieces of the stethoscope, he asked, "How about the fetus?"

"Its heartbeat is good and there's no bleeding from the vagina so I guess there's no danger of an immediate onset of premature labor," she reported. "The rate is a little fast, but the fetus was bound to have been shaken up considerably during the crash. How about the Princess?"

"She appears to be developing an extradural hematoma. With the blood pressure rising and her respiratory rate slowing, Ned Pierce will probably need to put some burr holes in the skull pretty soon to see what's going on inside it. In fact, if Ned doesn't get here soon, I'm going to put them in myself."

"I knew I could depend on you to handle the extraobstetrical emergencies," she said gratefully. "Meanwhile, I'd better talk to Sheik Almani if I can find him."

"I'm pretty sure I saw him arriving by limousine as I came into the ER. He's probably in the waiting room."

Dr. Thomas had cut the pressure bandage around Princess Zorah's head, revealing a laceration of the scalp in the left temple region about six inches long. Pulling on a sterile rubber glove from a tray Mrs. Burke had wheeled into place, he explored the scalp wound gently with his index finger.

"She's got a depressed fracture in the left temple area, Dr. Bronson," the younger doctor reported. "The bleeding that's knocking down the respiratory rate must be coming from that area."

Ted was moving toward the wall telephone at the nurses' station while listening to Thomas' report. Picking up the phone, he dialed zero and, when the operator answered, said, "Please see if Dr. Ned Pierce is still at home."

"This is Ted Bronson, Norma," he said when a woman's voice answered. "Is Ned there?"

"He's on his way to the hospital, Ted, and should be there any minute. What's wrong?"

"A plane from Arabia just crashed at the airport—"

"It was on the kitchen TV just now; the woman they took out of the plane appeared to be still alive. The reporter on the scene said she's the pregnant wife of Emir Hassim of Telfa. Is the baby okay?"

"Liz says so. I'm taking Princess Zorah down to Radiology. Ned's probably going to have to operate as soon as he gets here."

"I hope they both survive."

The telephone clicked as Ted pushed down the receiver and dialed the operator once again.

"When Dr. Ned Pierce comes in, please ask him to come to X ray," he said.

As Ted hung up the phone, he saw Liz MacGowan moving

toward him with the tall man he'd seen get out of the limousine just behind the ambulances.

"Sheik Yossuf Almani, Dr. Bronson," she said. "The Ambassador was waiting at the airport for Princess Zorah when the airplane crashed."

"This is quite a tragedy, Ambassador Almani," Ted said as he shook hands with the Arab.

"It's terrible, Doctor! Can you tell me anything about the Princess?"

"Only that she has a severe head injury with a depressed fracture of the skull and what appears to be some hemorrhage around the brain. Dr. Ned Pierce, our chief neurosurgeon, is on his way here now and I'm sure he'll have to operate immediately. Do you have the authority to sign a permit for emergency surgery on the Princess?"

"I'll do it and get the official permission later," said Almani crisply. "I've already got a call in to Telfa."

"Good!"

"Dr. MacGowan tells me the baby appears to be in good condition," Almani added. "I don't have to tell you that everything must be done to protect both Princess Zorah and the child."

"Sheik Almani thinks Princess Zorah is about twenty weeks into the pregnancy," Liz volunteered. "That's too early for a Caesarean section to offer much hope of saving the unborn child."

"Right now our main concern has to be with the mother and the head injury," said Ted. "What will happen to the pregnancy can be determined later."

"If the child is a boy, it is very important that it be kept alive," said Almani pointedly.

"It is very important to us as physicians that the fetus be saved no matter what the sex." Ted's voice had taken on a sharp, incisive note.

Yossuf Almani was not cowed by Ted's tone. "I quite understand the question of medical ethics involved in a situation such as this, Dr. Bronson. Nevertheless, a male offspring would ensure the line of succession for the Elzama family and, in Telfa, that fact could take precedence over any other consideration."

"You're not in Telfa now, Mr. Almani," Liz said firmly.

"Of course, Doctor. When I reach Emir Hassim by telephone today, I will tell him that every effort will be made to save both mother and child. Let us hope the need to distinguish between the welfare of one and that of the other will not arise."

Chapter Six

Dr. Ned Pierce came into the X-ray viewing room just as the first films of Princess Zorah's skull were coming out of the developer. Short, bald and with a small paunch, Pierce was not the ideal neurosurgeon envisioned by the public, yet was an acknowledged authority in the field of head injuries.

"What's going on, Ted?" he asked. "The operator said I was to hustle down here as soon as I arrived."

"I couldn't be happier to see anybody right now than I am you, Ned," Ted assured the neurosurgeon. "Princess Zorah is one of the wives of the Emir of Telfa, a small state in the Middle East that apparently floats on oil. She's pregnant and was being flown here in one of the royal aircraft so Liz MacGowan could determine by amniocentesis whether she's bearing a male heir to that emirate. The aircraft was destroyed when it crashed less than an hour ago while trying to land in that fog outside. Everybody aboard was killed except the Princess and the fetus."

"I heard about the crash on the car radio," said Ned Pierce crisply. "What else can you tell me about her?"

"Obviously, she has a depressed fracture of the skull and very probably a large extradural hematoma that's pressing on the brain. Liz says the fetus is doing okay but there's a complication there, too."

"If I ever have a patient again who's got a simple condition that I can cut and cure, I'll probably die of surprise." Ned Pierce was studying the X rays displayed on a panel of ground-glass screens in the viewing room. "What is it this time?"

"Princess Zorah is about five months pregnant and Emir Hassim of Telfa badly wants a male heir. Even if you save the mother but lose the baby and it turns out at autopsy to be a male, there's going to be hell to pay."

"Why not let Liz deliver the baby by Caesarean now?" Ned Pierce asked. "I've seen her operate and she could get the whole thing over with in ten minutes, leaving me plenty of time to find where the middle meningeal artery has probably been torn and put a metal clip on it."

"At this point Liz isn't even sure the baby is far enough along to survive life outside the uterus."

"The hell you say! In that case, it comes down to deciding who's more important—the mother or the child. In my opinion, there's no option—the mother comes first."

"I'm not denying that and neither is Liz," Ted told the neurosurgeon. "But you don't need second sight to realize that, in the mind of the father, Emir Hassim—and who knows, perhaps even in world history—the welfare of a male child who would be heir to one of the oldest thrones in the Middle East is paramount."

II

"Had your breakfast?" Ted asked Liz while Princess Zorah was being transferred from the X-ray table to the gurney that would take her to one of the upper floors devoted to operative surgery. With a competent neurosurgeon now in charge, their responsibility where Princess Zorah was concerned was temporarily in abeyance.

"No."

"Me neither. Let's grab a bite while Ned is getting ready to start the subtemporal decompression."

In the hospital cafeteria they selected Danish pastries and coffee and found a table in the corner of the doctors' dining room.

"Did you get any sleep last night?" Liz asked.

"I did after midnight. I worked on old hospital kidney transplant records until then."

"Find anything promising?"

"More than I'd even hoped for. I've already selected a dozen patients whose first and even second kidney transplants failed."

"Do you think you can convince them to undergo another operation?"

"I'll probably need my strongest powers of persuasion. But, if I were tethered to a dialysis machine, I'd jump at the chance to be whole again."

"How is Mike this morning?" Liz asked as she began to cut up a hot Danish pastry with her fork.

"His condition is surprisingly good—for twenty-four hours after major surgery. The hematocrit's still down but I've ordered another transfusion that should bring it up pretty quickly. Mike was a crack miler in track in college and Estrellita Mendoza told me he still runs six miles at least five days a week so he's got a good foundation of physical condition to build on."

"There's Arturo Corazon in the cafeteria line!" Liz exclaimed. "What would he be doing here this early—and alone?"

"I don't know," Ted conceded. "After I looked in on Mike this morning, I called Maria and told her he was doing even better than I had expected. . . . Mind if I bring Arturo over? He'll probably feel better in the company of friends."

"Bring him by all means. I didn't know the family let him go wherever he wants to go."

"Arturo did so well at the special school the family sent him to that, when he finished, Mike gave him a motorbike. He doesn't ride fast and he's never had an accident, so they let him go pretty much wherever he wants to go."

Ted crossed the cafeteria to the cashier's desk, where Arturo Corazon was just paying his tab.

"Come eat with Dr. MacGowan and myself, Brother," he said, using the affectionate nickname given the youngest Corazon by his family. "We're over here in the corner."

Arturo's round face broke into a pleased smile and his eyes shone with pleasure at the invitation. Carrying his tray, he followed Ted to the table where Liz was sitting.

"Good morning, Dr. MacGowan." Like most Down's Syndrome victims, Arturo's voice was somewhat overloud, especially when he was excited, as he obviously was now, and the words tended to run into each other. "Bet you can't guess why I'm here?"

"I give up," Liz told him with a smile.

"The hospital blood bank called me at home about an hour ago. They said my blood matched Michael's and that Dr. Ted here had ordered another transfusion this morning. Mama and my brothers hadn't had breakfast yet so I came right over on my motorbike."

"Have you already given the blood?" Liz asked.

"They took it a few minutes ago. It didn't hurt a bit! And they told me to eat a good breakfast to make up for losing the blood."

"You certainly obeyed orders. If I ate that much, I'd have to be on a diet the rest of the week."

"I was hungry." Arturo began to tackle a truly gargantuan meal consisting of two eggs, two pancakes, a double order of bacon, two glasses of milk and two glasses of orange juice.

"Besides, being able to help Michael made me happy and I always eat a lot when I'm happy."

"I think it's wonderful that you gave your blood to help save your brother's life," Liz told him.

"Do you really think it will?" Arturo asked eagerly.

"I'm certain it will."

"So am I," Ted Bronson agreed.

"That makes me feel good! Real good! After we got home last night, I went out to cut some flowers to bring to Michael's room this morning. A big moccasin was in one of the flower beds, must have come down the canal from the Everglades. But I stopped him right there with my rifle," he added on a strong note of pride.

"I'm glad it wasn't me that found a snake in your flower bed," said Liz. "I'm scared to death of snakes."

"I wasn't scared of this one," Arturo boasted, with his mouth half filled by hot cakes and bacon. "I just got my .22 and shot him in the head. That's the last time he'll get in my flower bed."

"I wish we could say the same about the man who shot your brother," Ted told him. "But human snakes are hard to destroy."

"When I pulled the trigger of the rifle last night, I told myself I was shooting the bad man that tried to kill Michael," Arturo confided. "If I could, I'd blow his head off, just like I did the snake's."

"The FBI will still get him," said Ted.

"I sure hope you're right, Dr. Ted, but just the same, I oiled the .22 yesterday. If Sam Gianno ever shows his face around my gardens, I'm going to shoot him just like I did the moccasin last night."

III

"We're monitoring the fetus and it seems to be okay," Dr.
Ned Pierce assured Ted and Liz, who were watching the operation on Princess Zorah from the glass-enclosed gallery overlooking OR 1. "I wish I could say as much for the mother,"
he added. "She obviously took a hard blow to the temple bone
to depress that section so deeply and I'm sure we're going to
find a lot of hemorrhage underneath, along with a good deal
of surface damage from contrecoup."

Neither of the two doctors needed an interpretation of the
word. In severe head injuries, the brain was not only bruised
beneath the area of the cranium where force was applied directly to the surface but was also driven against the opposite
side of the skull. This force, known as contrecoup, often
caused a contusion that could be as severe as the one in the
area where the original force had been applied.

"If the mother's head injury is fatal, Dr. MacGowan," one
of the medical students who now almost packed the gallery
asked, "do you think you're going to be able to save the fetus
by Caesarean section?"

"The *Lex Caesaris* says I must try." Liz named a law,
largely unwritten but sometimes appearing upon the statutes,
demanding that, when a mother died while a viable fetus was
in her uterus, surgery must be performed by anyone available
to remove the child and try to save its life. "Saving a baby as
early as the twentieth week is sometimes difficult, though,"
she added. "So let's be optimistic and hope the mother lives,
too."

"Is she really a princess?" a young woman student asked.

"So I'm told," said Liz. "Princess Zorah was being brought

here for amniocentesis in order to determine the sex of the fetus."

"I'm going to remove the depressed bone fragment," Dr. Pierce's voice came from the loudspeaker.

Through the glass wall of the gallery, the observers watched while he slipped a periosteal elevator—an instrument with a strong resemblance to a screwdriver—under the edge of the bone in one of the burr-shaped openings he had made by drilling away part of the skull along the fracture line itself. Nothing happened for a moment, then the observers heard a distinct crack and saw the fragment of bone that had been pressing upon the brain being lifted.

"We're obviously dealing with a large extradural hematoma." The neurosurgeon's voice was suddenly terse when a flow of dark blood appeared from beneath the bone fragment. "Evidently there's a tear in a blood vessel, usually the middle meningeal artery." As he spoke, Dr. Pierce reached for a heavy instrument called a rongeur. Its jaws mounted in a double-hinged fashion so as to transmit tremendous power to the biting end of the tool itself, the rongeur was capable of chopping off a finger or, more important, biting away sections of the skull.

Through the glass wall of the observation post, Liz and Ted could hear the crunch of the rongeur biting through the skull fragment pressing upon the brain. Moments later, the surgeon removed a section of the skull, roughly the size of a man's palm, discarding the bone. When he did so, the outer membrane—the dura mater—covering the brain came into view. In it the course of the middle meningeal artery could be seen, forming a treelike, branching pattern as it divided into many smaller channels.

"There's the laceration!" Pierce suddenly reached into the pool of blood filling the bony defect he had just created in the skull and pressed his finger against the small tear in the artery wall, staying the flow.

"Hemostat!"

When the instrument came into the surgeon's hand, he lifted his finger quickly and exposed the tear in the vital artery. Blood spurted in a tiny stream but he was able to clamp the artery with the hemostat, shutting off the flow. Two ligatures, above and below the tear in the artery, controlled the flow of blood and the surgeon began to remove the accumulation of blood clots against the brain with a suction tip. As he did so, the patient's pulse rate on the monitor declined steadily, while the respirations approached the normal rate.

"I'm going to remove all the clots I can toward the base of the brain stem with suction," Pierce explained to the gallery. "But since I can't get it all, I'll leave a rubber tissue drain in the wound when we close."

Picking up the microphone in the gallery by which it was possible to communicate with the surgeon below, Ted asked, "Could you look at the surface of the cortex, Ned?"

"I intend to," Pierce assured him.

Only a few minutes were required to open the dura mater over the immediate brain surface in a space large enough to see a portion of the convoluted brain cortex directly under the skull wound. Even those in the gallery could see from the appearance of the brain that the outlook was indeed grave. Normally white, its surface was quite dark from many small hemorrhages.

"If I were to expose the opposite side of the brain I'm sure it would look equally bad from contrecoup injury," Pierce commented as he placed a strip of rubber tissue deep into the space formerly occupied by the clots he had been able to remove. "The prognosis here is very poor, even with the improvement in respiration and heart rate from relief of pressure under the fracture."

IV

Sheik Yossuf Almani was waiting in Liz's office when she reached it, after reporting briefly to the newspaper and TV reporters waiting in the Lobby for news of Princess Zorah's injuries after the dramatic crash.

"I'm afraid I don't have very hopeful news for you, Mr. Ambassador," Liz greeted the tall, distinguished-looking Arab. "Princess Zorah suffered a severe head injury during the airplane crash with a depressed fracture of the skull and a large extradural hematoma. That's . . ."

"I'm familiar with the term, Dr. MacGowan," he said on a note of impatience. "Please go on."

Liz forced herself to be calm in spite of her irritation at his tone. "The hemorrhage has been controlled," she continued, "but the cerebral cortex was severely injured at the site of the skull fracture and almost certainly on the other side, too, by what is known medically as contrecoup. Dr. Pierce estimates her chances of recovery at considerably less than fifty-fifty."

"And the child—or fetus, as you call it?"

"We see no sign that it is in any danger."

"Wonderful!" Almani sounded genuinely pleased. "I'll tell Emir Hassim that, when I call him tonight. May I also tell him that you will remove the fetus by Caesarean section—"

"There is no indication for a Caesarean at the moment," Liz said firmly. "We have one of the finest neonatal intensive care units in the country here at Biscayne General but the fetus is still far better off within its mother's body than outside it. I intend to leave it there as long as possible."

"But you said Princess Zorah will almost certainly die," Almani protested. "Surely you wouldn't let the child die with the mother."

"Of course not, but as long as the mother's circulation is bringing oxygen to the fetus, there's no need to interfere surgically."

Yossuf Almani shook his head in apparent bewilderment. "The whole purpose in bringing Princess Zorah here was to discover whether she carries within her womb the legal heir to the throne of Telfa, Doctor. Plans were even made before she left Telfa for the appointment of a regent to ensure the rights of the infant, if it is a male. This child must live—"

"I have every intention of giving it the best possible chance to live, Mr. Almani." Liz's tone had become sharp. "Just as I would any other patient under my care."

"But if Princess Zorah dies—"

An idea popped into Liz's brain and she voiced it before Almani could go on: "Would you perhaps be the Regent of whom you spoke?"

"I am honored that Emir Hassim has enough confidence in my loyalty to him and to Telfa to consider me as guardian of a possible successor." Almani's tone was rough with anger. "Your insinuations—"

"Perhaps I owe you an apology," Liz admitted. "I remember now that Dr. Fraser said Emir Hassim is terminally ill."

"With leukemia," Almani confirmed. "For the past six months a famous Swiss hematologist has been living in the palace while giving the Emir injections of a powerful drug used in chemotherapy. For a while it seemed that the disease had gone into remission again, but within the past two weeks the state of the Emir's health has declined rapidly. In fact, Dr. Eckstein has informed the family that he doesn't expect him to live out the month."

"Oh, I'm sorry," said Liz sincerely.

"Perhaps you can understand now why determining the sex of the child Princess Zorah is bearing is so important. And why your delivering a live baby is essential, too. Why couldn't you accomplish both ends by immediate operation?"

"We could determine its sex, of course, if I removed it from its mother's body by section," Liz conceded, "but only by placing the life of the child at risk."

"I don't see why."

"Prematurely born infants are at considerably more risk outside the mother's body, largely because their lungs are not fully developed. Even when special ventilators are used to give them oxygen there is often difficulty in getting the oxygen through the lining membranes of the lungs and into the pulmonary circulation."

"I persuaded Emir Hassim to let me bring Princess Zorah to you so you could determine the child's sex by amniocentesis. Can't you still do that?"

"Amniocentesis takes only a few minutes," said Liz, "but the fluid we remove from the amnion—the sac in which the fetus develops—still has to be cultured for several weeks. During this period new cells develop from those shed from the fetal skin into the fluid. The final diagnosis is made by studying them under the microscope."

"Two weeks is far too long, Dr. MacGowan," Almani protested. "If Emir Hassim should die in the interval, a political vacuum—so to speak—could occur in Telfa, with enough factions vying for control to create a situation resembling anarchy. Is there no other way to determine whether a male heir to the throne exists?"

"We might try one other procedure—ultrasound."

"I know the term, Doctor. But how do you use it?"

"The technique is really quite simple. High-frequency sound waves are bounced off the fetus in the uterus and the image produced is photographed. Actually, I now use ultrasound when inserting the amniocentesis needle so I can see exactly where to place it. If the fetus is far enough developed, we can sometimes even see the genitalia themselves and determine its sex immediately."

"When can you do it, Dr. MacGowan?" Almani demanded eagerly.

"Perhaps as early as tomorrow afternoon, if the condition of Princess Zorah permits."

"Please proceed then," said Almani. "I will sign whatever forms you need before performing the procedure."

Chapter Seven

Liz's office telephone rang as she was about to ask her secretary to send in her first patient for the afternoon office hours. The voice in the receiver, when she picked it up, was masculine and very brisk.

"Dr. MacGowan?" the man asked.

"Yes."

"This is Steven Longaker at the State Department in Washington. I believe Princess Zorah from Telfa is a patient of yours in the hospital there."

"She is."

"The Ambassador from Telfa to the United Nations, Sheik Yossuf Almani, telephoned the Secretary a few minutes ago, but he was out of town and I took the call. The Ambassador says the Princess and her unborn child are dying in the hospital there. Is that true?"

"The Princess is gravely ill from a head injury sustained when her plane crashed," said Liz. "We expect brain death probably by tomorrow, but the fetus is very much alive and I expect to keep it that way."

"In an incubator, Doctor?"

"With our advanced life-support system we can keep a body functioning by keeping up respiration and heart action long after brain death occurs, Mr. Longaker. The best possible incubator for the fetus is the body of the mother and I plan to use it for that purpose."

"For how long, Doctor?"

"The latest reported case was, I believe, sixty-four days, but we have no idea that the fetus in this case will need to remain in the uterus much more than two weeks."

"Isn't even that period hazardous, Doctor?"

"No more hazardous than bringing it into the world before it has developed to where it can live without serious complications. I thought Ambassador Almani understood the situation."

"The Ambassador is in a rather difficult position," the man from the State Department explained. "Our Ambassador to Telfa has been in touch with the doctor who has been treating Emir Hassim for leukemia. The Emir is very ill and his physician says he may not last another week."

"I don't see how the illness of Emir Hassim could possibly justify my putting the life of the child at risk by doing an early Caesarean, Mr. Longaker."

"The situation is a very delicate one, Doctor. Emir Hassim has apparently told Ambassador Almani that, if the child the Princess bears is male, he will be appointed regent, making him practically the ruler of Telfa."

"He told me that, too," said Liz, "but I don't see why that should make any difference. In fact, I would think Sheik Almani would be even more anxious to see that the fetus has the best possible chance of survival."

"Politics in the oil kingdoms is always uncertain, Dr. Mac-Gowan," said Longaker. "No doubt there would be objections by some factions in Telfa to a takeover of the government by Ambassador Almani as regent. Frankly, Doctor, he is probably the most able man in Telfa, but far from being the most popular. And with Soviet and Iranian agents everywhere, an attempt to take over the present government without tangible proof of an heir to the throne might throw the Emirate of Telfa into turmoil."

"But it's such a small place, Mr. Longaker. Why are you so concerned?"

"Telfa is one of America's largest sources of crude oil, and its government is the friendliest to us of any on the Arabian peninsula. The country has been ruled for centuries by a family that treats its subjects well. For example, the per capita income of the people of Telfa is next only to the people of Kuwait, thanks to the policies of Emir Hassim and his family. The death of the Emir without a named successor and a strong government such as exists now—and which would no doubt continue with Sheik Almani as the regent representing the heir to the throne—could be very important to the stability of many other small countries on the Arabian peninsula, to say nothing of the price of oil. So you can see why this situation is very important to the United States."

"Are you telling me the future of an entire country may very well rest on whether the fetus Princess Zorah is carrying is male or female?"

"You said it better than I could, Dr. MacGowan."

"As a physician, the sex of the fetus is far less important to me than its life, Mr. Longaker."

"Granted," said the State Department official. "But under the law in Telfa, and almost anywhere else in the world, an unborn child is not a person. Even if the child is still in its mother's body, but known to be a male, Sheik Almani could take control in its name as Regent. His claim would be much stronger, however, if the child is a male and was already born."

"Are you asking me to put the life of the fetus Princess Zorah is carrying at risk by delivering it before I think it would be safe in even the most sophisticated incubators like the ones we have here, Mr. Longaker?"

"Certainly not, Doctor. But Sheik Almani tells me you could determine the sex of the baby."

"That's true," Liz conceded, "but there are certain dangers there, too. The least dangerous is by use of ultrasound, which we are satisfied now carries practically no danger to the fetus. The second is through amniocentesis, which, unfortunately, requires about fourteen to twenty-one days for the fluid removed from around the fetus itself to be cultured in order to provide growing cells. These can then be studied under the electron microscope to determine the presence or absence of the chromosome that determines sex."

"Which procedure would you prefer to do in this period of the pregnancy, Doctor?" Longaker asked.

"Unquestionably ultrasound first, hoping the fetus has developed far enough for us to identify the external genital organs."

"And the next?"

"Amniocentesis, but as I have warned you, even that requires at least two to three weeks before a final diagnosis can be made and Sheik Almani objects strongly to the delay."

"We do need a much earlier determination, Doctor," said Longaker.

"And one you're not going to get, unless I'm lucky enough to identify the fetal genitalia with ultrasound," Liz said flatly.

"We will abide by your decision, of course, Doctor, but please keep in mind that Ambassador Almani has served his country and its ruling family faithfully and well. The United States Government would be very pleased to have him in Telfa as a stabilizing force, whether in the official capacity as Regent—or some other."

"I'll keep you posted, Mr. Longaker," Liz promised and hung up the telephone.

11

At the moment that Liz concluded her conversation with the State Department representative, Ted Bronson was at the nursing station for the Critical Care section of the hospital studying the reports on the specimens of blood drawn that morning by laboratory technicians from Michael Corazon for chemical analysis. What he saw was in no way reassuring, however. Although the patient's temperature curve had been trending down under the influence of a powerful antibiotic, the blood chemistry reports were still going in the wrong direction.

While Ted was leafing through the sheaf of reports from the central laboratory, the chief of the Medical Service, Dr. Matthew Arnold, whom he had asked to see Michael Corazon, came into the small room back of the nursing station where red dictation phones were located so the doctors could immediately dictate notes after examining the patients on the floor.

"Glad to see you, Ted," said Arnold. "I examined your prize patient a few minutes ago and was going to call you."

"Did you see the latest blood chemistry reports?"

"No."

"Here they are." Ted handed the consultant the sheaf of reports and the head of the Medical Service leafed through them briefly before handing them back.

"There's nothing here I wouldn't expect from my own examination a few minutes ago. The alkaline phosphatase, serum bilirubin and transaminase are all elevated more sharply than you would expect from simple trauma to the liver from bullet wounds. So's the creatinine and I don't have to tell you what that elevated blood urea nitrogen level means."

"Impending liver failure." Ted's voice was grim. "The worst thing that could happen right now."

"I agree," said Dr. Arnold. "After being shot up like it was, I'd expect the liver to show some diminution in function for the first twenty-four hours but it ought to be coming back by now."

"And a lot farther than it has," Ted agreed. "I'll order the chemistry repeated tonight and we can see what those reports show in the morning. Do you have any other suggestions?"

"Are you sure the bleeding has stopped in the middle of the liver where that bullet penetrated?"

"Not entirely. I'm going to do a nuclear magnetic resonance scan on him in the morning to see what it looks like."

"Let me know when you start it and I'll try to get down there to see what it shows. That NMR machine is still a mystery to me."

"Good," Ted told him. "And thanks for seeing him this afternoon, Matt."

"Don't mention it," said Arnold. "I still think prosecutors like Mike Corazon are the only chance we have to make Miami a decent place to live in once again. Good night. If you need me I'll be at home."

III

Ted Bronson had finished seeing the patients who had been waiting in his office and was considering going to the hospital record room to continue for the rest of the afternoon his search of possible candidates for a second kidney transplantation when his secretary told him Estrellita Mendoza was waiting to see him. Going to the door leading to the outer office, he opened it and ushered her into the office.

"I'm glad you came," he told her. "Have you seen Michael this afternoon?"

"I just came from Critical Care. He's not doing very well, is he, Ted?"

"Not as well as I would like, but there's no real reason to be concerned too much yet. There was bound to be considerable reaction from the insult those bullets gave to his body."

"I had 'mono' when I was in college," said Estrellita, "so I'm quite familiar with the yellow tint of jaundice in the white part of the eyes. Mike is showing jaundice, too, isn't he?"

"Yes."

"What could that mean?"

"That his liver is not performing its functions and bile is being absorbed into the bloodstream," he told her. "We had proof of that in the elevation of the serum bilirubin in this morning's blood chemistry report."

"What if it continues to rise?"

"We'll fight that complication when, as, and if we come to it," he told her. "Right now I'm doing everything I know how to do."

"The family and I know we can count on you to do that," she assured him.

"Did you know Arturo gave blood for a transfusion for Michael?"

"Yes. He called me at the office shortly after they took the blood. He was very excited and happy about having been able to help Michael." She smiled. "And was talking so loud into the telephone that it almost ruptured my eardrums."

IV

When she finished talking to the man from the State Department, Liz dialed the office of Dr. Moses Harris in the Genetics Research Laboratory.

"I want you to solve a problem for me, Moe," she said.

"So? Just name it."

Liz gave the genetics specialist a quick summary of the sex determination question as far as Princess Zorah and the fetus she was carrying was concerned.

"You're an expert on amniocentesis, Liz, and I at least pass for one in genetics, so we shouldn't have any problem determining the sex of this fetus," said Harris. "What's worrying you?"

"Both the State Department and Ambassador Almani would like to know the result yesterday."

"So they're putting the heat on you; the clinicians do that to me all the time. What else is new?"

"The problem is I'm wondering just what we might be able to do to hasten the diagnosis here," Liz confessed. "If Emir Hassim is dying, it would be a tremendous boost for him to know he had fathered a son to perpetuate the dynasty that has ruled in Telfa for centuries."

"You'll think of something," Moe Harris assured her. "Just call on me if you need any help."

Chapter Eight

The stream of visitors to the Emergency Room of Biscayne General slacked off around four-thirty. Most of the "walk-ins" to whom the ER was the family doctor were seen by the first-year residents, giving them valuable experience in preparation for the day when they would start practice on their own or be employed in an established clinic. The rush of accident cases, both major and minor, produced by the five o'clock exodus of downtown office workers hurrying to homes in the suburbs had not yet begun so the Emergency Room staff, both nurses and doctors, were taking a breather.

The three-to-eleven nurse supervisor had been delayed by a dental appointment so Mrs. Burke, the gray-haired day supervisor, had stayed on after three waiting for the other nurse to come on duty. She was somewhat startled when a beefy man with a long scar on his face walked in, complaining of a headache.

Ushering the patient into one of the now mostly empty curtained-off cubicles, Mrs. Burke called Dr. Ed Thomas, the chief resident, knowing that a headache could possibly mean a sudden rise in blood pressure and an impending stroke. To her surprise, as she was directing the patient to sit on an examining table, she saw another man, almost the same size and build, come in and heard him tell one of the nurses that he, too, had a headache. As she turned to look at him, her foot struck a low stool next to the table, forcing her to grab the patient's shoulder for support. When she did so, she felt the unmistakable bulge of a pistol in a shoulder holster.

"Damn it, nurse, look what you're doing!" the man snapped angrily.

"Sorry, sir, the floor's slick." Pretending to be flustered, she turned to Dr. Thomas, who was entering the cubicle. "Things seem to be under control here," she said. "I think I'll take a short break now before the five-thirty rush."

"Go ahead," said the resident with a smile. "Bring me a cup of java when you come back—black with two sugars."

"Right." Heading for the door to the loading platform, the nurse dashed through another door nearby that led to the supply room. Seizing the first phone she saw, she rang the hospital operator.

"Do you have a phone in Critical Care assigned to the FBI detail guarding Mr. Corazon?" she asked the operator.

"Why, yes, Mabel."

"Ring it, please—and keep on until someone answers."

"What's up?" the operator asked. "You sound sort of tense."

"Never mind. Just ring that phone."

"Security detail," a firm, masculine voice answered on the first ring. "Patterson speaking."

"This is Mrs. Burke from the Emergency Room, Mr. Patterson," she said rapidly. "I think an attempt is about to be made against Mr. Corazon."

"Where are you?"

"In the supply room. I ducked out of the Emergency Room when I realized that a couple of patients who just came in complaining of headaches look like thugs. One of them is wearing a pistol in a shoulder holster, too."

"What were they doing when you left your station, Mrs. Burke?" Patterson's voice was suddenly tense.

"Dr. Thomas was taking the first one's blood pressure. The other came in as I was leaving but he's wearing a coat and his chest looked mighty broad to me so he may have a pistol, too."

"Don't go back to the Emergency Room."

"If they start shooting, my nurses, Dr. Thomas and a couple of students could be hurt."

"We'll protect them," Patterson assured her. "Obviously, if an attempt is to be made, it will be through the double doors between the Emergency Room and Critical Care."

"That's what I figured. I hope there isn't any shooting."

"The two men guarding the door from your department are carrying mace units," he told her. "They'll know what to do, but please stay where you are."

In the Emergency Room, the situation suddenly changed dramatically when the two men Mrs. Burke had warned the FBI chief about reached into their shoulder holsters and removed heavy automatic pistols.

"All you hospital people lie down on the floor and you won't get hurt," the one with the scar, obviously the leader, commanded.

Startled, all of them obeyed except one student. When he protested, he was promptly slugged by the second gunman.

"That door leads to the Critical Care ward where Corazon is, doesn't it?" the leader demanded of Dr. Ed Thomas, who was lying on the floor.

Thomas nodded, too surprised by the sudden turn of events to speak.

"We're going in there to get Corazon and we're coming back this way," the leader told those on the floor. "Stay down and you won't get hurt, but anybody that tries to stop us will stop a bullet instead."

In the Critical Care section Nick Patterson had ordered the two FBI agents guarding the door from the Emergency Room to move to positions on either side of the door. Each was now holding a pistol in his right hand and a chemical defense weapon, ordinarily known as mace, in the left.

When the two thugs charged through the double doors from the Emergency Room moments later, neither got a chance to fire the weapons they were carrying before the chemicals in the mace containers struck them full in the eyes, blinding them with a stream of the gaseous irritant. Crying out from pain, the gunmen promptly forgot any intention to use the pistols they were carrying; in a few seconds, the FBI agents had tackled them, throwing them to the floor and jerking their arms behind their backs where handcuffs were applied.

"What's happening?" Michael Corazon asked sleepily from the other side of the room, awakened by the cries of pain from the unwanted visitors.

"Sam Gianno sent some thugs disguised as Emergency Room patients to finish you off," Nick Patterson told him. "I'm pretty sure I recognize one of them as a hood from the Jersey mob who's on the FBI wanted list."

"Sounds like you were on the ball, Nick."

"You can thank the chief nurse in the Emergency Room," said the FBI agent. "If she hadn't suspected something was afoot when those two thugs walked in with minor complaints and she discovered that the leader was wearing a gun, there would have been a real battle when they rushed my men guarding the door."

"Was anybody hurt?" Michael asked.

"Only your would-be assassins," said Nick Patterson grimly. "And they'll have plenty of time in jail to recover."

Ted Bronson and Erasmus Brown, the hospital administrator, arrived on the Critical Care ward just as four Metro police officers were taking the still half-blinded thugs out to a squad car.

"What happened?" Ted asked.

"Sam Gianno must have decided he might as well finish up

the job of destroying the evidence against him and the bankers by killing your patient here on the ward."

"How did you know they were coming?"

"We didn't, until Mrs. Burke got suspicious of two walk-in patients complaining of headaches and slipped out of the Emergency Room to warn us. When the hoods came through the door, we were waiting for them with everything but the kitchen sink." Patterson's voice sobered. "We've got to move Mr. Corazon where we can guard him better, Dr. Bronson. I've been worried about this setup ever since he was brought back from the operating room."

"I agree," said Ted soberly.

"I'll authorize the use of one of those VIP suites on the tenth floor," said Erasmus Brown.

Dr. Peter Craig, the chief anesthesiologist, who was also in charge of the Critical Care department, had come into the room, too.

"Can you set up all the monitors we need up on the tenth floor, Peter?" Ted asked.

"I'm already getting one room on that floor equipped with monitors to follow the condition of the Arab princess who's a patient of Dr. MacGowan and Dr. Pierce. We're using monitors for both mother and fetus, so we can certainly get another set up to watch Mr. Corazon's vital signs."

Nick Patterson glanced at his watch. "The Metro Police downtown will be processing those thugs we just captured," he said. "If we can put enough pressure on them before Sam Gianno's lawyer can get a writ of habeas corpus from one of the local judges he's got on the payroll and spring them out on bail, we might get enough evidence together to justify arresting Gianno again."

"I'll second that," Michael Corazon said from his bed. "With another 'conspiracy to murder' charge against Gianno maybe you can convince a federal judge to hold him without bail."

II

Liz MacGowan was on the way from what was known as the VIP floor—because it was made up of luxury suites of two rooms each—to which Princess Zorah had been transferred from the operating room when she met Dr. Ned Pierce at the elevator.

"Any change in your prognosis, Ned?" she asked the neurosurgeon.

"The continuous electroencephalogram I ordered has shown a very poor picture of brain activity all afternoon, I'm afraid," he said.

"That's something you really can't do much about either, can you?"

"If the degree of contusion on the opposite side caused by the contrecoup injury is anything like what we could see when we opened the dura mater to examine it, she's almost certain to end up as a zombie—or a sleeping beauty. She must have been a real stunner."

"Emir Hassim seems to have had good taste in consorts," Liz agreed dryly. "The afternoon paper has some pictures of his other wives and most of them look like movie stars. Even so, none of them has managed to produce a male heir for him —unless he's inside Princess Zorah's uterus. Moe Harris and I hope to determine the sex of the fetus pretty soon, though."

"By amniocentesis?"

"Plus ultrasound, but I won't try either until you feel that it's safe as far as she's concerned."

"In your hands, Liz, puncturing the uterus for amniotic fluid couldn't possibly be much more of a strain on the patient than putting a needle in for an IV. Do it whenever you want to."

"Then we'll try tomorrow morning."

"I hope it's a boy and you can save it," said Pierce as the door to the elevator opened and he stepped inside. "Then maybe His Royal Highness will give some of his oil billions to endow a few scholarships for the Medical School."

III

Ted Bronson called Liz in her office shortly after five. Her secretary had left for the day but she was dictating some letters to be typed by the night stenographic pool from the cassettes in the tape recorder on her desk, ready for her to sign after making rounds.

"After the past two days and that near shoot-out this afternoon in the Critical Care section, I feel the need of something to calm my nerves before dinner," he told her. "How about joining me in the Dolphin Lounge?"

"Can you give me fifteen minutes? I still need to dictate two more letters so they can go out tomorrow morning."

"Sure. I'll gnaw on a dish of peanuts until you get there."

When Liz came in, Ted was at the bar of the popular lounge located adjacent to the hospital at the corner of the block, chatting with the bartender.

"I reserved that corner booth," he told her. "Bourbon and ginger okay?"

"Sounds good."

"I'll bring them over."

By the time Liz had settled in the booth, Ted came across the room balancing their drinks and a dish of pretzels on a tray held high in one hand. The room wasn't crowded yet with the evening rush of students, house staff and nurses, so several booths were empty besides the one where she was sitting. Handling the tray dexterously, he set it down on the table and handed her one glass before sliding into the booth close enough for his thigh to touch hers under the table.

"Glad to see I can still handle a tray," he said. "I earned spending money in medical school working in a beer joint down the street from the hospital. You look bushed but still beautiful. Been a rough day, hasn't it?"

"Yes, but mainly I'm worried about Princess Zorah. Ned Pierce isn't too optimistic about her prognosis."

"He told me she had one of the largest extradural hematomas he'd ever seen. It's always hard to get all the clot out from under the base of the brain where it can damage the major centers."

"The cerebral cortex was badly contused, too."

"Is the baby okay?"

"It was when I stopped to check the monitor on the way over here. How's Michael Corazon?"

"Conscious briefly between medication but he's getting a little jaundiced."

"Liver acting up?"

"*Not* acting is more like it; I'd be a lot happier if the bile produced by the liver cells was being poured into the small intestine where it's supposed to go instead of absorbed into his bloodstream." Ted's tone changed and became studiedly casual: "Have you talked with Sheik Almani in the past couple of hours?"

"No." Liz gave him a probing look. "Why do you ask?"

"Henry Letterman called me a little while ago. He'd just come from a conference with Almani in Erasmus Brown's office."

Liz didn't need to be told the possible significance of such a conference. As provost for medical affairs for the university, as well as chief administrator of the hospital, Brown occupied a very important position in the elaborate and complicated hierarchy of management characterizing most university hospitals and medical schools.

"Henry was on his way out of the hospital but he knew I would see that you were warned."

"Warned—?"

"Apparently, Almani is concerned about what will happen to Princess Zorah's baby."

"So am I, but for a different reason. I want to keep that fetus alive where it is now until it can be delivered by Caesarean section with the best possible chance of surviving."

"Why would Almani want anything else?"

"From what he says, Emir Hassim of Telfa is dying of leukemia and is very anxious to know whether or not he'll have a male heir to the throne—if that's what emirs sit on."

"That certainly is a natural concern."

"Of course, and I'm going to do everything I can to give him his wish," said Liz. "But Almani is pushing me to determine the sex of the fetus, even if I have to endanger its life by an immediate Caesarean section."

"Ned Pierce mentioned that the mother is probably near brain death. Why would Almani be putting pressure on you to remove it, then?"

"Apparently, the law in Telfa says a fetus isn't a separate individual until it's born, by whatever means," Liz explained. "From what Almani told me, Emir Hassim is going to make him Regent for the child, if it's a male. So the sooner the sex of the fetus is determined and it's delivered from the mother's body, the sooner Almani will be in the driver's seat to become the real ruler of Telfa when the Emir dies."

Ted whistled softly. "It looks like you're on the hot seat, darling. Can I do anything to cool down the situation?"

"Nothing but back me up. I'd rather lean on you than anybody I know."

"Now you're talking. If I can get you to lean on me enough, maybe you'll decide to make it permanent—and soon." He glanced at his watch. "I'd better grab a sandwich at the bar and run. I'm due for an interview on the educational TV channel at seven o'clock."

"About Michael?"

"The interview was scheduled weeks ago to talk about expanding the organ bank here at Biscayne General. But with so much having happened in the past twenty-four hours, I'm sure the question of Mike's being attacked will come up."

"I'm staying in the hospital tonight to be near Princess Zorah in case there's a sudden change in the EEG pattern and brain death occurs," Liz told him. "I'll watch you on TV in the doctors' lounge."

IV

At one minute before eight, Liz MacGowan settled on the sofa in the doctors' lounge facing the television set and switched the channels to the Miami educational television station. Ted had left for the ETV studios forty-five minutes earlier because of the heavy traffic on the Palmetto Parkway around Miami. From the credits to those corporations whose grants had made the program possible, the picture on the screen switched to a young blonde whose split skirt managed to afford the viewer an occasional glimpse of a shapely knee and lower thigh.

"Good evening and welcome to 'Here's to Your Health,'" she announced. "I'm Gwen Jones and tonight my guest is Dr. Theodore Bronson, Chief of the Organ Transplant Service at Biscayne General Hospital and Associate Professor of Surgery in the Medical School. Dr. Bronson, welcome to 'Here's to Your Health.'"

The camera switched to Ted, who looked a little self-conscious. "Thank you, Miss Jones," he said. "It's nice to be here."

"For starters, Dr. Bronson," said the interviewer, "suppose you give us a quick rundown on your professional preparation for the important post you now hold at Biscayne General."

"I studied premed at Harvard and received both my undergraduate degree and M.D. there. My hospital residency was in General and vascular surgery."

"Were you specializing in organ transplant during your residency, Dr. Bronson?"

"Not specifically, although as chief resident during my last two years, I assisted in a number of transplant operations. It was through them that I became intrigued with the problems of organ transplant today."

"Were you performing heart transplants?"

"By that time, most of the enthusiasm for heart transplants generated by Dr. Christiaan Barnard's first successful operation in South Africa had waned because of the unhappy experience of most transplant surgeons with organ rejection by the recipient. Only one group in California was doing very many successful heart transplants at that time, but for every heart operation that made the headlines even then, many more kidneys were being transplanted successfully. These saved the lives of people who would otherwise have been doomed to live a somewhat precarious life on kidney dialysis—or die."

"We visited a dialysis center once on 'Here's to Your Health,'" said Gwen Jones. "I don't remember seeing very many people there."

"The prospect of spending the rest of one's life tethered, so to speak, to a dialysis machine after both kidneys fail or a transplant has been rejected by the body is exceedingly depressing," Ted agreed. "Just today I received a letter from the mother of a young man upon whom I did a kidney transplant shortly after I came to Miami nearly two years ago. The transplant failed but, if you don't mind, I'd like to read the letter."

"Is it personal, Doctor?"

"It is, but I telephoned the writer late this afternoon and

she gave me permission to read it on the air because she believes this letter may help others to seek help rather than end their lives."

"In that case, please read it."

Ted began to read:

"Dear Dr. Bronson,

Your letter inviting my son, David, to come back to Biscayne General for a checkup and possibly a try at another kidney transplant with the new technique you describe came this morning—three days too late because we buried David just three days ago after he committed suicide. David did well for a year after you performed the transplant but then the new kidney began to fail. Several months ago he had to go back on dialysis but from the start he hated it and the bitter disappointment of having to return to it, I suppose, was too much for him to bear.

"Before the kidney failed, David had been able to return to college here at home. He was taking a premed course but once the transplant began to fail he realized that he would never be able to go to medical school. I'm sure he would have made a wonderful doctor, especially because he would have drawn upon his own experience with suffering and depression both before and after you did the transplant as he treated others. I pray that other kidney patients will receive your letters in time so you can use the new treatment on them and I will keep you and the great work you are doing in my prayers.

Sincerely,
Louise Worthington"

"What a pity!" Gwen Jones' voice was husky with emotion. "Do you remember David Worthington, Dr. Bronson?"

"Very well. He was one of the first kidney transplants I did when I came to Miami, a fine-looking college kid with an excellent mind and the eagerness to learn that a would-be doctor must have to succeed."

"Is suicide very frequent after transplant?"

"More often than you might think," said Ted. "A recent report in the Journal of the AMA last week cited a study of two hundred cases in Denver over a period of about two years. Fifty-four of them died within the study period, eight from suicide."

"Why, Dr. Bronson? I would think someone who'd had a successful transplant would be overcome with joy."

"We're talking about past experience, Miss Jones. As recently as a year ago, receiving a new kidney—or any other organ—meant taking large doses of several powerful drugs to suppress the resistance of the body's immune system to tissue that is not its own."

"For how long, Doctor?"

"Usually for life. Unfortunately, the same drugs that help prevent rejection also depress the natural immunity-producing forces in the body. As a result, the patient has little, if any, resistance to infection by ordinary bacteria which the body normally throws off easily. Most patients who die after transplant—whether heart, kidney, liver or even pancreas—do so because of infection."

"You're painting a rather disheartening picture, Dr. Bronson," said Gwen Jones. "If the picture is so bad, why would a highly trained surgeon like yourself choose the field of organ transplant?"

"Medicine—and surgery in particular—is a constantly challenging profession, Miss Jones—and nowhere more than was the case in organ transplant."

"I see that you are using the past tense, Dr. Bronson. Is that because any dramatic breakthrough has occurred in your field? Perhaps even one you hesitate to mention because of the well-known suspicion of the medical profession where new ideas are concerned?"

"Tonight, Miss Jones, I can assure you that a real breakthrough in the technique and the results of organ transplant in humans has already occurred. Briefly, a new drug called cyclosporin is literally revolutionizing the technique—and the results—of organ transplant. Using cyclosporin, along with small doses of the powerful steroids already in use, it will soon be possible to double the chances for life of a person receiving a transplant of almost any body organ."

"In your own experience, Dr. Bronson, which organ presents the most difficulty in carrying out successful transplant surgery?"

"Unquestionably the liver."

"But even that is still quite possible, isn't it? The newspapers are full of pleas for liver donors every day."

"And reports of successful operations," Ted agreed. "When we expand the organ bank at Biscayne General, I'm sure we will find many opportunities to save lives by liver transplant."

"One final question, Doctor, since we're about out of time. Is liver transplant suitable only for those very small children I've been reading so much about in the papers and watching stories about on television?"

"Not at all. In fact, I have an adult in his mid-thirties who may very well need one sometime in the next week or ten days in order to save his life."

"From what source, Doctor?"

"A gunshot wound."

"Let's hope you find a donor when the time comes," said Gwen Jones in closing. "With Miami seemingly in the race to become the murder capital of the country, the odds on success would seem to be good."

"I'm praying that they are," said Ted fervently, as the camera switched from him and Gwen Jones to the list of program credits.

"I didn't ask on the air"—Gwen Jones was unclipping the small microphone from Ted's necktie—"but the patient you mentioned just now must be Michael Corazon."

"Yes. But I'd rather you didn't—"

"We'll not mention his name, especially now when the pressure on you must be very great. But if the need for a donor in the Corazon case arises, you can be assured that those of us in television will be happy to help you in any way we can."

v

It was nine-thirty when Ted Bronson tapped on Liz Mac-Gowan's door in Biscayne Terrace. She had told him she was staying at the hospital but he got off the elevator on the off chance that she had decided to come home. When she opened the door, she was wearing a negligee over her night-gown and bedroom slippers on her feet.

"I was hoping you'd stop by for a nightcap," she told him. "Let me fix it; you look like you need one."

"Did you watch the broadcast?"

"Yes." She handed him a glass and a napkin.

"How did you think it went?"

"Very well. Gwen Jones is a very pretty young woman."

"I didn't notice. She kept me busy answering questions."

"Don't tell me you didn't even realize how high her skirt was split. I know you too well for you to get away with that."

"Well . . ."

"I'm glad you read the letter from Mrs. Worthington," she added. "It should convince anyone who's on dialysis that they should come to the hospital immediately for an evaluation."

"I'm hoping it will have that effect."

"There's one thing I wish you *had* mentioned, though."

"The possibility that Michael Corazon might need a liver transplant?"

"Yes."

"I didn't because I think my doing it might upset the family a great deal."

"Surely anyone familiar with his case—and that means practically everyone at Biscayne General—must know by now that the possibility of needing a transplant exists. That's not really what is worrying me, though."

"What's that?"

"If the people who already tried twice to kill Mike Corazon heard your broadcast tonight—and somebody's bound to tell them about it even if they didn't—they're going to realize that you are as much of a threat to them now as he is."

"How do you figure that?"

"Do you know any other surgeon here in Miami who has done a liver transplant?"

"Well . . . no, they're not exactly everyday affairs, particularly in adults."

"If Sam Gianno's crowd becomes convinced that Michael Corazon will die unless you find a donor and do a liver transplant, they could very well decide that with you out of the way, their worries are over."

Chapter Nine

Proof that Liz MacGowan wasn't the only one concerned over Ted's mention of a possible liver transplant during the broadcast came early the next morning. He was having a quick breakfast in the hospital coffee shop on the first floor when he saw Nick Patterson come in and join the serving line. When the FBI agent had paid for his selection, he came over to where Ted was sitting.

"Mind if I join you?" Patterson asked.

"Not at all. Have a seat."

"I was going to call you this morning after you saw Michael Corazon," the FBI agent said as he placed his tray on the table. "He's dying slowly from his liver wounds, isn't he?"

Ted studied the coffee grounds in the bottom of his cup briefly, as if hoping to find an answer to the immediate question there but didn't. "Both Dr. Arnold, the medical consultant, and I feel that Michael's liver is failing," he agreed. "Which means the only thing that could possibly save him is a transplant."

"You intimated that in your TV interview last night."

"I seem to have put my foot in my mouth that time," Ted admitted wryly. "I didn't think many people would jump to the conclusion that I was talking about Michael Corazon, but apparently they did. The young lady who was doing the interview mentioned it immediately afterward, and when I stopped by Dr. MacGowan's apartment later, she said the same thing."

"You practically invited Gianno to make a try at keeping you from doing a transplant," Patterson said bluntly. "From now on, we're going to have to guard two people instead of one."

"I'm sorry, Nick. I was so anxious to get people whose kidney transplants have failed to come in and let us do another operation that I guess I just wasn't thinking."

"The girl who interviewed you was clever," Nick Patterson assured him. "She practically led you to making a public admission that Mike is dying."

"And I swallowed the bait, hook, line and sinker."

"Don't feel bad about it," said the FBI team chief. "Letting doctors in the emergency rooms of hospitals in the whole South Florida area covered by that station know you may very well need the liver from a healthy young man or woman who dies from an accident soon should increase considerably the chances of your finding a donor before Mike is in such bad shape that even a transplant can't save him."

"There's still a chance that his liver may start doing its job of removing toxic wastes from the body again," said Ted. "Until I'm sure he's beyond that point, I couldn't really recommend a transplant anyway."

"Pray God you don't shave it too close, Dr. Bronson," said the FBI agent. "If you do, a year's work will probably go for nothing, besides the state and the country losing one of its most promising prosecutors."

"If I did operate too soon and the transplant failed, it would be tantamount to murder."

"But one you certainly couldn't be punished for."

"Except by my own surgical conscience. And that would be the worst punishment of all."

11

Liz MacGowan finished the operation she had scheduled that morning by ten o'clock and started rounds on the VIP floor. When she went to the nursing station, she found Dr. Ned Pierce dictating a note to the stenographic pool by way of the red telephone in the small doctors' office behind it.

"I tried to call you after I saw your prize patient a little bit ago, Liz," he said, hanging up the phone.

"I was in surgery."

"So the operator told me. I wanted to ask whether you would object to my ordering a bedside isotope angiogram on the Princess." Isotope angiography was a relatively sophisticated technique in which harmless radioactive elements were injected into the bloodstream. Their path through the body, particularly their concentration in certain organs, could then be studied by means of ultrasensitive electronic instruments.

"What are you looking for?" Liz asked.

"Her brain-wave pattern has been flat on the EEG monitors for the past several hours, so I'm almost certain that brain death has already occurred. I'd like to have it down as a matter of record."

"Her circulatory and respiratory systems seemed to be holding up pretty well when I examined her just now. And the fetal heart seems okay, too. Do you have any particular reason for doing the cerebral angiogram right away, Ned?" Liz was careful to keep her voice on a casual note, which far from reflected her own feelings.

"Well . . . nothing, except that I'd like to have the record complete . . ." Pierce's somewhat evasive answer confirmed Liz's suspicion that he wasn't giving her the whole reason.

Before she could speak, however, he slammed the chart from which he had been dictating down angrily.

"Damn it, Liz! I could never be an actor so I shouldn't try to fool you. The truth is that Henry Letterman called me this morning and asked me to order the angiogram."

"Did he say why?"

"Something about the State Department wanting to know the exact condition of Princess Zorah."

"What about the fetus?" Liz's voice had suddenly taken on a sharp note.

"Henry didn't say anything about the pregnancy. Besides, you know I wouldn't go barging into that area; it's your exclusive field."

"I'm glad somebody is convinced of that."

"Now, Liz." Pierce was red in the face and obviously flustered. "You know I wouldn't go behind your back—"

"Forgive me, Ned," she said. "It's just that I'm up to my ears with the State Department, Sheik Almani and the Emir of Telfa."

"If you don't want the angiogram done, I won't order it," Pierce offered.

"No, go ahead. If brain death has finally occurred, I want to know it as much as anyone else does. Jerry Rubin and Peter Craig need to know it, too, so the full Advanced Life Support Team will be on the alert."

"Why would the State Department be so concerned about the condition of the Princess anyway, when they know she's probably going to die from her injuries?"

"It's Almani who's got a case of the ants. Emir Hassim is dying of leukemia and, if the fetus is male, Almani thinks he will become Regent when Hassim dies. That's the nearest thing to being the sole ruler of Telfa I can imagine. If I know Almani, he'll manage to seize full control of the country and the revenues from one of the largest pools of oil in the Middle East."

"When can you determine the sex of the fetus?"

"I plan to examine the Princess' uterus today with ultra-sound in the hope of seeing the fetal genitalia clearly enough to determine its sex. If I can't, I'll go ahead with amniocentesis and get some fluid for Moe Harris to examine, but that means at least two weeks delay while the cell culture from the fluid grows. And I'm sure neither Almani nor the State Department will be very happy about that."

"How long do you plan to keep her on life support?"

"Until I'm sure I can deliver a viable baby by Caesarean section. That could be several weeks, depending on what measurements of the fetus we're able to do with ultrasound. With luck, they'll tell us the exact stage of development."

Down the hall from where the two doctors were standing opposite the chart desk, an elevator opened and two technicians from the Nuclear Medicine department emerged. They were guiding a large motor-driven machine on rubber-tired wheels and were followed by a tall young doctor in a long white coat.

"There's Tim Donovan with the camera oscilloscope now," said Ned Pierce. "We should have the answer to the question of brain death in a little while."

"I think I'll stay and watch," said Liz. "We don't do this sort of thing every day in my department."

"I've got to run now," said Pierce. "Will you call me when Tim can give us a report?"

"Sure. And thanks, Ned, for telling me about Henry Letterman's request."

III

Nick Patterson had been right, Ted saw when he came into Michael Corazon's room shortly after talking to the FBI agent at breakfast. The stark figures of the blood chemistry reports indicated a significant rise in by-products of normal body metabolism that could poison the whole system if they were not detoxified by the liver. Moreover, his patient's condition was even less encouraging.

Though he was sleeping from a hypodermic of Demerol recorded in the nurse's notes as having been given about five that morning for abdominal pain, the monitors recording respiration, pulse rate, EKG and blood oxygen levels were now all in the abnormal range. Even more significant was the lowered output of urine from the remaining kidney, an indication of decreased blood flow through the organ because of lowered efficiency of the circulatory system, no doubt produced by general body toxicity.

The abdominal wound had stopped draining and seemed to be healing normally. But when Ted lifted one of the sick man's eyelids, he saw that the yellow tint of the scleras—the white part of the eyeball—had deepened considerably since yesterday, a precise indication of further absorption of bile into the bloodstream from damaged liver cells.

Stimulated by the light shining in his left eye, Michael Corazon opened his eyes and tried to smile.

"Hi, Ted!" he mumbled. "Am I as bad off as I feel?"

"Depends on how bad you feel."

"Lousy! Everything looks foggy, too. Is that from the hypo I had earlier this morning?"

"Probably. Where was the pain then?"

"In here." Corazon moved his right hand—the left was held down by the strapping holding in place an intravenous needle through which a solution of glucose and saline was being dripped into a vein, along with an antibiotic solution from a plastic bag hanging from the same pole.

"The hypo took the pain away," said Corazon. "Would cocaine have done that if you were using it instead of Demerol?"

"Probably. Why do you ask?"

"I'm beginning to understand how some people who've had a long illness could get hooked on drugs."

"A few patients do but not very many; most start using the stuff for kicks."

"Nick Patterson told me last night that the case against Sam Gianno and the bankers who loaned the money for the drug peddlers is on hold until I'm able to testify against them."

"So you've got to hurry and get well," Ted told him on as cheerful a note as he was able to muster.

"*Am* I going to get well?"

"Of course." Ted hoped his voice was more reassuring than his convictions. "When you absorb as much lead in a few seconds as you did, it takes a little more time to get over the effects."

"How long, Ted? Be honest with me, please; it's pretty important that I know what to expect."

"I honestly don't know, Mike. Right now, your liver is still dragging its feet but the turnaround could come any day."

"Let's hope so. My being sick is especially hard on Mama and Brother; we've always been very close."

"Arturo is very proud that we used his blood for one of your transfusions. He keeps asking when he can give you more."

"Brother would give his life for me. I know that."

I V

Inside Princess Zorah's room, Liz watched from the foot of the bed while the technicians and Dr. Timothy Donovan, who headed the Department of Nuclear Medicine, maneuvered a huge camera into a position directly over the Princess' head and neck. It was hard even for Liz to believe the frail woman in the bed was legally dead, even if the test about to be performed showed that blood was no longer flowing through the arteries leading to her brain. Assisted by the ventilator, her respirations were regular and the EKG pattern moving across the monitor screen at the head of the bed was steady, although a little faster than normal.

When Dr. Timothy Donovan and his technicians had taken over, Jerry Rubin came over to where Liz was standing at the foot of the bed.

"You've had more experience with advanced life-support techniques than I have, Jerry," she told the tall young pediatric resident who was also head of one of the two advanced life-support teams in the hospital. "How long do you think we can keep heart action going?"

"The longest I've seen a patient survive—if you can call it that, once brain death occurs—on advanced life support is about three weeks."

"Who finally decided to pull the plug and let that patient die?" Liz asked.

"The family, thank God. By that time, I was beginning to feel a little like God and I'm sure that's a dangerous conviction for any doctor to develop."

"Did respirations go first after the plug was pulled?"

"Yes. The EKG pattern on the monitor was still strong for another five minutes, then it started to fade. Watching it slowly decrease as the heart muscle finally ran out of oxygen because it wasn't getting any from the lungs really shook me up. Particularly when I knew giving it oxygen would let it go much longer and I could have changed that by simply turning a valve."

"I can understand how you must have felt."

"When we have to pull the plug in this case, I hope you won't mind doing it, Dr. MacGowan," said Jerry. "The Princess must have been lovely when she was really alive, and I'll feel like a murderer if I have to stop the electric currents going to all the motors we use in the advanced life-support technique."

"I'm responsible for your keeping her technically alive for the baby's sake," Liz told him. "It's only fair that I take the final step when it has to be done."

At the head of the bed, Dr. Donovan was adjusting a heavy rubber band around the patient's head just above her eyes and ears.

"Why do you do that, Tim?" Liz asked.

"If you remember your anatomy, Dr. MacGowan, the external carotid artery comes off the common carotid below the lower jaw and supplies mainly the face and scalp. When the blood pressure is being maintained so well by advanced life support as it is in this case, there'd probably be some circulation through the external carotid, even if the brain itself isn't getting blood any longer. This rubber band acts as a tourniquet to stop blood flow outside the skull that might give us a false picture of what's happening to the brain itself inside it."

"Ingenious," said Jerry Rubin. "What next, Tim?"

"We're going to inject some Technetium Tc 99 in serum albumin as a bolus into an arm vein. The camera will pick up the radiation from the Technetium as it goes through the heart and is sent toward the arterial circulation of the brain."

"How long does that take?"

"We'll take serial images with the camera every three seconds for one minute to give us a picture of the entire brain circulation." Donovan moved to where one of the technicians was exposing the Princess' lower arm. Removing the sterile cover from the tray upon which lay a syringe and needle with the solution for injection, he prepared them both. Meanwhile, the technician tightened the tourniquet around the frail arm of the patient above the elbow, causing a vein in front of it to swell.

"Ready?" Donovan asked the other technician, who was manipulating the controls for the camera.

"Whenever you are, Dr. Donovan."

"Watch the monitor of the camera," Donovan told Liz and Jerry. "You'll see the flow of blood through the arteries to the brain, but if brain death has already occurred, it shouldn't go any farther than the base of the skull."

Deftly, Donovan injected the radionuclide into the patient's vein. Almost immediately a pattern appeared on the monitor screen of the camera as blood was pumped out of the left side of the heart and started flowing toward the brain. It went only a short distance, however, then suddenly failed to progress.

"You can see that circulation to the brain itself has ceased," Donovan told them.

"Fantastic!" said Jerry Rubin.

"We're photographing the images you're watching with the camera for the record, but the diagnosis is beyond doubt," Donovan assured them. "Brain death has already occurred."

"She's the responsibility of you and Peter Craig from now on, Jerry," said Liz. "I know you won't fail me."

v

The late morning conference in Ted Bronson's office on Michael Corazon's condition was not characterized by a cheerful note. Present were Dr. Matthew Arnold, chief of the Medical Service, Ted Bronson and Dr. Henry Letterman, chief of staff for the hospital representing the doctors from all of the combined services. For the benefit of Letterman, who was not necessarily familiar with the details of the case, Ted made a rapid summary of Michael Corazon's progress—or, rather, lack of it—since the assassination attempt.

When he finished, Dr. Arnold added, "We're obviously dealing with developing liver failure here. The increased levels of alkaline phosphate, bilirubin, creatinine and serum trans-aminase, plus the clinical symptoms of increasing jaundice, all indicate that Corazon is dying slowly because his liver appears to be damaged beyond repair."

"But why?" Letterman asked. "The hemorrhage into the liver itself seems to have ceased following Ted's surgery."

"I don't have the answer," Ted was forced to admit.

"What about the damage from the bullet you took from beneath the skin of Corazon's back?" Letterman inquired. "Apparently it penetrated the liver completely and such wounds ordinarily are not fatal."

"I don't know," Ted admitted frankly, then his face bright-ened. "But there's a way to find out."

"How?"

"Nuclear magnetic resonance; I don't know why I didn't think of it before. If there's a spreading hematoma inside the liver itself, we ought to be able to see it clearly with that examination."

"Then by all means do it," said Letterman.

"I'll call the laboratory right away," said Ted. "This is enough of an emergency to justify scheduling it as quickly as possible."

In the viewing room of the Biomedical Analysis Laboratory, Dr. Harvey Chung and Ted Bronson watched a technician cross the room carrying the films containing images of Michael Corazon's abdomen, centered upon the liver. Shortly before, Corazon had been transferred to a movable stretcher before a huge machine whose heart was a giant doughnut-shaped magnet. The center opening was large enough for the body to be rolled inside the ring by pushing the trolley upon which he lay into the desired position for the particular part of the body being studied.

When the technician placed the films upon the brightly lit viewing screen, several cross sections of Michael Corazon's body were visible. In them, the liver, amounting to more than half of the abdominal contents at that level, was sharply delineated—and obviously not normal.

"I know this picture is supposed to be produced when the nuclei of chemical elements inside the body are lined up by the magnetic field into a parallel position, then kicked into a quarter turn by a shift of the magnetic field," Ted Bronson admitted. "And then, when that shift is released, an image is produced and the computer accentuates it. But I'd still rather think it's magic."

"Scientific magic—and damned expensive," said Chung. "This particular gadget costs over a million dollars and they're building better and more expensive ones every day that are going to make it obsolete in a few years."

"If nuclear magnetic resonance can tell what's going on inside the body and save putting patients through what we used to call exploratory surgery, just to see what's going on inside his belly or chest, then it's worth every nickel of it," said Ted.

"I agree." Picking up a pointer from the counter before which they were sitting, Chung used the end of it to delineate the outline of the liver on the films. Many of the organ's larger blood vessels were actually shown in different colors, since each element involved in the magnetic effect produced its own characteristic image.

"Something's going on inside that organ, something that's pretty big," said the biomedical expert. "My guess would be that it's also pretty dangerous to what is left of the normal liver, after those two bullets went tearing into it."

"The center of the liver is much darker than the rest," Chung added, "so a considerable amount of blood has probably accumulated in that dark area, mixed with bile produced by whatever cells are still able to function."

"The bullet that went entirely through the liver must have damaged some branches of the hepatic artery, causing enough hemorrhage to close off small branches of the duct system carrying bile to the common duct and the gall bladder on the way to the small intestine," said Ted.

"That sounds reasonable," Chung agreed, "especially since the gall bladder isn't at all distended. Which must mean that a certain amount of the normal production of bile is leaking back into that hematoma in the center of the liver."

"I guess that leaves me no choice except to see if I can remove the pressure against the bile ducts by aspirating blood from that hematoma and hopefully decreasing some of the jaundice Mike is showing." Ted rose from the stool where he'd been sitting. "Pray for me, Harvey. I'm going to need a lot of help and I'll accept it from any source that's willing to provide it."

Chapter Ten

"You've got a visitor," Liz's secretary told her when she returned to her office after watching the angiogram that had made the diagnosis of brain death for Princess Zorah beyond question.

"Almani?"

"Yes. You don't have any other appointments this afternoon, though, so you can sneak out without seeing him if you'd like. I'm pretty good at telling lies."

"Thanks, Lillian. Until Princess Zorah's case is settled, Sheik Almani is going to be my cross, so I might as well bear it."

"Good afternoon, Dr. MacGowan." Almani rose when Liz entered. "I apologize for intruding but I understand that Princess Zorah is near death and—"

Liz gave him a startled look. "How did you learn that?" she asked.

"In hospitals, what I believe you call the 'grapevine' is faster"—Almani produced a half-smile—"than, shall we say, a speeding bullet?"

"I've never known it to be quite that fast, Mr. Almani," Liz said on a somewhat frosty note, "but I won't quibble. The angiogram Dr. Pierce ordered this morning after pressure on him by Dr. Letterman, at the request of the Department of State and no doubt yourself . . ."

Almani shrugged. "I am required to remain in contact with them, Doctor."

"Of course. Well, getting back to what we were saying, the angiogram did establish the validity of a diagnosis of brain death. Before I explain the medical meaning of the term, however, I should also explain something else that, in my estimation, is very important. Statistics from thousands of cases prove that a fetus delivered at twenty-five weeks gestation has a thirty-eight percent chance of survival. Even one additional week in the uterus raises that chance to sixty-one percent, and at twenty-seven weeks the likelihood of survival is seventy-six percent, doubling the twenty-five-week figure. With this in mind I'm sure you can understand that increasing the period during which the fetus remains inside the mother's body—granted that her heart and lungs are kept functioning by means of what is called advanced life support—becomes extremely important as far as ensuring that a live child can be brought into the world at, say, twenty-seven weeks gestation."

"Twenty-seven weeks! But Princess Zorah's pregnancy has only lasted twenty-four weeks."

"We can't be certain of that," said Liz. "Estimation of the gestation period is often in error by as much as four weeks because of the difficulty of determining when menstruation stops."

"Just how long do you plan to keep the Princess' body alive, Doctor?"

"Until recently we assumed that keeping the fetus alive with the mother on life support measures might be limited to perhaps two or three weeks. Recently, however, a report has appeared indicating that the fetus can safely be kept alive in the uterus as long as sixty days after the diagnosis of brain death in the mother has been made."

"Surely you don't expect—"

"No. In this case, I would think three weeks would be enough to ensure that the fetus has developed to where it can be delivered by Caesarean section with every hope of surviving."

"You said just now that Princess Zorah already shows brain death, didn't you?"

"Yes."

"But her heart is still beating. I saw the EKG picture on the monitor when I was in her room."

"It is beating, and I hope it will continue to do so without our having to stimulate it. Until recently, the established criteria for death were a fixed pupil, with no reaction to light, cessation of respiration and the inability to hear a heartbeat with the stethoscope. In the past several years, however, we have learned that the brain can die, yet the rest of the body— what we call the somatic portion—can continue to exist. This is particularly true when the body is maintained on measures we call advanced life support, a highly technical and complicated regimen by which the circulation and the flow of oxygen through the lungs to the cells of the body—and in this case the fetus—is maintained."

"I'm afraid I have some difficulty in understanding the difference between two kinds of death, Dr. MacGowan. And even as intelligent a man as Emir Hassim would be even more confused by the distinction."

"I imagine he would," Liz conceded. "In fact, some doctors are against using life-support techniques after brain death occurs. Its main use is to preserve organs such as the heart or the liver until they can be transplanted into another person but, in this case, my sole reason for using it is to give the fetus every chance to survive."

"Thank you, Doctor." Almani rose to his feet but stopped with his hand on the knob of the door leading to the outer office and waiting room. "I can understand your concern for the welfare of the fetus, but I cannot understand your reasons for making the father wait perhaps three weeks longer to know whether or not he will have an heir. It seems to me that, in this case, the wishes of a dying man should be respected whenever possible."

"The Emir is always free to turn his wife over to another obstetrician, Mr. Almani."

"True, but what I can only regard as your intransigence, Doctor, puts me in a very difficult position. I was the one who recommended bringing Princess Zorah to Miami, at the suggestion of my friend Dr. Paul Fraser. If anything should happen to the child she bears—particularly if it is a male—I could be criticized very sharply in Telfa for not insisting that the child be removed from Princess Zorah's body before her death."

"Brain death, Mr. Almani," said Liz. "That can be very different from somatic death."

"A difference, I believe, you would have difficulty explaining to a father who had lost an heir because of your stubbornness."

"Will you let me know whether Emir Hassim wishes to place the Princess under the care of another obstetrician?" Liz asked stiffly.

"Of course, but I shall advise him against it. I'm sure you are a compassionate person, Dr. MacGowan. When you've had time to think about this particular situation, and particularly easing a dying man's concern about the succession to his throne, you will change your opinion about the operation."

II

Storming out of the elevator at the seventh floor of the Biscayne Tower, where the offices of the surgeons were located,

Liz almost knocked Ted Bronson down as he was about to enter it.

"Why don't you look where you're going!" she demanded, before recognizing whom she had bumped into.

"Wait a minute!" Ted was holding her a little closer than was quite necessary to keep her from falling.

"That damned Almani! He's impossible!"

"There's a coffeemaker in the utility room on this floor that's absolute proof of perpetual motion," he said soothingly. "How about stopping for a cup before you run somebody else down and find yourself sued for damages."

"All right," she said. "I need to blow off some steam anyway before I start seeing patients or I'm liable to chew out some young society mother who's gained a few more pounds than she should."

In the utility room, Ted brought her a steaming cup of coffee from the urn and took a seat on an adjacent stool. "Get it off your chest now, while you've got someone to listen who loves you," he suggested.

"This time Almani went too far—bribing a special nurse on duty with Princess Zorah to let him watch the monitor."

"Relatives sneaking looks at hospital charts are a normal hazard."

Liz took a swallow of coffee and controlled herself with an effort. "But Almani isn't even a member of the Elzama family—"

"He does represent Telfa in the United States, doesn't he?"

"Yes, but that doesn't give him the right to tell me how I should treat a patient."

"What does he want you to do?"

"Emir Hassim has leukemia and is probably near death. If I can make sure the fetus has a chance to develop inside the mother's uterus for a few weeks longer, it will considerably increase its chances of survival."

"How far along is the pregnancy now?"

"Twenty weeks, from the information we have. The Arabic nurse who's been with the Princess since she became pregnant was killed in the crash, so we don't know exactly what level of gestation we're dealing with."

"Which means the fetus could be a month farther along in development than you think it is—or vice versa?"

"Not less than twenty weeks, judging by the size of the abdomen, and probably a week or two more. What really burns me up is that both Almani and the State Department are more concerned about the sex of the fetus than they are about its welfare."

"How certain could you be of determining fetal sex at this stage of gestation using ultrasound?"

"Practically none; it depends upon actually seeing the genital organs of the fetus. What I can do though," she said thoughtfully, "is use the ultrasound film record to judge the stage of the pregnancy by measuring the fetal BPD—"

"What's that?"

"BPD stands for the biparietal diameter of the fetal skull. By measuring that on the ultrasound picture, plus other fetal dimensions, it's possible to make a pretty accurate estimate of fetal development."

"And maybe decide to do the section somewhat earlier?"

"It's possible—but not likely."

"So what it all comes down to is this," Ted suggested. "You won't lose anything by using ultrasound, right?"

"Yes."

"And even though you probably won't discover that the next ruler of Telfa is inside his mother's uterus, you·can at least find out the degree of development and plan your strategy accordingly."

"You're right," Liz conceded. "I'll go ahead with the ultrasound examination as soon as I can schedule it in the laboratory. While I'm at it, too, I might as well have a tray ready for amniocentesis in the Sonar Laboratory and put the needle in under direct vision." She leaned over to kiss him.

"What's that for? Not that I didn't like it."

"For keeping my red-haired temper from getting the best of my common sense," she told him.

III

On the VIP floor, Ted found the Corazon family in the adjoining room to Michael's. Arturo was sitting next to his mother holding her hand, and they both looked up expectantly, even hopefully, when Ted came in.

"How is he, Ted?" Maria asked.

"The aspiration I just did proved that the diagnosis we made with the scan this morning was correct. He has a large hematoma—that's a collection of blood inside the liver."

"Does the fact that he has only one kidney left have anything to do with that?" Manuel Corazon asked.

"If everything was working as well as the left kidney, I wouldn't be concerned at all," Ted told him.

"You can give him one of my kidneys," Arturo stammered eagerly. "Giving Michael blood didn't bother me at all and I'm ready to give more anytime."

"The trouble now is almost entirely with the liver," Ted explained.

"What does that do except make gallstones?" Maria asked. "I had to be operated on a few years ago for those."

"The liver has two extremely important functions," said Ted. "It produces bile that helps digest fats in the body, and sometimes stones, largely of cholesterol, do form from the chemicals in that bile. But the liver is also the major agent in detoxifying the by-products of metabolism, as well as any harmful substances that are accidently taken into the body."

"Is that why people who drink a lot develop what's called cirrhosis of the liver?" Maria asked. "One of our neighbors died of it recently."

"Cirrhosis is usually produced by too much alcohol," Ted agreed. "In Michael's case, though, the trouble appears to be from the bullet that passed all the way through the liver. We presumed that it didn't do much real damage, but it must have struck a fairly large blood vessel inside the organ. The bleeding seems to have stopped, but not before a considerable amount of liver tissue was damaged as well as some very tiny ducts that carry bile. After the NMR examination this morning showed a dark shadow inside Mike's liver, I put in a large needle and removed quite a lot of old blood and bile that had accumulated there."

"What else can you do?" Manuel asked.

"At the moment nothing but support Mike's general condition with fluids and more blood if he needs it and probably do another scan tomorrow, too. If that shows more hemorrhage inside the liver from the through-and-through bullet, I might have to go back in and open up the large clot and pack it, the way I did the area where the bullet fragment injured liver tissue."

"Could he survive such an operation in his present condition?" Manuel asked.

"A lot better than he could a few days from now." Ted took a deep breath before he spoke again. "The problem now is liver failure—and I might as well tell you there's only one treatment for it—a transplant."

IV

When Liz rang the telephone in Princess Zorah's suite, Jerry Rubin answered.

"Have you started the patient on advanced life support yet, Jerry?" she asked.

"We're almost ready, Dr. MacGowan. I was going to call you and ask whether you were planning to use ultrasound—"

"I am—but how did you know?"

"Ambassador Almani was asking about it but I clammed up until I could talk to you."

"Do you think it's safe to move the patient to the Sonar Laboratory? If I can't find out what I want to know with ultrasound, I'm going to put in an amniocentesis needle, using the ultrasound image to guide me."

"A portable ventilator will keep the respiratory movements going," Jerry Rubin assured her. "I'll bring along a portable pacemaker-defibrillator, too, just in case we need to use it."

"Good! Please take her down to the Sonar Laboratory then and let me know when everything's ready," said Liz. "Meanwhile, I'll have the OR send down the amniocentesis tray."

Connie Matsumoto, the technician in charge of the Sonar Laboratory, called Liz about thirty minutes later. "The Princess is on the table, Doctor." The Japanese-American technician's voice sounded worried. "Her pulse is pretty fast and her breathing is shallow but Dr. Rubin is here and he says everything's going to be all right."

"I'll be there right away, Connie."

Connie Matsumoto had been right in being apprehensive, Liz saw when she came into the Sonar Laboratory where Princess Zorah was lying on a cushioned table. At one side was the apparatus for recording the high-frequency ultrasound waves that would bounce back from the tissues inside the body being examined with this extremely valuable diagnostic tool. Except for the gross mound of her abdomen produced by the pregnant uterus and the turban of bandage around her head, Princess Zorah could almost have been without life. Her respirations were being maintained by a portable ventilator, and her pulse, visualized on the small monitor of the portable pace-maker-defibrillator, was thready.

"I'll make this examination as short as possible, Jerry," Liz promised.

Switching on the sonar machine, Connie Matsumoto picked up the scanner, by which it was possible to send the ultrasound waves deep into the body. When they bounced back, they were recorded upon the monitor screen of the apparatus, in brilliant black and white in the darkened laboratory and also on film for hospital clinical records.

Delineated in exquisite detail upon the small screen of the monitor, as the technician moved the scanner back and forth, were the head, neck, arms and chest of the small occupant of the uterus. Starting at the lower limits of the rib cage, however, a shadow came between the viewers and the rest of the small body, except the lower legs and tiny feet, which, jack-knifed as if they were folded against the lower body, were visible above the top limit of the obstruction to vision.

"Damn!" said Liz. "The placenta is attached on the anterior surface of the uterus."

"You probably won't be able to identify the genitalia anyway, Dr. MacGowan," said Connie Matsumoto. "With the breech jammed down into the lower part of the uterine cavity, the fetus is practically sitting upright."

"That placenta isn't going to make a Caesarean section any easier when you get ready to do it, Dr. MacGowan," Jerry Rubin commented.

"Or putting in the amniocentesis needle without penetrating the placenta and, worse still, maybe jabbing it into the head or thorax of the fetus," Liz agreed. "What's your estimate of the stage of gestation judging by the size of the fetus, Connie?"

"I'd say twenty-four weeks or maybe even longer, Dr. Mac-Gowan."

"It's a good-sized one all right," Jerry Rubin agreed. "With luck, it won't cause many problems for me in the Neonatal ICU, after you deliver it by section a few weeks from now."

"The fetus does appear to be at maybe twenty-four weeks of development at least," Liz agreed. "Thank God the head isn't obscured by the placenta; we ought to get a pretty accurate figure for the BPD when you measure it from the films, Connie."

The technician flipped a switch, and somewhere inside the sonar apparatus a Polaroid camera photographed the image of the screen. At the same moment, the fetus inside the uterus suddenly clinched tiny fists and appeared to launch a blow against the confining walls of his mother's womb.

"Look at that!" Connie Matsumoto exclaimed. "It even has a temper."

"Which means it's probably a female," said Jerry Rubin.

"Whatever it is, pray God it keeps its temper under control for at least two weeks and doesn't start premature labor," said Liz. "I'm going ahead with the amniocentesis, Connie."

Only a few minutes were required to paint the overlarge abdomen of the frail patient with antiseptic and cover it with a sterile sheet in which a window had been cut through which minor surgery could be performed. While Connie Matsumoto held the ultrasound scanner steady, Liz inserted a long needle with a stylet in the center to give it rigidity. Watching the ultrasound picture of the fetus inside its protective cocoon of membrane and fluid, Liz carefully directed the point of the needle through the muscles of the abdominal wall, then those of the uterus, until the point penetrated the inner cocoon just at the top edge of the placental shadow inside the front wall of the uterus.

"Nice going!" Jerry Rubin was watching the monitor. "It looks like you missed the placenta entirely, Dr. MacGowan."

"We'll see." Liz removed the stylet from inside the needle and attached an empty sterile syringe to the flanged outer end. She pulled back gently on the plunger, hoping to see some slightly opalescent amniotic fluid spurt into the syringe; instead, however, bloody fluid appeared.

"Damn!" said Liz. "A bloody tap."

"That's probably placental blood with maybe a little placental tissue," said Connie Matsumoto. "If you push the needle in a little farther, Dr. MacGowan, you might still get clear fluid."

"We'll get a specimen from this area first." Liz continued her pull upon the plunger of the syringe, drawing into the needle some of the bloody material it had entered just inside the muscular layer.

"Be sure and send this specimen down to Dr. Harris, Connie," she directed. "Even if I don't get any clear amniotic fluid, there may be enough fetal cells in it for him to get a culture."

Reinserting the stylet into the needle, Liz gingerly pushed it about a centimeter deeper. And this time, when she removed the stylet, clear fluid dripped from the end of the needle.

"It looks like we hit a very small jackpot," she said as she attached an empty syringe to the end of the needle and drew a syringeful. "Dr. Harris will be happy to see this. I'm sure he can easily culture the cells he will need to determine the sex of the fetus."

"Be sure and label both specimens for Dr. Harris," Liz told the sonar technician as she was leaving the room. "And thanks for your help, Connie."

"You don't ever have to thank me, Dr. MacGowan," said Connie. "One of these days, I'm going to have a baby myself —God willing—and I don't want anybody but you to deliver it."

"Please go ahead and put the Princess into the advanced life-support routine, Jerry," Liz told the tall, handsome young resident. "I think I'm going to treat myself to the luxury of a drink."

"I'll have her on full automatic life support within the next thirty minutes," Jerry Rubin promised.

Chapter Eleven

Outside the Sonar Laboratory, Ted saw Liz walking down the corridor to the elevator. "Leaving for the day?" he asked.

"Yes. I'm bushed."

"That makes two of us. Going anywhere this evening?"

"Home."

"Is there any chance that I might seduce you into having a quiet drink first in the Dolphin Lounge?"

"I'm not much in the mood for gaiety tonight but I could certainly use some of that bourbon you talked me into stocking in my private stock. Why don't we enjoy a drink while we relax in the breeze from Biscayne Bay on my balcony?"

The sun was hot as they crossed the thoroughfare to Biscayne Terrace, but inside the lobby the air conditioning was a welcome change. At Liz's apartment door, she handed Ted the key and he opened it, standing aside for her to precede him.

"Fix us a couple of highballs," she said, crossing the living room toward the two bedrooms in the back. "I'll be back in a minute."

"Sure you don't need unhooking or anything?"

"Nice try, but no thanks." She flashed him a smile. "I'm just going to get out of this dress and into a negligee."

"Wear the one I gave you last Christmas," he suggested.

"And look like the center-fold spread from *Playboy?* No thanks."

In the small bar adjoining the kitchen, Ted took down a bottle of bourbon from a cabinet and poured two jiggers for each of them. Taking ice cubes from the freezer atop the refrigerator and dropping them into the glasses before adding ginger ale, he selected a half-filled jar of cocktail peanuts from the refrigerator. Pouring these into a dish and placing them on a silver tray along with the drinks, he moved into the living room and a coffee table before the sofa facing the wall of glass and the broad expanse of Biscayne Bay to the east. As he finished these chores, Liz came out of the bedroom wearing a long, blue silk hostess gown zipped up the front.

"I'm beginning to think you'd make a fairly good husband," she told him as she joined him on the sofa and held up her glass to touch his. "To luck with both of our sickest patients."

"I'll drink to that, and it looks like I'm going to need it pretty badly," Ted said soberly.

"Why?"

"I'm beginning to doubt my own surgical ability."

"Nonsense! No surgeon in Miami could handle a liver wound better than one accustomed to transplanting whole organs. Besides, with a through-and-through wound, you had every reason to expect the liver tissue would close around the bullet path, stopping the bleeding."

"I hope you're right." Ted kicked off his shoes and put his feet up on the coffee table. "What was your day like?"

"Very good—until I had the run-in with Sheik Almani I told you about earlier."

"He does seem to be your *bête noir.* Anything new?"

"Not really. The ultrasound study this afternoon showed that the pregnancy is probably several weeks farther along than we had judged from the small amount of information we had from Almani. While we had the Princess in the Sonar

Lab, I did an amniocentesis under direct vision but I'm afraid that didn't help much either."

"Why?"

"When I first put the needle in, I got a bloody tap—probably because I was too close to the placenta, which is located on the anterior surface of the uterus—"

"When you have to do the section some time later, it's going to be pretty rough, going through an inch or an inch and a half of placental tissue in order to reach the amnion and the fetus," he commented.

"Fortunately, I was able to push the needle in a little farther and obtain some clear amniotic fluid that Moe Harris can culture."

"Did you tell Almani that?"

"No. I called Princess Zorah's room but he wasn't there. He's probably calling the State Department, trying to put more pressure on me to do an immediate section so he can find out right away whether he's going to be the Regent."

"Do you really blame him?"

"Possibly not," Liz conceded. "In all fairness to him, I guess he antagonized me from the start by giving me the impression that he had some doubts about whether a woman would be able to handle a case as difficult as the Princess'. He's a pretty authoritarian individual to start with, and with that sort of an attitude, he could easily have rubbed me the wrong way."

"By the way." Ted's voice took on a deliberately casual note. "Henry Letterman talked to me this afternoon—about the Princess."

"Why?"

"The gist of what he said is derived from a very frank conversation between him and Sheik Almani. The essence of it is that, if things turn out all right and you deliver a viable male child, Emir Hassim will donate a few of his oil millions to the Biscayne Research Foundation as an indication of gratitude."

"Almani hasn't mentioned anything like that to me."

"I doubt if he would. A man in his position as an intermediary between a Middle Eastern monarch and the country that buys most of the oil his country produces is bound to be up to his ears in intrigue. That being the case, he wouldn't hesitate to influence you and others by a direct approach—money."

"Why did Henry Letterman talk to you?" Liz's voice was suddenly taut.

"Everybody in the hospital knows about our relationship," Ted protested. "Maybe I shouldn't have said anything about it now, but I didn't want the dean of the Medical School to hit you with it unexpectedly tomorrow."

"Lay it on the line," Liz commanded. "You know better than to try to beat around the bush with me."

"Here's the nitty-gritty. The expanded organ bank I've tried to get going ever since I came to Miami is in line for the next large gift to the Biscayne Research Foundation. Unfortunately, though, there haven't been any large gifts for the past six months."

"Go on," said Liz grimly.

"Almani has assured Dean Charmyn that, if the fetus Princess Zorah bears is a male and is alive when it's delivered, he can practically guarantee that Emir Hassim will donate several million dollars to the Foundation."

"With your expanded organ-bank project the ultimate beneficiary?"

"That would appear to be the way the cookie crumbles, but believe me, darling, I didn't buy it. I told Letterman this very afternoon that nobody was going to influence you through me. For one thing, the welfare of the fetus comes first in your estimation and, for another, there's the fact that the baby has only a fifty-fifty chance at the most of being a male."

"You don't think I'm holding out against Almani because

he rubbed me the wrong way from the beginning, do you? And because everybody in Telfa who's involved seems to regard Princess Zorah as nothing more than a brood sow."

"My God, no! Besides, she's a queen."

"Not in Telfa—and I guess that's something else I resented. The only title Emir Hassim gave her was that of Consort with the rank of Princess, and from what Almani tells me, the country must be full of those. Only if the child she bears turns out to be a male—and therefore directly in line to rule in Telfa—would Princess Zorah have any chance of ever being named Queen."

Ted had finished his drink and looked questioningly at Liz, but she shook her head.

"The things you've told me require some serious thinking, and the kick this stuff has after a second round doesn't promote much mental clarity," she admitted.

"Do you want me to go home, then?"

"Why don't you go down to the Pizza Hut on the corner and bring one home? While you're gone, I'll fix us a salad and we can discuss this whole problem a little more intelligently and rationally after we've finished eating."

"Second best news I could have had today," he told her.

"What's the first—no, don't answer."

"Someday I'm going to write a paper on the aphrodisiac qualities of a mixture of 101-proof bourbon and a pizza supreme with anchovies and Italian sausage from Pizza Hut," he said with a grin as he opened the door to go out. "So I still can hope not to sleep alone tonight."

"I've never known you to need any aphrodisiac."

"Just call me Old Rough and Ready."

"Ready, but never rough," she assured him. "I guess one of the reasons I love you so much is that you're the tenderest man I've ever known."

"And I hope one of the few you have—or will—in the biblical sense."

Just after midnight, Liz awoke, warm, comfortable and loving in Ted's arms, where she'd fallen asleep after a particularly active bout of lovemaking. When she turned to face him, he didn't awaken, but the arm across her tightened unconsciously, pressing her naked body gently against his own.

She didn't awaken him for almost half an hour, though, while she reviewed in her mind—with a detachment she hadn't been able to achieve while the events were happening —the last forty-eight hours. Finally, however, when her thinking was finished, she touched Ted's shoulder.

"Wake up," she said. "I've got something to tell you."

Ted reached farther across her shoulder as he drifted into wakefulness, drawing her lovely bare breasts against him while he gave her a sleepy kiss.

"I've been thinking about the whole question of Princess Zorah, her baby, Emir Hassim and the Emirate of Telfa," she said. "And I'm sure you were right about my getting my back up because Almani rubbed me the wrong way. Now that I've gone ahead with the ultrasound examination and the amniocentesis, I'm going to let this situation develop as it will."

"I think that's the simplest way." Ted was wide awake now. "Are you certain?"

"Absolutely. Now, go back to sleep."

"You deserve a reward for that decision," he told her. "A kiss, at the very least."

But the very least was not enough for either of them for quite a while.

Chapter Twelve

On the VIP floor, shortly after eight the next morning, Ted Bronson studied Michael Corazon's chart and could find nothing encouraging in what he saw. The patient, he'd been told, had been taken down to the Biomedical Image Analysis Center earlier, where the examination of yesterday was being repeated with the NMR scanner as Ted had requested.

"I see that Dr. Groover was in this morning for the consultation I requested," Ted told the special nurse who was busy making up Michael Corazon's bed, "but there's no note of his examination on the chart."

Dr. Max Groover headed the Department of Gastroenterology and Hepatology, the latter specialty dealing with the liver and its diseases.

"He was here early this morning and dictated a long note, but it probably hasn't been typed up yet by the stenographic pool," the nurse told him.

"I'll call him as soon as I finish rounds." Ted hung the chart over the bracket at the foot of the bed, where it normally stayed. "How long ago did Mr. Corazon go down to the Biomedical Image Laboratory?"

"Nearly a half hour ago. They had plenty of help so I came back to make up the bed and straighten the room before they bring him back."

"The scan is probably finished by now; I'll run down and take a look at the films. If the Corazons come in, tell them I'll be back to talk with them later on in the morning when I have the blood chemistry and other reports."

"Of course, Doctor."

In the Biomedical Image Laboratory, Michael Corazon was just being transferred to a hospital gurney from the mobile platform upon which he had been lying while the magnet of the NMR scanner was accomplishing its scientific miracle of looking inside him with a meticulously probing eye. He smiled when he saw Ted, but his eyes were bright from fever.

"How's it going, Mike?" Ted asked. "Having much pain?"

"No. I slept most of the night without a hypo but this damn itching is driving me crazy. Can you help a little?"

"It's coming from the jaundice and the bile pigment in your skin," Ted explained. "I'll order something that may help."

In the viewing room of the Biomedical Analysis Laboratory, Dr. Harvey Chung was studying a reproduction of the images that had just been produced by the NMR machine.

"Can you see any change in the picture from yesterday, Harvey?" Ted asked.

"The mass inside his liver is considerably smaller. How much blood did you remove from that hematoma yesterday?"

"Something over two hundred cc's—both blood and bile."

"It doesn't seem to have filled up at all during the night." Chung indicated the film on the view box before them. "That probably means the hemorrhage has stopped."

"I hope you're right, but his serum bilirubin is still up sharply, as well as the BUN and several other indicators of liver function. Max Groover saw him early this morning; I'm going to stop by his office and see what he thinks."

"As early as Dr. Groover gets up, he's probably done a whole day's work by now," Chung said with a smile. "The grapevine says the Research Foundation is probably going to get quite a lot of money for research from the husband of one of Dr. MacGowan's patients and you'll be the lucky one."

"I made a presentation to the Foundation yesterday for some funds to expand the organ bank but I'm afraid they're going to be contingent upon a number of things. One is whether the fetus Princess Zorah is carrying turns out to be a male and the other whether Liz is able to get it out of the uterus alive and able to survive."

"She can do it if anybody can," said Chung. "I hope you don't have to wait as long to get funds for your organ bank as we did to get the money for the nuclear magnetic resonance scanner."

On the floor devoted to the medical service, Ted stopped at Dr. Max Groover's office. The digestive-system specialist was on the telephone when he came in.

"Has my note on Corazon's chart been typed up yet?" Groover asked when he hung up the phone.

"No," said the surgeon. "A typist would have had to get up in the middle of the night to have it ready. You must rise at the crack of dawn, Max."

"I'm running usually before sunrise. Incidentally, have you ever seen the sun rise across Miami Beach and the Bay?"

"Once or twice—when I was going home from an emergency operation or a night on the town."

"You and Liz ought to get married." Groover was in his sixties, with a flock of children and grandchildren. "The trouble with smart women in medicine is that, if they've got enough on the ball to get ahead, they're often career crazy and don't want to marry. Or they're not ready to have children until they're old enough to run the risk of kids having Down's Syndrome."

"I've been telling Liz that for a year now but I haven't gotten anywhere. . . . What did you think of Michael Corazon's condition when you examined him this morning?"

"His liver is losing ground fast," said Groover.

"Do you have any idea what's happening inside him?"

"Probably no more than you have after your experience in Pittsburgh with liver failure in patients being prepared for transplants."

"Most of those were children with congenital biliary atresia. This is different."

"Maybe not as much as you think. In both cases you're dealing with a liver that's failing."

"That much almost anyone can see now, but I still don't understand why. Especially since the hemorrhage inside the organ seems to have stopped."

"I guess you're stymied then. Which means your only recourse is going to be a liver transplant."

"I'm beginning to wish I'd kept my damn mouth shut and not mentioned it on TV. To transplant a liver—if you're lucky enough to find a donor—you've got to take out a liver. And I can't convince myself yet that this one is past redemption."

"Maybe not past," said Groover bluntly, "but damn near it in my opinion."

"I guess that's really what I wanted you to tell me, Max." Ted got to his feet. "I haven't wanted to make a public appeal yet for a donor but it doesn't look like it's going to be safe to put it off much longer."

"With that, I agree," said Groover. "How are you going to handle it?"

"I suppose the best thing to do is to call a press conference and put the whole southern half of Florida on the alert. That way we can hope to get a crack at the liver of any young person who's unlucky enough to undergo brain death after an accident."

II

Liz MacGowan entered the lobby of Biscayne General shortly before nine and went directly to the VIP floor and Princess Zorah's room. Jerry Rubin, who was adjusting the controls to the ventilator, looked up and smiled.

"Morning, Dr. MacGowan. I hope you slept well."

"Like a top." Liz moved across the room in order to see the monitor closely. "Those heart contractions are certainly stronger than they were in the Sonar Laboratory yesterday afternoon."

"When we brought her back from Sonar yesterday afternoon and started connecting her up to the life-support apparatus," said Jerry, "I called Pete Craig and suggested that we add some digoxin to the IV solution. It slowed the heart almost immediately and stepped up the blood pressure, too."

"When are you going to start intravenous alimentation?" Liz asked.

A comparatively new technique by which concentrated nourishment that was far more effective than the glucose and saline solutions ordinarily used for intravenous injection could be injected directly into the bloodstream, the procedure called intravenous alimentation was widely used now in preserving as well as enhancing the strength of patients who were seriously ill for some time.

"We'll probably start it today," said Jerry. "The fetus has been kicking a lot. Maybe it's hungry."

"I'm counting on you and Peter Craig to keep it kicking," said Liz. "From the looks of the fetal monitor, though, you won't have much trouble."

"The monitor registering the fetal pulse has an alarm system of its own, and if the rate becomes markedly slower or faster, the alarm will sound," Jerry assured her. "With that much warning, we ought to be able to notify you of any serious change in its condition immediately and give you plenty of time to get the fetus out of the uterus by Caesarean section."

"Have you seen Sheik Almani this morning?" Liz asked.

"He was here for a while after we brought the Princess back from Sonar yesterday afternoon, but I haven't seen him today," said Jerry. "He told me he studied both electronics and petroleum geology at M.I.T. a long time ago, so he understood everything I told him about the advanced life-support apparatus."

III

"You've got a visitor—and a present," Liz's secretary told her when she went to her office after making rounds that morning. The visitor was Arturo Corazon, beaming happily and holding a fairly large flat package.

"Arturo!" she greeted him warmly. "How nice to see you!"

"Nice for me, too." Still beaming, Arturo turned the flat package he was holding around so she could see it.

"It's lovely!" Liz cried when a framed painting of a spectacularly beautiful orchid in full bloom was revealed.

"I painted it several days ago," he told her. "It reminded me of you so I want you to have it."

"I love it! Can you tell me its name?"

Arturo took the chair by her desk. "It's called 'Southern Moon.'"

"I'm going to hang it on the wall of the office where I can see it every day—and think of you," Liz assured him.

"I'd like that." Arturo beamed even more happily. "Will you be my friend?"

"Of course. I'll be happy to be your friend."

"Dr. Ted is a good friend, too."

"I know. He often speaks of you and your family. He thinks of them just like his own."

"Dr. Ted is going to save Michael."

"Dr. Ted is a very fine surgeon. I'm sure he will."

"Are you going to marry him?"

"That's a secret," Liz said laughing. "But because you and I are such good friends, and friends should always tell each other their secrets, I'm going to tell you—the answer is yes."

"When?"

"As it happens, Dr. Ted and I are working on very important projects right now," she explained. "He's trying to find people who had kidney transplant operations that failed so he can give them new ones that will succeed. I'm trying to save a baby who hasn't been born yet. If it's a boy he'll be a king."

"A *real* king?"

"An emir, which is what the rulers of small kingdoms are called. So it's just like being a king."

"When you've done that, are you going to marry Dr. Ted?" Arturo asked.

"We'll probably set up a date as soon as all this is settled," she promised. "Will you be an usher at our wedding?"

"I would like that. Michael and Estrellita are going to be married one of these days. They want me to be an usher for them, too."

"It looks like you're going to be very busy," Liz told him. "And I'm sure you'll be happy because you enjoy so much doing things for your family and for those who get to be your friends." Liz held up the lovely painting to look at it again. "I'm going to treasure this all my life, Arturo. Not just because it's so beautiful, but because you painted it especially for me."

IV

Shortly after ten that morning, Ted Bronson's office telephone rang while he was going through the morning mail.

"Mr. Corazon's nurse said you wanted to be notified when
the family came into the hospital," said the operator. "She
says they're in the room adjoining Mr. Corazon's now."

"Thanks," Ted told her. "I'm on the way."

Estrellita Mendoza was with Maria and the three brothers.
"Did the examination you were going to do earlier this morning tell you anything new, Ted?" she asked.

"Only that the bleeding inside the liver seems to have
stopped," he said, trying to summon up an optimistic note he
was far from feeling.

"I've been busy trying to get the indictments against Sam
Gianno and his crowd processed so we could keep them off
balance until Michael gets well enough to take over, so I
haven't been able to visit Mike as much as I would have liked.
Frankly, I was stunned to see the change for the worse in his
condition this morning."

"All the tests we've done over the past several days confirm
that he's going downhill fairly rapidly from liver failure," said
Ted. "A certain degree of suppression of liver function could
be expected from an injury as severe as the one Mike sustained, but we've been hoping it would start coming back."

"Then it hasn't?"

"No. If it were going to happen, we should already see
some signs of lessening in the amount of jaundice."

"That's even worse," Manuel commented.

"Are you willing to say his condition is past the point of no
return?" Estrellita asked the question Ted had been dreading.

"Not yet, but that point might not be far in the future."

"What then?"

"His only chance would be a transplant." Ted had decided to put the truth bluntly.

"But that's the last resort!" Estrellita cried in horror.

"Very much so," Ted agreed. "That's why I'm not yet willing to recommend it."

Arturo had been listening while clinging fast to his mother's hand. Now he suddenly buried his head against her breast and his shoulders shook in a spasm of sobbing. Maria tried to comfort him, and Estrellita, of whom he was very fond, reached over to take his hand, but he continued to sob.

"I would think any further delay would jeopardize the chances of success for a transplant," said Estrellita.

"It does," Ted admitted soberly. "And it also shortens the time available to find a donor."

"I don't exactly understand you," said Pedro. "You're a transplant surgeon, aren't you?"

"Yes."

"Then why can't you give him a new liver?"

"For a successful transplant, we would need a liver from someone dying from trauma," Ted explained patiently. "The most likely prospects are usually found in emergency rooms when people brought in with severe head injuries undergo what we call brain death."

"I know about that," Estrellita told him. "As Assistant State's Attorney, I've prosecuted cases where the final verdict depended almost entirely upon just when brain death occurred."

"According to the afternoon paper, a diagnosis of brain death was made on that princess from Telfa," said Maria. "The one who was injured in a plane crash at the airport the day after Michael was shot. Do you think—"

"Princess Zorah is carrying a fetus in her uterus," Ted said firmly. "Besides, she's much too frail and too small for her liver to be selected for Michael, even if she wasn't pregnant."

"Then what do we do?" Estrellita asked.

"Pray," said Maria in a voice without hope. "Pray that Michael's liver can still regain its function. And, failing that, for a donor to turn up in a hospital emergency room somewhere nearby before it's too late."

"Shouldn't you notify the media, Dr. Ted?" Estrellita asked. "That way doctors in nearby emergency rooms could be on the alert for a possible donor."

"I'm not entirely satisfied in my mind that Michael is yet at the point where nothing but a transplant can save him," Ted admitted. "If a liver did become available, I'd be in a position of having to go on with it when I'm not absolutely certain that surgery still cannot be avoided."

"It looks like we're putting you between a rock and a hard place," Manuel Corazon agreed.

"Suppose we see how Michael does over the weekend," Ted suggested. "Patients awaiting liver transplant often go for weeks before a donor is found so we shouldn't lose much ground, in case his liver still refuses to start coming back."

"That sounds reasonable," Estrellita conceded. "If he doesn't improve over the weekend, you can always call the press and be sure the media will give it wide coverage."

Chapter Thirteen

About midafternoon, Liz received a call asking her to come to the Genetic Research Laboratory. She took the elevator to the hospital basement at once, and when she went in, Dr. Moses Harris shoved an electromicrograph across his desk and handed her a large magnifying glass.

"Tell me what you see, Liz," he said.

"It looks like a Y chromosome."

"That's exactly what it is," the plump geneticist with the graying beard assured her. "Congratulations on recognizing it."

"I've seen enough electromicrographs to be able to recognize something as large as a chromosome, Moe," she said, a little tartly. "What the hell is this all about?"

"Remember that bloody tap you sent me for examination yesterday?"

"Of course. I started to discard it."

"It's a damn good thing you didn't. When it arrived here in the laboratory, I put it into the ultracentrifuge. One of my technicians stayed after hours last night to make up a paraffin preparation of the cells at the bottom of the tube so I could examine them this morning."

"That's a lot of trouble for a simple blood contamination of amniocentesis fluid," said Liz. "Do I detect an element of mystery here?"

"Not a mystery, but the solution of one."

"Am I supposed to guess? Or are you going to tell me?"

"All in good time," the pudgy doctor assured her. "Don't spoil my triumph by being in a hurry."

Liz had a sudden inspiration. "Are you telling me the Y chromosome I just saw is from a body cell of the fetus Princess Zorah is carrying?"

"There you go, wrecking my playhouse," Moe Harris complained. "I should have known better than to try keeping a smart gal like you on the hook. The evidence is irrefutable; your Princess is carrying the only male descendant of the Emir of Telfa."

"Who may well rule one day over the largest pool of crude oil in the Middle East." Liz's eyes were shining with delight and excitement. "Wait till I tell Sheik Almani about this!"

"I suppose this means the Emir will come through with that offer of a sizable donation to the research fund," said Harris, a little wistfully.

"I don't see why not; Almani practically promised Henry Letterman the donation if the fetus turned out to be a male."

"Did you know Ted's project for enlarging the organ bank here at Biscayne General may hang on the Emir's gratitude?"

"He told me last night. How did you learn about it?"

"I was at the meeting of the Foundation Committee yesterday afternoon—with my hand out asking for funds to use in trying to find a gene in families with an inherited tendency toward cancer. But with the promise of cyclosporin in transplant surgery, I can understand why Ted's project should be first. Incidentally, how long do you think you can keep Princess Zorah on advanced life support before you deliver the royal infant?"

"I'll settle for two weeks but even that is iffy. Jerry Rubin and Pete Craig are geniuses at maintaining advanced life support, but you can never tell when something could go wrong. In that case, I'd have to get that fetus out of the Princess' uterus in a hurry."

11

Liz found Yossuf Almani in the adjoining room of Princess Zorah's VIP suite on the tenth floor of the Biscayne General Tower. He was looking very glum.

"Cheer up!" she told him. "I have good news for you."

"What could that be? Princess Zorah is dead in spite of all that complicated apparatus you're using to make it seem that she's alive. When I tell Emir Hassim, he's going to blame me for insisting that she be flown to Miami."

"I've already explained to you that brain death and somatic death are not the same thing," Liz said sharply. "Weren't you listening?"

"Frankly, I find these philosophical distinctions you doctors make between the stages of death unconvincing," said the tall Arab with a shrug. "If the brain is dead, the personality—and therefore the soul—is dead, too. So what remains?"

"A body that can be kept functioning by artificial scientific procedures for some time," Liz told him. "In the case of one pregnant woman reported in medical literature just recently, her body was kept functioning as the best possible incubator for a live fetus for more than sixty days."

"Did the baby live?"

"The report said the child was quite healthy. The doctors in charge carried it almost to term, but with the Princess, the best I'm hoping for is perhaps two more weeks. With experts in advanced life support like Dr. Craig and Dr. Rubin in charge, we shouldn't have too much trouble accomplishing that."

"Culturing the cells from the amniotic fluid you removed yesterday will take two weeks, will it not?"

"That's the usual time, yes."

"Since you won't be determining the sex of the child any earlier either way, what do we gain that might help prevent possible turmoil in Telfa?"

"I came to tell you something else." Liz made no effort to hide the note of triumph in her voice. "On the basis of the fluid I drew from the uterus of the Princess yesterday morning, Dr. Harris has just assured me that the fetus is a male."

"Can you be certain of that?" Oddly enough, Almani did not appear to be as exuberant over the news she'd just given him as she would have expected.

"Dr. Harris says he'd stake his professional reputation on the diagnosis. And that—in case you don't know—is worldwide. Will you notify Emir Hassim that he has the son you say he wants so badly?"

"Of course."

"Be sure to tell him there's a healthy, viable fetus—inside its mother's body. And that we're going to keep it alive and developing normally long enough to make sure it gets the best possible start in life."

The Arab shook his head in obvious doubt. "Emir Hassim believes strongly in tradition and adheres to the older ways, Dr. MacGowan. I had enough trouble convincing him that by sending Princess Zorah to you, the sex of the baby would be determined long before normal birth could be expected. How can I explain to him what you propose to do with the body of the Princess?"

"Why tell him anything about brain death?"

Almani stroked his gray beard in thought before he said: "American newspapers are widely circulated in Telfa, Doctor MacGowan, so by tomorrow at the very least news of what you plan to do in the case of both mother and child will be known there. When Emir Hassim calls me tomorrow and asks for details, how can I assure him that his son may not die inside his mother's womb?"

"I'm not going to let that happen," Liz said firmly.

"I'm sure you mean what you say, Doctor." Almani did not appear to be reassured very much by Liz's promise. "But when the reigning Emir dies—which could be at any time— there is no government unless a living successor in the royal line exists. Under the laws of Telfa, an unborn child is not a successor to the throne."

"Do you want me to deliver the fetus, when doing that might endanger severely its chances of survival?" Liz asked bluntly.

"You spoke of complications. How serious could they be?"

"Serious enough to determine whether the baby lives or dies."

"The decision is a medical one," Almani surprised Liz by saying. "I will leave it to you."

"I'm glad we agree on that," said Liz. "You can depend on my choosing the course that seems best for the fetus; no doctor could promise more than that."

III

In her office on the seventh floor of the Biscayne General Tower, Liz put through a call to Mr. Longaker, the State Department officer with whom she had talked earlier. By that time it was shortly after five and she reached him in the limousine bearing him from his office to his home in Georgetown.

"What's happening down there, Doctor?" Longaker asked. "Anything serious?"

"I wouldn't have bothered you but you did tell me to call you whenever I thought you needed to know something."

"My apologies, Dr. MacGowan. I've got several other headaches in the Middle East besides Telfa, and it's always difficult to establish priorities for them."

"I don't know about the priority for this one, but I did think you'd like to know we've determined that the fetus Princess Zorah is carrying is a male."

"That *is* news, Dr. MacGowan. Have you informed Ambassador Almani?"

"Yes, I just finished talking to him."

"He should be quite pleased."

"He is, with the sex of the fetus. But I had difficulty explaining to him why it should not be delivered immediately."

There was a moment of silence, then Longaker asked, "Would you mind explaining it to me, too, Dr. MacGowan?"

"Not at all. When I talked with you shortly after Dr. Pierce operated upon the Princess' brain, I told you, as I remember it, that he gave no hope of her survival."

"I remember that, too."

"Yesterday morning we determined that brain death has already occurred, but I hope to maintain the condition of what I suppose you might call artificial life for perhaps as much as two weeks, in order to allow the fetus to develop more."

"Would it be safer to deliver the baby now by Caesarean section or to allow it to remain in its mother's body for that period? I'm not questioning your decision, Doctor, I just don't exactly understand it."

"What it comes down to, Mr. Longaker, is roughly this. Delivered two weeks from now, the baby will have twice as much of a chance for survival without serious complication than it would have if it were delivered now."

"Did you tell Ambassador Almani that?"

"Yes."

"What did he say?"

"He questioned, as you appear to be doing, the advisability

of not delivering the fetus by Caesarean section now. But his reasoning is based purely on political considerations."

"I might as well tell you the State Department is inclined to agree with the Ambassador in this case, Dr. MacGowan."

"That's a bit like playing Russian roulette with an unborn fetus that can't help itself," said Liz sharply. "I'll have no part of it."

"Did you tell Ambassador Almani that?"

"Yes."

"What did he say?"

"He left the decision up to me as a doctor."

"I guess we'll have to do the same thing," said Longaker. "Will you keep me informed about the progress of the Princess and the fetus?"

"Of course."

"Just one more question, Dr. MacGowan," said Longaker. "There's a phrase I hear every now and then when cases like this are being discussed on television or written about in the news magazines. What happens if someone, to quote the phrase, 'pulls the plug' on the Princess' advanced life support?"

"Nobody's going to do that here at Biscayne General," Liz said firmly.

"But if it should happen? Say from a power failure?"

"The apparatus has a battery that would keep it functioning at least long enough to give me time to perform a Caesarean section. I'd rather not be forced to do that but we do have one of the finest neonatal sections in the country. So even if the baby were more premature than we'd like it to be, the odds are that it would survive. I can give you my word, though, that nothing like this is going to happen."

The phone clicked off and Liz slammed her own receiver down on the cradle, letting the anger she'd held in during the conversation with Almani and also with the State Department officer explode.

The telephone rang almost immediately and, jerking the receiver from the cradle, Liz snapped, "Yes!"

"Wow!" It was Ted Bronson. "You sound riled."

" 'Riled' isn't the word for it. Where are you?"

"In the lobby. I was going to invite you to have a drink with me in the Dolphin Lounge before dinner."

"I'll be there in ten minutes."

"I'll get us a booth. It being Friday, a lot of people will be getting a start on TGIF."

Liz didn't need any explanation of the acronym. She arrived at the Dolphin Lounge to find the place teeming with happy people. When Ted waved to her from a booth in the corner, she saw that he already had two glasses on the table between the seats.

"What's worrying you?" he asked when she slid into the seat beside him.

"The usual—Sheik Almani and the State Department."

"I'd think knowing the fetus is a male, thereby making certain that the succession to the throne of Telfa would continue for at least one more generation, would please both of them."

Liz put down her drink suddenly. "How did you know that?"

"I met Moe Harris in the lobby just now and he told me about it. Finding a growing cell in a bloody tap wouldn't happen again in a thousand tries; I'd think you'd be happy about it, too."

"I am—or rather I was, until I talked to Almani and to Mr. Longaker at the State Department. Do you have any idea what they want me to do?"

"Something you don't want to do, I can see that."

"Both Almani and Longaker want me to deliver the baby right away."

"I won't ask you what your answer was, but I can guess."

"I acted like a lady," she told him. "But it damn near killed me."

"What did they say?"

"Both of them told me the decision is mine—I guess they could see it was going to be anyway."

"Did they promise not to put any more pressure on you?"

"No. And I don't believe for a minute they'll stop at merely putting the burden of decision on me."

"Probably not," he agreed. "The trouble is, you don't know just where it will come from, do you?"

"Not from Paul Fraser; I can be sure of that. But I'm a little less certain about Henry Letterman." Liz put down her drink and reached over to cover his hand with hers. "Forgive me, I have no right to dump my troubles on you—"

"I don't know of anyone who has a better right."

"You've got enough to worry about with Mike Corazon losing ground steadily," she said. "He *is* heading for liver failure, isn't he?"

"I'm afraid he's already there," Ted admitted. "When I talked to the family about noontime, Arturo broke down and cried. He's taking the poor outlook for Mike harder than the rest; I suppose because he's nearer childhood than they are, both in age and in his intellectual development."

"He seemed to be very happy when he brought me a lovely painting of an orchid for my office this morning."

"That must have been before I saw him in the Corazon suite."

"I'm sure it was because he told me you're going to save Michael."

"I guess it hit Arturo pretty hard when I had to tell the Corazons and Estrellita that I couldn't be certain Michael is going to make it."

"I've had to do that a few times myself," she said. "It's a burden no doctor can put on anyone else."

"I'd like to take you out to dinner," he said, "but I'm going to work late in the record room again, finishing up the letters to the transplant failures."

"I can't get far away from the hospital anyway," said Liz. "The OR staff set up a special sterile tray that will be kept in the Princess' room from now on. Jerry Rubin set the parameters for the fetal monitors, too, so a warning will sound at any significant change in its heart rate. If that happens, I'll have to be there in five minutes, so I'd better not get very far away."

IV

Liz was having a hamburger in the hospital coffee shop when the pager she wore pinned to her long white coat sounded its strident call. "Mr. Brown would like to see you in the administrative offices, Dr. MacGowan," the operator said.

Knowing that if Erasmus Brown was working after six o'clock—and it was already seven-thirty—it must be on something important, Liz decided to go immediately to the administrative offices, occupying the entire top floor of the tower. The four men in the spacious office of the chief administrator rose when she was ushered in by a secretary.

"Thank you for responding so promptly, Dr. MacGowan," said Erasmus Brown. "I believe you know everyone here."

"Hello, Mr. Nathan," Liz said as she accepted one of the comfortable chairs. "Aren't you working a little late for Friday afternoon?"

"Reporters are always on call for newsbreaks, Dr. MacGowan." Tall, gray-haired and handsome, Robert Nathan was the science editor of the Miami *Herald*. Usually he limited his reporting to news on medical and scientific subjects, making him a familiar figure around the great hospital. The other two men were Ed McIntire, head of Hospital Public Relations, and Nero Staige, liaison officer between the hospital and the broadcast media.

"In case you're wondering why I asked you to join us, Dr. MacGowan," said Brown, "did you happen to watch the national news on television at six-thirty today?"

"No."

"Late this afternoon, the U.S. State Department issued a news release describing what appeared to be an abortive attempt at a coup by a dissident group opposing the rule of Emir Hassim of Telfa. The coup failed but the Emir barely escaped assassination."

"I talked to Mr. Longaker of the State Department shortly before five, and also to Sheik Almani," said Liz. "Neither of them mentioned anything about political turmoil in Telfa."

"Apparently the news didn't reach the State Department until after five o'clock," the Miami *Herald* reporter volunteered. "As soon as State released it to the news-service tickers, I tried to call Ambassador Almani at the Dupont Plaza. The hotel said he checked out less than an hour earlier, taking a taxi to the airport and probably bound for New York."

"Was there anything special about your conversation with the Ambassador, Dr. MacGowan?" Mr. Brown asked.

"Very special! I told him Dr. Harris had just established that the fetus Princess Zorah is carrying is a male."

"And heir to the throne of Telfa!" said Nathan. "With Almani as Regent?"

"I understand," said Liz, "that according to Telfa law, in order to be actually in the line of royal succession, the baby must be alive and outside the mother's body when Emir Hassim dies."

"Dr. Pierce and Dr. MacGowan put Princess Zorah on advanced life support yesterday, Bob," said McIntire.

"What about the fetus, Dr. MacGowan?" Robert Nathan asked.

"The fetal pulse is strong and it's moving actively inside the uterus."

"How far along is the pregnancy?" Nathan was scribbling on a roll of copy paper such as reporters always carry with them.

"When she was admitted, we were told by Sheik Almani that the gestation period was probably twenty to twenty-two weeks," said Liz. "However, measurements taken while studying the fetus with ultrasound yesterday morning seem to indicate several weeks longer."

"Enough to make it viable if you did an emergency section now?" Robert Nathan asked.

"Viable, certainly," Liz admitted, "but also prone to serious complications. With the mother's body functioning as an excellent incubator for the fetus, I saw no reason to reduce its chances of surviving by doing a Caesarean section now, even though Sheik Almani and the State Department officer I talked to both seemed to want me to do it."

"How long do you plan to leave the fetus in what you consider such an excellent incubator?" Nathan asked.

"I estimate that two more weeks of intrauterine life would double the chances of delivering a viable child without much likelihood of complications," said Liz.

"What if you learned that Emir Hassim is dying and wants to know that a male successor is in existence, Doctor?" Erasmus Brown asked. "Wouldn't that affect your decision not to operate now?"

"My first concern is with the life of an unborn child, whether it's royalty or a black fetus from the slum," Liz said pointedly. Then a possible reason for this conference suddenly struck her. "Who's been pressing you to get me to change my mind, Mr. Brown?"

"What makes you think that?" he countered.

"Just a hunch—but I'm right, aren't I?"

"A high official in one of the major oil companies did call

me about an hour ago," Brown confessed. "He offered to make a substantial donation to the Research Foundation of the hospital if the Elzama baby were delivered alive."

"Weren't you surprised?" Liz asked.

"Of course, until he admitted that Ambassador Almani had called him and requested that he talk to me."

"Now we have international oil involved," said Nero Staige. "This story is getting more sensational every minute—and more unbelievable."

"Sensational, certainly, but maybe not unbelievable," said Robert Nathan. "During the oil famine imposed on the U.S. by the Arab producers several years ago, I flew to the Middle East and spent some time there filing a series of articles on the crisis."

"Did you visit Telfa?" Liz asked.

"Yes, along with several other of the emirates and the larger producers of oil. There were rumors then that one man controlled the entire output of oil from the fields of Telfa and determined the price."

"Yossuf Almani!" Nero Staige exclaimed. "It's all beginning to fit together, like the pieces of a jigsaw puzzle."

"I think you're right, Nero," Nathan agreed. "Did Ambassador Almani tell you he'd already been appointed Regent for the Emir's son if Emir Hassim dies, Dr. MacGowan?"

"As I remember the word he used, it was designated," said Liz. "But he was quite confident that he *would* be Regent."

"As Regent for a newborn successor to Emir Hassim, Almani could seize control of the government of Telfa as a virtual dictator," Erasmus Brown observed.

"I don't think so," said Liz. "He was particularly emphatic about the fact that Telfa law required the baby to be delivered alive and healthy before he could act as Regent."

"And with you refusing to deliver it until you were sure it was viable, Almani was trapped," said Nathan. "No wonder he tried to force you to operate immediately by having one of his client oil company heads call Mr. Brown and offer to make a donation."

"Did the oil company executive name a figure for that donation?" Liz asked Erasmus Brown.

"Yes. A million dollars."

"Wow!" said Ed McIntire. "Almani really *was* anxious!"

"My guess would be that there's more to it than that," said Robert Nathan. "When you told Almani this afternoon that the fetus is a male, Dr. MacGowan, did he seem to be very pleased?"

"That was what surprised me most about this whole affair," said Liz. "I expected him to be ecstatic, after the way he'd been insisting that it be delivered at once so its sex could be determined. But the news merely seemed to make him nervous."

"You've described Almani's reaction exactly as if he'd known that a plot to kill Emir Hassim was already in progress," Nathan told her.

"But that's absurd!" Erasmus Brown protested.

"Maybe not; listen to this scenario and tell me how it sounds," said Nathan. "Yossuf Almani has controlled the output of oil from Telfa for years, making contracts with American oil companies and no doubt getting a cut from the proceeds before they're paid to Emir Hassim. He probably has millions stashed away in Swiss bank accounts like a lot of other Arabs who've made fortunes in oil, but with Hassim dying of leukemia, he can now see an end to his cut. The logical thing for him to do, then, is to gain control of Telfa itself."

"How could he do that?" Erasmus Brown asked.

"The easiest way would be by being appointed Regent for an infant who is officially a successor to its father. So he convinces Emir Hassim to let him bring Princess Zorah to Miami, where Dr. MacGowan could determine the sex of the baby in advance. And, if it turned out to be male, persuade her to deliver it at once. That way he could be sure that a dying father would be grateful enough to appoint him Regent, to take office at the death of the Emir—which we hear could happen any day."

"Your scenario is ingenious," Liz told the newspaperman, "but I can see one serious fault in it."

"What's that?"

"Sheik Almani is no doubt smart enough to have known before he brought Princess Zorah here that the odds favored the fetus she was carrying being female."

"Why do you say that?" Erasmus Brown asked.

"In the ordinary course of events, human conception produces females more often than males—plus the fact that all the offspring Emir Hassim has fathered until now are females."

"I've an idea Almani is smart enough to have had another ace in the hole too," said Nathan. "With his cut in Telfa's oil millions, he has probably put together a political group that stands ready to seize control of Telfa if the Emir dies without an heir—"

"Then why is he so anxious for the baby to be born now that he's willing for its life to be in danger?" Liz asked. "As Regent, you'd think he'd want to make sure the child was viable and healthy."

"Almani's appointment to that office isn't official yet," Nathan reminded her. "Emir Hassim could always change his mind."

"I follow you," she said. "Please go on with your scenario. It gets more fascinating every minute."

"At this point, Almani's neatly laid plan gets fouled up," Nathan continued. "First, the Princess is fatally injured. Second, you tell him that at least two weeks will be required after amniocentesis so fetal cells in the fluid you remove can grow to where they can be identified as male or female."

"This time luck was with us," Liz reminded him. "We were

able to determine in twenty-four hours that the fetus is a male."

"You still refuse to deliver the baby before you consider it safe to do so," Nathan reminded her. "Emir Hassim seems to be losing ground more rapidly from leukemia than anyone expected and might well die before you consider it safe to deliver the child, leaving Telfa without a government."

"That was one of the arguments Ambassador Almani used to try to convince me to go ahead with the section," Liz said.

"Thank you for making my story even more creditable," Nathan said with a smile. "If Almani has to wait the two weeks you insist on and Emir Hassim should die before the heir to the throne is actually born, somebody in Telfa could step in and take over the government. So Almani takes no chances; before Princess Zorah comes to Miami, he hires a pack of the assassins who are always ready in Arab countries to kill anybody for a price. Their job was to assassinate the Emir when Almani gave them the word, and afterward he could claim a promise by Hassim to make him Regent if the child turned out to be male. That way he could keep the situation confused until you deliver the baby and an actual successor under the laws of Telfa is in existence—with Almani not only Regent but also virtual dictator."

"He's been playing both ends against the middle," Liz exclaimed. "But according to the news bulletin from the State Department you mentioned, the attempt to assassinate Emir Hassim failed. Where does that leave Almani?"

"I doubt that Almani ordered his minions to make the assassination attempt quite as soon as they did, but he is still in the driver's seat," said Nathan. "The only person who might let Emir Hassim in Telfa know he has sired a son before Almani can get there to deliver the news in person is the State Department official you talked to this afternoon, Dr. Mac-Gowan. I believe you said you reached him by a mobile phone in the limousine taking him home."

"Yes."

"Washington being what it is late on Friday afternoon, that means the State Department won't take up the matter of the succession in Telfa before Monday. I'd bet that Almani won't stop in New York, except to change airplanes before he heads for Telfa to take over in person."

"Planes, even on overseas flights, are pretty well filled on Friday afternoons," Ed McIntire objected.

"With a diplomatic passport, the Ambassador to the United Nations from even a small emirate like Telfa could bump somebody off the first plane heading across the Atlantic and take the seat," said Nathan. "Can anybody find holes in my scenario?"

When nobody did, the newspaperman headed for the door. "If you'll excuse me, I just have time to write the story for the morning edition."

"Along the lines of your scenario?" Liz asked.

"Not yet. This will be the first of a series I hope to develop as this affair breaks, now that you've given me the lead," Nathan said from the open doorway. "But to give you some idea of the turn it will take, I'll quote you the headline for the one that will appear tomorrow morning:

'DOCTOR FIGHTS TO SAVE UNBORN CHILD. DELAYS ROYAL BIRTH.'

"Don't be surprised to see your picture on the front page tomorrow morning, Dr. MacGowan," he added. "It won't damage my story a bit, either, that you're about the most photogenic medico anybody would want to see."

Chapter Fourteen

The sun was just rising over Biscayne Bay at six o'clock Saturday morning when Liz MacGowan started to cross the almost deserted thoroughfare between Biscayne General and her apartment in the Terrace. She had slept in the adjoining room of Princess Zorah's hospital suite but had not been disturbed. And when she'd looked in before leaving for her apartment, the advanced life-support apparatus had been functioning so smoothly it was hard to believe that, without it, the frail mother would have been dead.

"The little fellow's pulse has slowed down to normal and he's been kicking a lot during the night," the special nurse on duty for the eleven-to-seven shift had told her.

"Let's hope he stays active. If anything goes wrong, I'll be across the street getting a shower and some fresh clothing."

It had rained for a while during the night, giving the air the fresh smell of flowers from the gardens surrounding both the hospital and the Terrace, a pleasant aroma that would shortly be displaced by poisonous exhaust fumes from the morning traffic rush. The security guard outside the hospital lobby looked up from his desk and smiled.

"You're on the front page again with that Arab patient of yours, Dr. MacGowan," he said. "I'm glad I don't have the responsibility of keeping that mother and child alive until it can be born, but everybody here knows you can do it."

"Just part of my job," said Liz.

Dressing after her shower, Liz considered cooking breakfast and decided against it. In the hospital, the huge cafeteria was beginning to come alive with people, the oncoming shift grabbing coffee and a quick breakfast before the 7 A.M. change. She was surprised to see Dr. Ned Pierce at an empty table and took her tray over to join him.

"We don't often see you here on Saturday morning, Ned," she said. "Don't you usually play golf on weekends?"

"Not this morning," said the neurosurgeon. "The brain-tumor patient I operated on yesterday started having seizures about two hours ago. I came in to check on him."

"He wouldn't be a young adult with possible brain death, would he?" Liz asked quickly. "Ted badly needs a liver for Michael Corazon."

"No such luck, though there'll probably be several candidates before the weekend is over. Has Ted decided a transplant will be necessary?"

"Unless Mike shows a change for the better by Monday noon, Ted's going to make an appeal on TV and radio for a donor."

"What brings you out so early?" Pierce asked.

"I'll be sleeping in the hospital as long as Princess Zorah is on advanced life support."

"I glanced at the headlines of the morning paper when I came through the lobby—"

"I'm determined to save that baby, Ned—"

"Judging from the *Herald* story, you're going to have everybody from the U.S. State Department to the Emir of Telfa in your debt if you do. My brain-tumor patient is on the tenth floor, too, and I glanced into the Princess' room while I was up there. It looks like both mother and baby are doing fine on life support."

"Jerry Rubin and Pete Craig are tops in making the dead seem to live."

"Nevertheless, there's a lot of discussion nowadays about keeping people alive when they're dead by all the standards we used a few years ago," Pierce said soberly. "A lot of doctors seem to think body function should be preserved as long as possible without regard to the brain, even though it's a very costly process—"

"The Emir of Telfa is said to be one of the richest men in the world."

"Granted that the cost question doesn't apply in this particular case, some pretty important thinkers—both inside medicine and outside it—are questioning the wisdom of putting extremely ill patients on long term life support."

"I'm making it as short as possible this time, while sparing the fetus many of the complications we know happen to very premature babies. But I still haven't forgotten how many premies became blind later from retrolental fibroplasia because of the large amounts of oxygen we used to give them."

"That's one of the things that makes me doubtful about initiating life support in many cases—particularly the newborn. The probability of complications in the child long after the neonatal period are pretty sobering."

"It's still better than dying, Ned."

"Maybe. But when I see a child with Down's Syndrome, plus a neural tube defect like spina bifida and hydrocephalus, I can't help feeling that both patient and family would have been a lot better off if somebody had done amniocentesis during the first trimester of pregnancy. Once the diagnosis of Down's is made from studying the chromosomes, a syringe full of concentrated saline injected into the uterus can make it empty itself in a harmless abortion with no more danger than having a wisdom tooth pulled."

"I could argue those points with you, Ned, but we would be wasting time that could be better spent," said Liz. "My guess is that the question of prolonged life will be discussed for years, especially since some family members have started suing doctors accused of pulling the plug too soon."

I I

By Monday morning, eight days after the attempt on Michael Corazon's life, it was obvious even to a nonmedical observer that his damaged liver had passed the point of no return. And that without a replacement in the form of a transplant, the sick man was doomed.

"The only thing that can save Mike is a transplant," Ted told the Corazon family when he finished his morning examination. "And since he can't give me permission to broadcast a call for donors and operate immediately, if one becomes available, you as the family must do it."

"Doesn't the donor have to be dead before you take the liver from the body?" Estrellita asked.

"Only a diagnosis of brain death is required," Ted explained. "Actually, when we take the liver from the donor, we prefer for the heart to be still beating—"

"But the donor would still be alive!" Maria protested.

"Medically not," Ted told her. "It has been shown in hundreds of cases that no patient will live once the electric currents that accompany brain activity cannot be measured."

Arturo had been listening, but a look of bewilderment had steadily deepened in his eyes and on his face.

"Is Michael dying, Dr. Ted?" he asked.

"What I'm saying, Arturo, is that there's no way to keep him alive unless the liver of another person can be found in time to transplant it in the place of his own."

"Then do it!" In his concern, Arturo's voice had risen almost to a shout, and when Estrellita reached for his hand to comfort him, he clung to it with a grip that must have been painful. "Don't let Michael die!"

"What course do you propose to follow now?" Estrellita asked.

"I'd like to call a press conference before noon today, so we can hit the noonday radio and television news programs. At the same time, I'll notify the emergency room personnel of all hospitals in Miami and also within a few hours flying time that we badly need the liver of a person about Michael's age and size. If a liver is made available from an accident case or other injury, I will fly directly to the hospital and personally remove it and bring it to Miami as quickly as possible."

"Shouldn't you get on with the press conference, then?" she asked.

"I'm waiting only for the family's approval, but I wanted to be sure all of you understood the situation."

Maria looked at her sons and turned back to Ted. "We trust you," she said. "If anybody can save him, we're sure it's you."

"My plane will be available twenty-four hours a day to fly you wherever you want to go," Pedro assured him.

The press conference was called just before noon and the small teaching auditorium of the hospital was half filled with media representatives when Ted came on the platform.

"I have asked you here because a grave change has occurred in the condition of Mr. Michael Corazon," he said. "As you know, an attempt on his life failed about ten days ago, largely due to prompt action by technicians of the Rescue Squad who answered the emergency call to Mr. Corazon's home last Monday. A bullet that went completely through Mr. Corazon's liver apparently did enough damage inside the organ to cause what is known as liver failure. It is the opinion of both the surgical and medical staffs of this hospital that, unless a healthy liver can be obtained for transplant shortly, Mr. Corazon will not survive."

"What do you mean by a healthy liver, Doctor?" a reporter on the front row asked.

"Ideally, the organ we need would be that of a healthy male or female accident victim, preferably with a head wound, in whom brain death has been determined by electroencephalography."

"Am I right in assuming that you called this conference to launch a search for a transplantable liver in time to save Mr. Corazon's life, Doctor?" another reporter asked.

"Yes. You are correct."

"May I ask what other steps have been taken?"

"Since about ten o'clock this morning, I have personally telephoned every hospital within the city as well as those within a few hours flying time," Ted answered. "I have asked the chiefs of their emergency services to alert all their personnel to watch for an accident patient who fulfills our requirements."

"Which are what, besides brain death?" a woman reporter asked.

"Someone preferably between the ages of perhaps eighteen and forty-five."

"With the same blood type as Mr. Corazon?"

"We no longer believe a difference in blood type between donor and recipient is necessarily a barrier to successful transplant."

"Suppose you do find a donor and you operate and perform a technically successful transplant operation but Mr. Corazon does not survive?" said another reporter. "Would his death still be legally classified as homicide?"

"Legal authority will have to establish that. My whole concern is for Mr. Corazon's life, and I am asking all of you to do whatever you can to publicize the fact that we need a donor. Hopefully, the family of some accident victim who might be suitable will hear of our need and make an intact liver available before it's too late."

The conference broke up as the reporters hurried to get their stories into the press and on the air. Ted had not seen Liz come in at the back of the auditorium but, when he came up the aisle in the wake of the departing media representatives, he was glad to see her standing there.

"I didn't see you come in," he told her.

"I thought one of the news people might ask why Princess Zorah cannot be used as a donor, since the onset of brain death was announced several days ago."

"How is she?"

"Functioning beautifully as an incubator, which is all I want her body to do. But suppose I offered to deliver the baby now and let you remove Princess Zorah's liver immediately to save Michael Corazon's life?"

"It wouldn't work."

"Why?"

"For one thing, the difference in blood vessel size is too great. For another, we don't know how much the fact that you have her on advanced life support may have diminished her vital functions."

"You just took a load off my mind," she told him as they left the auditorium. "I was afraid that if no donor turned up soon, you might suggest using Princess Zorah and I would have to say no because of the fetus."

"You've already said no once; I'm glad I won't have to ask you to say it again. By the way, what is Ambassador Almani doing?"

"Cooling his heels in New York or Telfa as far as I know, waiting for me to put the next Emir of Telfa in his care as Regent."

But there, as it happened, Liz was wrong.

III

Just before eight, Liz dismissed her class of young mothers—
and the few fathers dragooned by their wives into attending—
intended to prepare them not only for the rigors of childbear-
ing but, even more important, for its responsibilities. Fairly
certain that Ted would be at work in the hospital records
room, she stopped by and found him hunched over the keyboard of the master computer. With it, he was studying the
hospital records of patients in whom kidney transplants had
been rejected, both before and during the two years in which
he had been chief of the Organ Transplant Service.

"It's time you took a break—for the night," Liz told him.

"The prospects of nights alone aren't exactly exhilarating
when you've been studying your own failures—and those of
others—since six o'clock," he told her somewhat ruefully as
he switched off the computer. "Even during the last two
years, when the whole thing has been my responsibility, there
have been a lot more failures than I have let myself realize."

"How about the old days—before you came here?"

"I shouldn't really criticize the surgeons involved and I
don't. They were certainly as good in their operating techniques as I am."

"I doubt that. A surgeon gains proficiency in operative
technique by experience. You've had plenty of that in Pittsburgh and during the two years since you've been chief of
service here. How is your search for kidney transplant failures
going?"

"The last of the letters will be in the mail tomorrow," he
said.

"Any answers yet—besides the one from Mrs. Worthington?"

"Not yet—but they should start coming in soon. How's your human incubator doing?"

"As perfect as I could wish. The fetus looks great on the monitors, too."

"I wish I could say as much about Mike."

"No leads yet for a possible donor?" she asked, but he shook his head.

"No; and I'm afraid the waiting is going to be tough on the family, particularly Arturo. He doesn't seem to understand just why I can't take a liver from anyone who dies, no matter what the cause."

Both of them were startled when the phone beside the computer keyboard rang sharply. Ted picked up the receiver.

"There's a call for you, Dr. Bronson," said the operator. "He says it's long distance—about Mr. Corazon."

"I'll talk to him, Mary." Ted's voice was suddenly tense as he put his hand over the telephone receiver and told Liz, *sotto voce*, "It's about Mike—long distance."

There was a brief pause while the connection was made, then a masculine voice came on the line.

"Dr. Bronson?"

"Yes."

"This is Dr. Jonas Ellington in Everglades City—about sixty miles west of you off the Tamiami Trail."

"I know where Everglades City is, Doctor. One of the faculty here at Biscayne General keeps his boat there. I went with him on a fishing trip out of Everglades last year."

"Then you know how to get here. I heard on the radio that you're looking for a liver donor."

"I certainly am, Dr. Ellington." Ted's pulse had jumped at the other doctor's question. "Do you have one?"

"I may have, Dr. Bronson. A deck hand on one of the fishing boats here was in an accident this afternoon as he was going home. His motorcycle ran off the road and struck a tree, smashing his head right hard. He's been in coma ever since and in my judgment he can't live much longer. When I told the family you were looking for a liver donor for Mr. Corazon, I was able to talk them into letting me call you."

"Do you think they'd give permission if we can establish brain death?"

"I believe they might, if you come here and talk to them."

"Couldn't the injured man be brought to Miami by ambulance?"

"I suggested that but they didn't like the idea. Said they couldn't see the point in hauling him sixty miles or so to Miami when he was going to die anyway, and then only have to haul him back. If you're coming, better bring your instruments and everything you'll need to take the liver out as soon as he can be pronounced dead."

"I can be there in an hour and a half—"

"He should live that long, I've got him on a respirator. I run an emergency clinic at the city limits on the road into Everglades City from the Tamiami Trail. You can recognize it by the electric sign."

"I'll be there in no more than an hour and a half, Doctor," Ted told him. "And thanks."

"That was a Dr. Ellington in Everglades City," Ted told Liz as he hung up the phone. "He has an accident case there who is probably about to suffer brain death and thinks the family will let me remove the liver."

"How far is Everglades City?"

"About fifty-five or sixty miles west of here and a few miles south of the Tamiami Trail. Dr. Ellington said if I come right away, he thinks he can keep the patient alive on the respirator until I get there. And, if the family gives me permission, I can remove the liver right there and bring it to Miami in a cooler. I'll leave as soon as I can get a sterile laparotomy tray fixed from the OR—"

"I've been keeping one in Princess Zorah's room in case I had to do a section. You can save time by picking it up and the night OR crew will fix another one for me. Are you going to fly?"

Ted shook his head. "Pedro Corazon offered me the use of his plane, but I can get to Everglades City in my Porsche in an hour or less and we'd lose that much time getting the plane engine warmed up and filing a flight plan. All I have to do before I leave is pick up your tray and a large cooler from the blood-bank area in the basement and put some ice into it. After I remove the liver, the trip back shouldn't take more than an hour and a half and that's well within the safe limits for transplanting the organ."

"You could use some surgically skilled help in removing the liver," she told him. "How about letting me go with you?"

"What about Baby Elzama?"

"I slept in the hospital last night because I needed to be sure it would be stable with the princess on advanced life support. The fetus is doing fine and any trouble it will get into won't happen for several days at least, when it might start absorbing some toxic products with the state of artificial metabolism we've created in the mother's body with advanced life support. We'll be back by midnight anyway."

"Fine. I'll pick you up in the parking garage across the street in twenty minutes."

Liz was waiting when Ted drove his sleek Porsche down the exit ramp of the parking garage. She was wearing slacks and a knit top with a blue bandeau around her hair. Opening the right door of the Porsche when he braked it to a stop, she slid inside, shutting the door.

"I'm glad you took time to attach the CB antenna." Liz fastened her seat belt as he guided the car out into the westward traffic. "I always feel safer traveling at night if I know the CB is handy and I can call for help if I need it."

"In that outfit, I'd better keep you out of sight when we get to Everglades City," Ted told her. "If the donor's brain isn't completely dead, the sight of you might wake him up and we'd lose any chance of getting a transplantable liver."

Darkness had fallen well before they reached the Dade County line. As the traffic on the Tamiami Trail thinned, Ted was able to step up the speed of the sleek Porsche above the legitimate fifty-five miles per hour. The terrain here was flat, the level expanse of the Everglades—aptly known as the "River of Grass"—broken only by clumps of trees on slightly higher ground known as hammocks. With the windows of the low-slung car shut, the two were isolated in a small, air-conditioned space craft, so to speak, hurtling westward on what, until the development of another trail to the north with the colorful name of Alligator Alley, had been Florida's best-known road.

When the "Leaving Dade County, Entering Collier County" sign flashed by, Liz reached for the off-on switch on the CB radio set attached beneath the cowl board and turned on the power.

"Why don't I talk on Channel Nine to the Florida Highway Patrol in Miami?" she said. "Maybe they have a trooper stationed in Everglades City who could escort us back to Miami. Once we remove that transplant, the sooner you get it into Mike's abdomen and connected up to his circulation, the better it will be for him."

"Good thinking," Ted approved. "By all means try raising the police."

"Sergeant Peters, Florida Highway Patrol," a firm, masculine voice answered Liz's call and she handed the microphone to Ted.

"This is Dr. Theodore Bronson from Biscayne General, Sergeant," he said.

"Heard on the six o'clock news about Mr. Corazon needing a transplant, Doctor. What can I do for you?"

"I had a call about an hour ago from a Dr. Ellington in Everglades City, Sergeant. An accident victim there appears to be dying from a head injury and the doctor believes I can talk the family into letting me use his liver as a transplant for Mr. Corazon."

"A near-fatal accident in Everglades City, did you say?"

"Yes."

"We've had no report of it."

"Dr. Ellington said a crewman on one of the fishing boats operating from there was riding a motorcycle, apparently from the docks to his home, and ran into a tree. It's possible that nobody thought of it as the kind of accident that should be reported to the Highway Patrol."

"You're probably right," the policeman agreed. "We have a trooper who lives in Everglades City, Doctor. Right now, there's been a bad pileup on Okeechobee Road in Hialeah, but when the traffic gets going again I'll check with him. Can we do anything else to help you?"

"If the injured man dies and I'm able to convince the family to let me remove his liver, I'd like to have a police escort at least from the Dade County line to Biscayne General."

"As soon as you have the organ for transplant, Doctor, call Trooper Harold Muldoon. He'll escort you all the way to the hospital. His number in Everglades City is five-five-five-one-two-one-two."

"Thank you, Sergeant. I'll call him when we're ready to leave for Miami."

"Good luck, Doctor."

Chapter Fifteen

Outside the limits of metropolitan Miami, traffic on the Tamiami Trail thinned out noticeably and Ted put the Porsche up to seventy miles an hour. Nobody passed them and only very rarely did they see the taillights of a car ahead before rapidly overtaking it.

"The Trail was a busy thoroughfare when I first started spending Christmas vacations in Coconut Grove with the Corazons about fifteen years ago," Ted told Liz. "Much of the traffic nowadays goes by way of a new road called Alligator Alley. It cuts straight across the Everglades about thirty miles north of here and runs from Naples to Fort Lauderdale. Even though it's a toll road, it's cheaper than wearing out tires on the Trail, unless you have to come this way as we're doing tonight."

"We seem to be following what looks like a canal," she observed. "In some places the water doesn't appear to be more than fifteen or twenty feet from the edge of the road."

"When the land is as flat as this is and largely covered by water much of the time, except for the hammocks, it's easy to dig a canal and pile up the dirt for a road beside it—the way they did in the twenties when the Tamiami Trail was built. Naturally they called the canal Tamiami, too."

"Is it very deep?"

"Deep enough for cars that veer off the road for any reason to go into the canal, sometimes not to be discovered for years. I certainly wouldn't want to be driving on this road with much alcohol in my bloodstream."

"Will we have to travel beside the canal all the way to Everglades City?" she asked.

"No. The Trail veers north and leaves the canal not far from a place called Paolita Station. We ought to be there in another twenty minutes or so."

"I'll be glad to see that damn canal disappear; it gives me the willies. Are there any alligators in it?"

"Plenty," he said. "Mike and I often saw a lot of gators when we fished along the canal during vacations. Hunting them to get their skins for shoes and women's handbags was pretty profitable back in the twenties and thirties, and so many gators were killed that the state government had to step in and protect them. They breed pretty fast, though, and lately so many of 'em have been crawling out of Florida streams and up through storm drains into people's yards, those who live near the water, that the state started allowing the taking of some skins. Mostly they catch dogs or pigs, but for a really big gator, even a man is easy prey."

Liz had been staring out the window as the dark ribbon of the road with the canal beside it—the water shut away sometimes for as much as a quarter of a mile by stands of Australian pines that often grew between the water and the roadside —flashed past. Now she leaned forward suddenly and pulled down the sun visor that was folded up against the windshield by night. In the center of it was a small mirror for women to use in repairing their makeup and this she moved carefully, staring into it intently.

"We won't get to Everglades City for at least another thirty or forty minutes," Ted told her. "There's no point in worrying about fixing your makeup yet."

"I thought I saw the flash of a headlight from your rear-vision mirror just now," she said. "I see a car in this one; it looks like it's overtaking us."

Ted glanced up at the rear-vision mirror and then at the side mirror located just in front of the door. "He's really making time, too. We're doing eighty-five and he's overtaking us fast, so he must be doing ninety or ninety-five."

"Who would be driving out here in the wilderness at that speed and at night?"

"Search me. One thing we can bet on, though, it isn't a highway patrolman."

"How can you tell?"

"If it was he would have turned on his flasher long since, warning us to pull over."

Moments later the approaching car, as silently as a panther stalking its prey, started going past them.

"And mighty close, too," Ted conceded.

As the other car crept halfway past, they were able to see that it was a Jaguar, as powerful a vehicle as the Porsche and easily capable of outrunning them at a much higher speed.

"I've got all I can do to hold the Porsche on this old road at the speed we're going, but try to get a good look at the driver of the Jag and at the tag when it gets past us," Ted told Liz. "We can report it to Trooper Muldoon when we get to Everglades City."

"The glass in the side door has a very dark tint." Liz had turned in her seat and was studying the passing car. "I'll be able to see through the back window, though, as soon as he gets well past us and your lights shine through it into the inside. Why don't you slow down and let him go?"

"I'm slowing but he is, too—and veering toward us." Ted's voice was suddenly taut and the Porsche swerved a little to the right as he guided it closer to the often crumbling edge of the blacktop marking the roadway. The passing car swerved, too, however, and there was a sudden grinding sound of metal scraping against metal as the front fenders momentarily touched, setting off a shower of sparks.

"I just got a glimpse of people in the Jaguar," Liz reported. "It's two men and one of them is holding a rifle or a sub-machine gun."

"Get down on the floor but try to reach up and switch on the CB and get the microphone."

"I've got it," she reported moments later from a position on the floor of the Porsche.

Ted gripped the wheel and braced himself as the two swiftly moving cars ground against each other again, producing another shower of sparks and forcing the Porsche to swerve dangerously.

"They're trying to kill us by driving us into the canal!" Liz cried.

"Where we might not be found for years," Ted added grimly. "Call Channel Nine on the CB," he directed as the other car, having given up the strategy of forcing them off the road and into the canal, began to pull ahead.

"Come in Channel Nine! Come in Channel Nine!" Liz's voice was high-pitched with fear at this attack upon them on a deserted roadway at night.

"Channel Nine, Sergeant Peters," a welcome voice sounded.

"This is Dr. MacGowan with Dr. Bronson, Sergeant. We're somewhere on the Tamiami Trail and a Jaguar is trying to run us off the road into the canal."

"Can you see his license plate, Doctor?"

"Yes, they failed to push us into the canal so they're pulling ahead. The license plate is in our headlights now; it's DRU 724, Dade County."

The Jaguar was ahead of them now. In the glare of the Porsche's headlights, Liz saw a man lean out of the right-hand window. He was holding an automatic rifle, aiming back at the Porsche.

"Stay down, Liz!" Ted warned as he took his foot from the accelerator, hoping to widen the distance between the vehicle and make it a more difficult target. "He's shooting at our tires."

A sudden burst of fire came from the barrel of the gun ahead and bullets ricocheted off the fender and the hood.

"Brace yourself, Liz!" Ted shouted. "If he hits the front tire—"

A loud crack penetrated even the metal protection of the smaller car's body as its right front tire exploded from a bullet penetrating the rubber tire.

"I can't hold it!" Ted shouted as the Porsche swerved sharply to the right. "We're going into the canal!"

Even as he was speaking, the Porsche left the roadway and hurtled across the shoulder, heading inexorably to the dark, brooding waters of the Tamiami Canal.

II

Crouching on the floor of the car, Liz was tumbled about as it bounced across the narrow portion of unpaved shoulder and plunged beneath the surface of the canal. Still clinging to the cord of the CB microphone, although it could help them no longer, she fought her way to an upright position in the car as it started settling. And feeling Ted's arms closing about her when he slid over to her side, she clung to him with her left hand, reaching instinctively for the right-hand door latch.

"Don't try to open it!" His voice was hoarse with tension.

"But it's the only way we can escape!"

"You couldn't open that door now against the pressure of the water outside no matter how hard you tried," he said. "Just pray that the Porsche settles on the bottom of the canal still upright and deep enough for the CB antenna to be hidden."

"Why? When we're going to drown anyway?"

"We won't drown if we keep our heads on." His voice was intendedly sharp, trying to jolt her out of her immediate terror. "The water is already rising through the floorboards but this car is tightly built. If we hold on while it fills, enough air will be trapped inside the metal roof for us to be able to breathe for quite a while."

"When the Jaguar pulled ahead so the man with the automatic rifle could get a shot at a tire, our headlights lit up the inside." Liz had gotten control of herself, with the security of Ted's arm about her. "It was Sam Gianno."

"Are you sure?"

"I delivered his last child, so of course I could identify him."

"Then save your breath; we're going to need it. Breathe normally and you'll use up less oxygen in the air that's being trapped under the roof. Once the pressure inside gets anywhere near that outside, we can open the door and swim to the surface." His words were interrupted by a sudden jolt as the wheels of the car struck bottom. "If you've ever prayed, do it now."

"Hold me tighter, darling. If we're going to die, I want it to be in your arms."

"We're not going to die," he assured her. "The car has settled to the bottom in an upright position. If the air trapped inside the roof lasts long enough for those two outside to decide we've drowned and give us up for dead, we've got it made."

For perhaps ten minutes—although it seemed like an eternity—Ted sat bolt upright in the Porsche with Liz in his arms. The pressure of the trapped air was making breathing much more difficult as the level of water rose to their shoulders and then up to their chins in the steadily narrowing space under the roof of the car.

"How long has it been?" Liz asked.

"Maybe twenty minutes."

"Twenty minutes! The water's up to my chin."

"Turn your head back and keep your nose above it as long as you can," he advised. "Each minute that we can stay submerged increases the chance that Gianno and his gunman will decide to leave. Thank God I insisted on manual controls for the windows," he added. "Even if we can't get the door itself open, I can always run down the glass and leave us enough space to escape through and swim to the surface. When I push the door open," he added, "crawl out and swim toward the back of the car and as far away as you can before you surface. Then head for the bank on the roadside; the weeds and grass growing along the edge there may keep them from realizing we've escaped."

"Say when." She kissed him before drawing in as much air as her lungs would hold. Taking a deep breath at the same time, Ted shoved down on the latch of the door, pushing it outward. It opened slowly, and when he judged the opening to be wide enough for Liz to escape, he shoved her out through the narrow space and followed her.

The turbulence of her rapidly kicking heels against his face told him she was swimming as far away from the car as she could before being forced to the surface to breathe. Following close enough behind her to touch her heels occasionally, he surfaced when he could hold his breath no longer. As he emerged, he seized a clump of weeds growing down across the edge of the canal bank. And when he reached out in a sweeping motion, seeking Liz, his hand touched her breast. She caught his hand and he pulled them both along, seeking to get as far away as possible from the spot where the car had plunged into the canal by clutching the tendrils of grass and weeds along the bank at the water's edge.

By pulling himself up to the level of the bank for a brief moment, Ted was able to see where the Porsche had gone over. The two men were using the powerful beam of a searchlight to sweep back and forth along its edges, obviously seeking to discover whether the two they had sought to kill could possibly have escaped.

"It's been a half hour since they went over the bank, Sam." The speaker's voice had a distinct Jersey accent. "Nobody's ever been down this long and lived."

"I guess you're right," the other man admitted.

"Then let's get the hell out of here before a car comes along and someone sees us. Unless a fisherman finds those two maybe years from now, nobody's going to know what happened to them."

"I just hope for your sake that you're right, Abe," the man named Sam, who was obviously in charge, agreed. "This could be the third time you've failed. First, you didn't manage to kill Corazon—"

"I put two bullets into his liver, according to the newspaper stories," the Jersey accent said indignantly. "Corazon's going to die in a few days and you'll be in the clear, so what the hell are you worrying about? When that surgeon at Biscayne General turns up missing, everything you want to accomplish will be over."

"If you'd aimed six inches higher that morning in Coconut Grove," the man called Sam interposed, "we wouldn't have had to worry about anything."

"Anybody can spray a lot of bullets around with a machine gun," Jersey accent protested, "but it takes a real sharpshooter to put one where it counts."

"All right, so you're a professional," the man called Sam said. "Let's get the hell out of here."

Listening from a position close against the bank of the canal, while Ted's left hand gripped the roots of an Australian pine growing beside the canal, they heard the engine of the

Jaguar start. It was followed by the squeal of tires as the driver reversed the car, turned and sent it hurtling back along the Tamiami Trail toward Miami.

Using all the strength he could muster, Ted managed to drag himself over the bank of the canal to a place on its grassy border. Reaching down, he pulled Liz up beside him and they lay in a close embrace for a long moment, savoring the joy of being alive and together, in spite of the chill from their wet bodies that was rapidly bringing goose bumps. Finally, Ted pulled himself to his feet and drew her up.

"We're so far from the road that any car coming past might fail to see us," he told her. "Besides, we've got to get help to take us on to Everglades City so I can get that liver and take it back to Miami."

"You mean you're still going there after what just happened?" Then she answered her own question. "But of course you are—being you."

"Even if that call from Dr. Ellington was a fake—and it probably was—to get me where Sam Gianno could get rid of me by leaving my body in the canal, I can't deny Mike his only possible chance to live."

"I guess we'd better start walking then," Liz said resignedly.

Walking along the Trail toward Paolita Station, where Ted hoped to find help, they had gone less than a mile when they saw the headlights of a car approaching from the west. It was moving at a high rate of speed and, when Ted saw the flashing light identifying it as a police car, he pulled a sodden handkerchief out of his back pocket and waved it frantically. The car passed them but the sudden squeal of brakes told them they'd been seen. Moments later, the police car turned around and stopped beside them. Leaving the lights glaring, the driver opened the door and came around the car. He was a tall young trooper in uniform and Ted couldn't remember when he'd been so glad to see a policeman.

"Dr. Bronson?" the trooper asked.

"Yes. This is Dr. MacGowan."

"I'm Sergeant Muldoon from Everglades City. Where's your car?"

"In the canal."

The trooper gave them a startled look. "Run that past me again, please."

"The car is submerged," Ted explained, "but fortunately I remembered something I read a long time ago about how to handle a situation like this. We stayed inside my Porsche while it filled and were able to breathe the air trapped under the roof. When the air pressure inside and the water pressure outside became equal, I opened the door and we swam out."

"It's a miracle," said the policeman in a tone of awe.

"Dr. Bronson does miracles every day, Sergeant," said Liz. "What about that accident patient in Everglades City whose liver was going to be donated for Mr. Corazon?"

"There never was an accident patient—"

"But Dr. Ellington—" Ted protested.

"Nor a Dr. Ellington either," the trooper added. "Someone faked a call from Everglades City to lure you out on the Trail tonight, Doctor, where you could be killed and your car, with your bodies inside it, hidden in the canal."

"How did you . . . ?"

"When Sergeant Peters called me about giving you an escort back to Miami tonight with the transplant, I told him there was no Dr. Ellington in Everglades and no near-fatal accident this afternoon. The Sergeant and I decided that the whole thing was a trap planned by the criminal organization Sam Gianno heads in Miami to kill you so you couldn't save Mr. Corazon, even if a donor is found in time. He tried to raise you on your CB to warn you, but your radio didn't answer."

"I must have switched it off after we talked to Sergeant Peters as we were leaving Miami," said Liz. "I remember now that I had to switch it on again so I could call him to tell him we were being passed by another car that was trying to force us off the road."

"I'll call Sergeant Peters and tell him to set up a roadblock at the Dade County line," said Muldoon. "What kind of car were they driving, Doctor?"

"A red Jaguar. You'll find some paint scraped off the right fender where the cars rubbed together."

"With luck, that scraped paint will send your would-be killers to the electric chair," said Sergeant Muldoon as he went to the police car and picked up the receiver of the radio.

"Muldoon calling Dade Central," he said. "Muldoon calling Dade Central."

"This is Dade Central," a distant voice answered. "Go ahead, Muldoon."

"I'm a few miles east of Monroe Station with Dr. Bronson and Dr. MacGowan. They're safe."

"Then their car didn't go into the canal?"

"It did but they used their heads and let it fill before opening the door and swimming out. Dr. Bronson says the people who were trying to kill him were driving a red Jaguar and some of the paint from his car ought to be on it." Muldoon turned to Ted, who was standing with his arm around Liz, who was now shivering from the cool night air on her wet clothes. "What color is your car, Doctor?"

"A sky-blue Porsche. We scraped fenders with the Jaguar twice before they passed. Afterward, a man with an automatic rifle leaned out of the right-hand window and shot out my right front tire, sending my car into the canal."

"When you catch them, look for sky-blue paint on the right fender of the Jag," Trooper Muldoon told the Miami officer.

"Good work, Jimmy," he said. "We'll set up a roadblock on the Tamiami Trail at the Dade County line. Bring Dr. Bronson and Dr. MacGowan directly to the Dade County Sheriff's Office. I'd like to get their statements on record so we'll have them if we're lucky enough to catch those hoods at the road-block. Did either of the doctors see the two men in the car well enough to identify them?"

"I—" Liz started to speak, but Ted quickly shook his head and she didn't continue.

Hanging up the microphone on its hook, Muldoon opened the back door of the police car and brought out a large rain-coat. "This will feel like a tent, Dr. MacGowan," he said, holding it for her to slip her arms into the sleeves, "but it will keep you from getting a chill. If you will show me where you went off the road into the canal, Doctor, I need to get some flash pictures before it rains and washes out the tracks."

The spot was easily determinable when they reached it, about a mile east of where Ted and Liz had met the trooper from Everglades City.

"It must have taken a lot of muscle to hold that wheel and maneuver it between two of those Australian pines growing close here," Trooper Muldoon said as he was photographing the scene. "If you'd happened to hit one of them at that speed instead of going into the water, both of you would no doubt have been squashed inside your Porsche." Going back to his car, the trooper took a round object from it and brought it back to where they'd been standing along the roadway. "I'm going to put a firepot here to mark the area where you went off so we can find it early in the morning. I'll bring a wrecker out here then and pull your car out."

"Do you think there's any chance you might find the bullet that punctured the right front tire inside it?" Ted asked as the policeman was lighting the wick on the firepot.

"We'll certainly look for it, Doctor. If Sergeant Peters catches those two in the Jaguar, the ballistics laboratory may be able to match the bullet to the weapon that fired it and we'll have them in a real bind."

III

At the Dade County Sheriff's Office in Miami, Ted and Liz had to wait briefly while a court reporter was brought in to transcribe their stories of what had happened earlier that evening. While they were drinking coffee in an empty office, Liz asked, "Shall I still keep quiet about recognizing Sam Gianno driving the Jaguar?"

"I'd rather you did."

"Mind telling me why?"

"Sergeant Peters told me just now that only the hired killer with the Jersey accent was caught in the Jaguar by the police roadblock. That means Sam Gianno managed to drop off somewhere on the Trail west of it and he's certain to have prepared an alibi before he followed us out of Miami and, if he's arrested tonight, his lawyers will have him out on bail before morning. You're the only person a jury would believe, if your testimony places him under the wheel of the Jaguar tonight. With the criminal resources Gianno and his lawyer could command, your life wouldn't be worth the proverbial plugged nickel once he was free."

"I didn't think of that."

"If Gianno would go to the lengths he went to tonight to kill me just because I might be able to save Mike Corazon—if we ever find a liver donor—he certainly wouldn't hesitate to have you killed. I don't want to be going to your funeral before our wedding."

"I still don't feel exactly right in letting him go free."

"Neither do I, but I think the circumstances justify it." Then he brightened. "Tell you what—the police say the Jersey hood who was using the automatic rifle was turned over to Nick Patterson and the FBI. After we tell our stories for the Dade County authorities, I'll call Nick and talk to him about what you should do."

"I'll feel a lot better if he agrees with you," she said.

The court reporter appeared just then and they spent the next hour telling the story of their adventures that night—without any mention of Sam Gianno. As the reporter was leaving, Nick Patterson came into the office where the interviews had been held.

"I guess you two know how lucky you were tonight," he said in a tone of mild reproof. "I've chewed out the agent who was guarding you, Dr. Bronson, even though he tells me you told him he could wait in the lobby while you were working in the record room. How did you manage to get out without his seeing you?"

"I forgot all about him," Ted confessed. "I picked up an ice chest at the blood bank in the basement of the hospital and left by the loading platform where the morticians pick up bodies. Sorry."

"Please let us know before you blunder into another trap. It's too bad neither of you got a good look at the man who was driving that Jaguar."

Liz gave him a startled look. "I thought they only caught one."

"We did, but a Jaguar isn't the easiest car to drive when you're not accustomed to handling powerful foreign cars with a stick shift. The thug the police caught was doing a lousy job of driving when they nabbed him at the roadblock. He tried to turn around but got into reverse instead."

"Which means?" Ted asked.

"In your statement just now, you said you were making about eighty-one when the Jaguar passed you. In Dr. Mac-Gowan's statement she described the man with the automatic rifle quite well and said he was leaning out the right front window when he shot out the tire of your Porsche. That means someone else was driving but managed to drop off on the Trail west of the roadblock. Want to tell me why you didn't describe the second man, Dr. MacGowan?"

Liz looked questioningly at Ted, who answered for her:

"She made a positive identification of Sam Gianno, Nick, but I told her not to mention it because if she did she'd be his number one target."

"I thought that might be it," said the FBI agent. "Are you sure of your identification, Dr. MacGowan?"

"No question about it. Our headlights were shining through the back window of his car and I saw him plainly, when he turned his head."

"Do you know him that well?"

"Right after I came to Miami, I delivered his last child," Liz explained. "The family even had me out to their estate in Coral Gables for dinner after Mass one Sunday."

"That should convince any jury when the time comes for you to testify," Nick Patterson told her.

"But not now," Ted insisted.

"I agree," said Patterson. "Guarding both of you would take more agents than I could muster, anyway, but the hired gun who was caught tonight probably handled the weapon in both assassination attempts. When he finds out the evidence we have against him, he'll probably want to make a deal."

"Would you let him off that easy?" Liz inquired. "With two charges of attempted murder against him—three in all— if you count us as two tonight?"

"Hired guns are available these days to anybody who's willing to pay from twenty-five to a hundred thousand dollars for someone to spray bullets on citizens who are getting close after crooks. It's the fellows at the top who employ the gunmen we're after and this time it looks like we'll be able to put Sam Gianno where the Family in Jersey he represents down here won't be able to get him off."

"I hope so," said Liz. "For a few moments, while the water was creeping up my body toward the small amount of air trapped underneath the roof of the car, it was pretty rough being face-to-face with my Maker."

"You're lucky Dr. Bronson remembered what to do," Nick Patterson told her. "In your place, I think I'd try to keep him close by from now on."

"You can depend on that, Mr. Patterson," said Liz firmly.

"Right now, a gaggle of reporters and TV people are waiting outside to grill you both. But considering the number of times you've been on the front pages and featured on the six o'clock news lately, I'm sure neither of you is camera shy."

IV

At the press conference, Ted told their story, beginning with the telephone call from the fictional Dr. Ellington in Everglades City and ending when they hid themselves from the approaching car after escaping from the Porsche submerged beneath the dark waters of the Tamiami Canal.

"Could you identify the man who shot out the tire and sent the car into the canal, Dr. Bronson?" one of the reporters asked.

"I was too busy hanging on to the steering wheel," Ted answered.

"How about you, Dr. MacGowan?"

"I saw the man with the rifle plainly in the headlights of our car," said Liz. "Mr. Patterson tells me my description exactly fits the one who's been turned over to the FBI by the Sheriff's Office."

"Somebody had to be driving the Jaguar," the reporter insisted. "Could either of you see him clearly?"

"At eighty-five miles an hour, a flat tire is something you don't want to have to cope with very often," Ted answered. "I was pretty busy at the time."

"The driver had the back of his head toward us," Liz added. "Anyway, the police tells us there'll be even better evidence in the right front tire of the Porsche, once it's been pulled from the canal and they dig out the bullet that punctured it."

"What was it like sitting there waiting for the car to fill with water before you could escape, Dr. MacGowan?" a woman television reporter asked.

"Pure hell!" Liz said without equivocation. "Even a few minutes in that sort of situation can seem an eternity."

Chapter Sixteen

Ted and Liz's adventure had ended too late for the morning papers but the brief local newscasts during the network morning shows featured tapes from the press conference at the Sheriff's Office. By the time they reached their offices in the morning, the whole hospital was already buzzing with the news. Ted was busy all morning talking to two patients whose kidney transplants had failed and who had taken advantage of the hospital's offer to evaluate their condition and the possibility of a second operation. It was almost noon when his secretary told him Estrellita Mendoza was outside and wanted to speak to him.

"Send her in, please," Ted told the secretary.

"I apologize for bothering you, Dr. Ted, but I wanted to talk to you for a minute before you saw the rest of the family," said Estrellita. "Even I can see that there's been no change for the better in Michael's condition."

"We're still hoping a donor will turn up in one of the hospital emergency rooms in the city or somewhere within flying range."

"I wanted mainly to talk to you about Arturo. He's taking Michael's illness very hard."

"I noticed that yesterday."

"Arturo and I are closer than the others, perhaps because

we're more nearly the same age. He worships Michael and I'm afraid he's having trouble understanding that his brother is dying."

"When you're as sensitive as Arturo is, I guess it must be hard to understand why nothing can be done to help." Ted gave Estrellita a probing look. "Something else is troubling you, though. What is it?"

"I'm afraid Arturo might become violent," she admitted. "It's been a long time since he's shown any signs of that and maybe I'm overly apprehensive because I've seen a few Down's Syndrome patients get into trouble with the law during violent episodes. Arturo doesn't talk much to the others but this morning he told me he would like to get the rifle he uses for killing snakes and go after Sam Gianno."

"Did Nick Patterson talk to you this morning?"

Estrellita nodded. "He told me why Dr. MacGowan didn't reveal the fact that she can make a positive identification of Sam Gianno as the driver of the other car. I agree, but you don't have to be any more intelligent than Arturo is to figure that Gianno was behind the attempt to kill both of you last night."

"I guess not."

"Or that he'll try to get you again. Nick Patterson also told me he's doubling your protection."

"The way things are going, I'm afraid I'm not much of a threat to anybody."

"Your surgical ability still represents Michael's only possible chance at life," she told him. "When I think of how close you and Dr. MacGowan came to drowning in the Tamiami Canal last night, it makes me shudder."

"I had some nightmares myself," Ted admitted. "The important thing, though, is that Liz did recognize Gianno in the Jaguar and can testify that he was driving—if you legal eagles ever do bring him to trial."

"Neither our office at the state level nor the federal Task

Force wants to have Gianno arrested again and let his lawyers know all the details of the case we have against him—especially after last night. Getting back to Arturo. He thinks a lot of you and I thought maybe you could talk to him sometime today and try to calm him a little."

"Of course, I'll go up right away."

"Incidentally," she said from the doorway, "how did Dr. MacGowan know Sam Gianno well enough to make such a positive identification?"

"By an odd coincidence, she delivered his last baby. She says he and his family are charming."

"Sicilians often are—and some Spaniards." Estrellita laughed. "I almost married one before I came back home and fell for Michael. He's Juan Perez, anchorman on the news programs for a TV station here that broadcasts in both Spanish and English, mainly to Cuban refugees. After Juan and I broke up, he married my best friend in the Cuban émigré community and we're still very close friends."

Ted had a sudden inspiration. "This is no reflection on the Cuban émigré population, but I have the impression that there's more violence in Little Havana than in the rest of Miami."

"You're right—especially since Castro let the Marielos leave Cuba."

"Do you suppose your friend would let me make an appeal on one of his news programs? It might help us locate a donor."

"I can find out right away." Reaching for Ted's desk phone, Estrellita dialed nine and then a local number. When it was answered, she said, "This is Estrellita Mendoza. May I speak to Juan Perez?"

Moments later, a rapid interchange occurred in Spanish, none of which Ted understood. When it was finished, she put her hand across the receiver and turned to Ted.

"Juan will be happy to put your message on the air—in Spanish."

"But I don't speak the language."

"All you have to do is dictate what you would say in English to him over the phone. Then at the proper moment during the six and also the eleven o'clock news broadcasts, Juan will pick up a telephone before the TV cameras at the studio and have a conversation with you—faked, of course."

"Fine. When do we do it?"

"Right now." She handed Ted the receiver. "Keep it short, Juan's going to slip your message into the news broadcast but it will have to be brief in order not to interfere with the commercials that are already set up for the program."

"*Buenos dias*, Señor Perez," Ted spoke into the phone.

"Your Spanish is execrable, Doctor," a masculine voice replied in perfect English. "I graduated from Harvard four years after you and Mike Corazon. Just tell me the message you want broadcast and when the time comes, you'll hear it in colloquial Cuban Spanish. When I say 'Now,' give your request in as few words as possible."

"Right," Ted agreed.

"Now," came the voice over the phone and Ted began to speak, imagining he was in a TV station looking directly at the camera and voicing the plea that, with luck, might save his friend's life.

"This is Dr. Theodore Bronson from the Organ Transplant Service of Biscayne General Hospital in Miami," he began. "Unless sometime in the next few days I am able to transplant the liver from an accident victim who has no chance to live, Michael Corazon, who heads the federal task force seeking to control the drug traffic in the United States entering Miami, will die. I implore any of you with a relative, male or female, who is injured in an accident and whose progress is considered hopeless by the physicians in charge to give us permission to transplant the liver into the body of Michael Corazon."

"That was short and to the point, Dr. Bronson," Juan Perez's voice came on the phone again. "Give me a telephone number where you can be reached at all times. It will appear on the screen following your appeal."

Ted gave him the hospital switchboard number.

"Watch the six o'clock news and the eleven o'clock rebroadcast," Juan Perez told him. "You may not be able to understand your fervent appeal for the life of our friend, Mike, in Spanish, but you'll know I'm giving it my best."

II

Liz MacGowan visited Princess Zorah's VIP suite shortly after nine while making morning rounds. Jerry Rubin was checking the life-support apparatus which, she saw, had become much more complicated since she'd seen it shortly after midnight.

"How do you do it?" Jerry asked with a smile.

"Do what?"

"Manage to look like you're on your way to a society luncheon. If I had gone through what you did last night—according to the early morning news reports—I'd still be shaking."

"I'd be, too, if I'd been alone," she told him. "I'm all for women's lib, but I must admit that having a man around at a time like that was definitely comforting."

"Not just any man," said Jerry. "More than any kind of doctor I know of, a transplant surgeon needs the proverbial nerves of steel. And Ted Bronson has them."

"How are things going here?"

"Couldn't be better. We haven't needed to stimulate her heart once with the catheter-electrode Pete Craig put in through the subclavian vein last night as a precaution. The blood chemistry reports look good, too."

"When did you start intravenous alimentation?"

"This morning. The little fellow was kicking so hard, I thought maybe he was hungry. It's working like a charm, too."

"I should think you and Pete Craig would feel at least like lesser gods in cases like this, Jerry," said Liz. "After all, you really are maintaining life in two people."

"The second I'm sure of, the first I don't know. In some cases—not this one, of course—I sometimes feel like we're interfering in God's purpose by preserving life when a non-functioning brain couldn't possibly find any pleasure in being connected to a body that doesn't even know it's alive—and never will."

III

In the doctors' office at the main nursing station on the VIP floor, Ted Bronson closed Michael Corazon's clinical record and slid it into the rack where they were kept available for the physicians in charge of patients to examine them and make notes.

"We're losing the fight, Cheryl," he told the special nurse he'd asked to have assigned to Michael's case, as he often did for his more serious cases. "And the worst part is that I can't do a damn thing to control it. Do you know where the family is?"

"They went down to dinner—except Arturo. He insisted on staying here and they didn't try to make him go. As upset as he is, he's gotten to be pretty stubborn about doing exactly what he wants to do."

"Miss Mendoza is afraid Arturo might have one of those unexplained outbreaks of violence that seems to attack people with Down's Syndrome when they run up against things they can't handle."

"If it does come, I'm not sure it will be what you call an unexplained burst of violence," said the nurse. "I was talking to Arturo just now and got the distinct impression that he would possibly react in a much more logical way than you would expect."

"What do you mean?"

"I don't exactly know," the nurse admitted. "I guess I'm particularly interested because I'm taking a course, the Psychology of Criminal Personalities, at Nova University in the mornings before I go on duty. Somehow I get the impression that we're playing out the scenes of a typical Greek tragedy here, one where nobody can do much to either predict or prevent the inevitable end."

"Miss Mendoza is afraid Arturo might take some sort of overt action against the men responsible for Mike's condition. She thinks I might be able to talk him out of it."

"He was in the room next door a few minutes ago, listening to Cuban music from a foreign-language station that's very popular in Little Havana."

"I've known Arturo for perhaps half of his life and I've never seen anyone who loves his fellow man as much as he does," said Ted. "But that's often the case with Down's Syndrome people, and the fact that their intelligence level is below normal causes many people to shun them. I'll talk to him before I leave the floor and try to determine whether he's as near a breaking point as you and Estrellita Mendoza seem to think he is. I'd hate to see him get involved in any sort of violence and possibly be arrested. When that happens, a lot of people jump to the conclusion that the person is actually dangerous and insist that they be locked up in a mental institution."

When Ted came into the adjoining room he saw Arturo standing by the window looking down at the street. The radio was playing overly loud and when the disc jockey made his announcement, it was in Spanish.

"Michael's dying, Dr. Ted." Arturo turned from the window.

"Your brother is very sick, but I haven't given up—"

"I heard Juan Perez on the radio just now." Arturo's tone was loud and even more hesitant than usual, proof, Ted realized, that he was under a considerable strain. "He said you told him Michael will die unless somebody gives him a new liver."

"I'm afraid that's true," Ted admitted, "but we're hoping Juan Perez's broadcasts on radio and TV will help us find a donor from one of the shootings that happen so often in Little Havana. Or from an automobile accident."

"Why can't it be me?" Arturo blurted out.

"That's impossible, without a liver you would die."

"But Michael would live?"

"Probably, but we can't even consider that. To kill one person so another can have his liver would be murder."

"Suppose it was somebody like Sam Gianno?"

"Gianno has to be tried and convicted before the state can execute him in the electric chair," Ted explained. "That would take a long time."

"Then you can't do anything?"

"Not until someone provides us with a liver I can transplant into Michael's body. But cheer up; with as much violence as we have here in Miami, that could happen any minute and I'm hoping it will."

Arturo didn't answer but turned back to the window. His shoulders were slumped in an attitude of deep depression. And when Ted told him good-bye, he didn't even answer.

I V

Hoping to find the Corazon family there, Ted stopped by the cafeteria before leaving the hospital for his apartment across the street. He didn't see them, though, and since nothing was to be gained by going back to the VIP floor in the hope of finding them, he left the hospital and crossed to Biscayne Terrace, entering through the parking garage. Liz Mac-Gowan's Mercedes was in its stall so he stopped at her floor and rang her doorbell. She answered it immediately.

"I called Mike Corazon's room and asked for you a few minutes ago but Cheryl said you'd just left," she told him. "I was going to invite you to have a drink and maybe we'd send out for a pizza afterward."

"I'm glad I stopped then," he said, putting an arm around her and drawing her close for a long kiss.

"This is a better treatment for depression than anything I know," he said when she pushed him away, a little breathlessly. "I'll also take a shot of that fine bourbon you store for thirsty visitors."

"Go into the living room and watch the six o'clock news while I fix the drinks," she told him. "I heard Juan Perez on the radio just a little while ago; he's still reporting your plea for a liver donor. If you get that Spanish-speaking TV station you might hear your plea—in Spanish."

"Arturo told me he heard it on the radio this afternoon." Ted was standing in the doorway to the small but efficient kitchen in her apartment watching Liz as she expertly mixed their drinks. Just being there lessened some of the depth of his depression after visiting Mike Corazon and his talk with Arturo.

"I'm looking forward to doing just this every evening for

the rest of my life," he told her when she handed him the glass.

"Be careful, I'm a very militant feminist," she said, laughing. "Serving as a slave to a man just isn't allowed in our philosophy."

"I'll mix the drinks before dinner and see that the children do their homework," he promised. "As long as you're their mother."

"If I forget to take the pill again, as I did last night after I got home from the Sheriff's Office, you'll probably have to go to work on that job a lot sooner than you expect," she told him.

"That suits me to a tee! I'll even diaper the babies into the bargain."

"Now there's a prospect that tempts me," she said. "Find any more prospective kidney transplant patients today?"

"I've got several lined up but I hesitate to tie myself up for three to four hours with an operation in case a donor becomes available for Mike and I need to start on that in a hurry."

"Dr. Taylor can always take over the kidney operation if you're caught."

"That might not work; some of the patients could have been operated on by him in the first place. Even though the failure wasn't his fault, the patient might not be very happy about it. While I think about it, what would you say about my selecting Cheryl Rubin as the transplant coordinator for Biscayne General?"

"You couldn't do better. She's far too competent to be limiting her work simply to nursing."

"Jerry Rubin's appointment as Assistant Professor of Neonatalogy—when he finishes his residency next July—is up for approval at the next meeting of the hospital trustees. I'm sure it will be approved, and if I give Cheryl the job at a good salary, they might decide to stay in Miami."

"I hope you can do it. Jerry's much too valuable to the

Neonatal ICU alone for us to let any up-to-the minute medical group lure him with a salary of sixty-five thousand a year or more."

"Unfortunately, the university can only pay him around thirty-five and he could make twice that, and perhaps more, with one of a dozen groups through the country," said Ted. "Just as you could make twice what you're asking in private practice."

"Which I don't want," Liz assured him. "Besides, if I hadn't come to Biscayne General and the University Medical School as an associate professor of obstetrics a couple of years ago, I might never have known you."

"And I would never have been able to limit my work to transplants if I hadn't taken the same route you've taken in teaching instead of private practice," he agreed. "A surgeon who limits his work to organ transplants isn't going to be worth much to a group these days."

"One who is at home in the chest, abdomen or in any operation involving microsurgery to connect arteries, blood vessels and nerves together can name his own price. Have you ever been sorry you limited yourself strictly to the transplant field?"

"Only on days like this when I have to watch my best friend die. By the end of the week I'm sure I'll have a dozen kidney transplants lined up for the next month using cyclosporin. Yet I can't even find a single liver to save the life of my very best friend. If you could have seen the look in Arturo's eyes just now, when I had to admit that Mike is probably going to die, you'd feel as helpless as I do."

Chapter Seventeen

Ted Bronson made rounds early Tuesday morning and was in his office talking to a possible kidney transplant patient when the morning-shift nurse called him from Michael Corazon's suite.

"The Corazon brothers are here, Dr. Bronson," she said. "They would like to see you."

"I'll be up there in a few minutes," he promised. "Is Arturo with them?"

"No, Doctor. They said he and Mrs. Corazon were still at home but might come by after lunch."

Finishing the physical examination of the kidney patient, Ted sent him to the laboratory for blood chemistry tests as a beginning of the intensive study necessary before deciding whether the chances for success justified further surgery. Taking the elevator to the tenth floor, he went into Michael's room and glanced at the nurse's notes briefly before going into the adjoining room where Manuel and Pedro Corazon were waiting.

"We can see that Michael isn't any better, Dr. Ted," said the older brother.

"I'm afraid he's worse."

"How much longer can he last?" Pedro asked.

"A week, perhaps ten days. Did you watch the TV program last night?"

"Yes. After we had supper downstairs, we went home to watch it and then drove to the cathedral. Mama wanted to talk to Father Mulcahy about administering last rites to Michael."

"It hasn't come to that yet; we could still find a donor. I'm counting on Juan Perez's TV appeal to alert the Cuban community to our need."

"We all know you've done everything you could to save Mike's life," said Manuel. "Father Mulcahy said whatever happens now will be God's will, but it's hard to understand why a just God would let our brother die."

"How did Arturo take that?" Ted asked.

"He didn't go with us. When we came back, he asked us what Father Mulcahy said, but I'm afraid that only upset him more. He had nightmares during the night and kept us all awake."

"Once or twice Mama heard him crying in his room, too," the younger brother added.

"I'm not surprised," said Ted. "Last night Arturo asked me point-blank whether Michael wasn't dying and I had to tell him the truth. He talked of trying to kill Sam Gianno so we could take his liver to save Mike but I think I explained why that wouldn't work."

"Arturo told Mama what you said," Manuel assured him. "We hope it will keep him from trying to do anything dangerous. Mama stayed at home with him this morning in the hope of calming him down some."

"I wish there was something I could do for Arturo," said Ted, "but I guess there isn't."

"Like the priest said last night, what happens now is God's will. All we can do is try to understand it."

Liz had two operations scheduled on Tuesday morning. When she finished, it was almost lunchtime, so she showered and changed to a street dress. Knowing how Ted must be feeling as the hours passed and the likelihood of being able to save Michael Corazon grew more and more bleak, she didn't feel like eating. Instead, she settled for a cup of coffee in the nurses' lounge on the VIP floor, where a coffee machine perked constantly. Her only consolation was that Princess Zorah and the fetus were exhibiting a textbook pattern of effective advanced life support, with every prospect that the patient's body functions could be kept going smoothly for the next two weeks.

As Liz was finishing her coffee, the door to the lounge opened and Miss Boardman, the seven-to-three nurse on duty with Princess Zorah, stuck her head in. "There's a long-distance call for you on the telephone in the adjacent room of the suite, Dr. MacGowan," she said. "I believe it's from New York."

"Sheik Almani?" Liz voiced the first thought that came into her mind.

"I don't think so," said the nurse. "But I'm not sure."

Leaving the lounge, Liz moved quickly down the corridor to the second room of the Princess' suite and picked up the telephone there. "This is Dr. MacGowan," she said.

"This is Gordon Tallant in the United Press International Office in New York, Doctor," a brisk male voice said. "I believe you're looking after Princess Zorah of Telfa and her baby in the hospital there."

"Her *unborn* child to be exact, Mr. Tallant."

"Of course, Doctor. We carried a story on how you are handling Princess Zorah's pregnancy a few days ago. Have you delivered the baby yet?"

"No, Mr. Tallant, but it's doing fine with its mother on advanced life support. May I ask why you called?"

"Our correspondent in Saudi Arabia went to Telfa right after the attempt on the life of Emir Hassim Elzama was made recently. He has just filed a story about the situation there which is still a little unclear. Did you know Emir Hassim is dying from leukemia?"

"Yes. Sheik Almani told me before he left for New York—"

"And Telfa. Our correspondent saw him there over the weekend. Do you have any idea why Almani left Miami so suddenly, when we understand that he was responsible for bringing the Princess there in the first place?"

"The Princess was brought here so we could determine the sex of the child she is bearing," Liz explained. "Sheik Almani left for New York—and Telfa from what you tell me—right after I told him we had established beyond question that the fetus is a male."

"And the successor of Emir Hassim," said Tallant. "Our correspondent learned that much in Telfa."

"I assumed that Sheik Almani went to Telfa to give the good news to the Emir," said Liz. "He had apparently been promised the appointment as Regent when Emir Hassim died."

"Did you say 'promised,' Doctor?" Tallant asked.

"So he told me."

"Our correspondent in Telfa was notified a few hours ago that Prince Khalil Elzama has been appointed Regent for the child. Khalil is the Emir's youngest brother and has been in the United States for the past four years, as a student at M.I.T. We tried to reach him in Cambridge but got no answer, so I suppose he may be on the way to Miami to enter upon his duties as Regent for the baby."

"But the child isn't even a person yet, according to the laws of both Telfa and the United States."

"I understand that, Doctor. If Prince Khalil turns up in Miami, I'd appreciate your asking him to call us here at UPI in New York."

III

After the connection to New York was broken, Liz studied the silent telephone for a long moment. Then, leaving the room, she took the elevator to the seventh floor, where her office was located.

"Please get me Mr. Robert Nathan at the Miami *Herald,* Lillian," she told her secretary as she passed through the outer waiting room, which had not yet filled with the patients for the afternoon.

Liz's office phone rang a few minutes later and a feminine voice said, "This is Mr. Nathan's secretary, Dr. MacGowan. He hasn't come in yet. Shall I have him call? Wait a moment, please," she added. "I think I hear him outside in the hall."

Robert Nathan came on the line a moment later. "You must be psychic, Dr. MacGowan. I was going to call you in a few minutes."

"I just finished talking to a Mr. Tallant in the UPI office in New York—"

"We're still on the same psychic beam, Doctor. I have a fresh UPI dispatch on my desk that came in over the wire service a few minutes ago. Did Tallant tell you Prince Khalil Elzama, a younger brother of the Emir of Telfa, has been appointed Regent for the baby you're maintaining on life support?"

"Yes. It certainly looks like you called the shots correctly with your scenario the other afternoon in Mr. Brown's office. Maybe you're the one who's psychic."

Robert Nathan laughed. "I claim no such talent, Doctor. Ten years with the Associated Press in the Middle East gave me a pretty broad understanding of the Arab mind. Tallant didn't tell you when Prince Khalil will be coming to see about his little nephew, did he?"

"He doesn't even know where the Prince is. Or Sheik Almani either."

"Just a minute, Doctor. My secretary just handed me an Associated Press dispatch about Telfa. It's much longer than the UPI one and apparently has considerably more detail about what's happening over there. Will you hold while I read it?"

"Of course."

"According to this dispatch, the situation in Telfa is still clouded," Nathan said when he came back on the line a few moments later. "Apparently, something like a palace revolution must have occurred since the attempt on the life of Emir Hassim the other day. The Elzama family seems to be moving to be sure somebody not of their blood doesn't take over the government."

"Sheik Almani told me the family has ruled in Telfa longer than any other monarchy in world history."

"They seem determined to keep on doing just that. Emir Hassim is said to be in coma, possibly terminal, but he did rouse up long enough to name a cousin, General Armin Elzama, as chairman of a three-man Governing Council. I know Armin very well; he's head of Telfa's small army and is absolutely trustworthy. The two others are both Elzama's kinsmen and were already high up in the government. Those three apparently decided to make the younger brother, Khalil, technically the Regent, although it looks like the Council will actually rule the country in the name of Emir Hassim's male offspring, who's in your care."

"Does the AP dispatch say anything about where Prince Khalil is?" Liz asked.

"No. Almani has been kicked out of his job at the UN, though, so it stands to reason that General Armin must have learned of his part in the plot to kill the Emir and take control."

"Just like you predicted the other night, Mr. Nathan," said Liz. "Please look in your crystal ball and tell me what will happen next."

"I can't help you there, but since our conference in Erasmus Brown's office I've been consulting with some friends in the Middle East. They say that for years Almani has been taking a large cut out of the millions American oil companies were paying for Telfa crude. As smart as he is, I'm sure he's stashed most of that loot in Swiss banks, so he might still be able to buy enough support to gain control of the government of Telfa. Failing that, he will no doubt head for a country with whom Telfa doesn't have an extradition treaty and live there in the lap of luxury for the rest of his life. One thing you can be pretty sure of, Doctor—he won't be getting into your hair anymore."

But there, as it happened, the newspaperman was wrong.

IV

Ted was leaving the room where he had talked to the Corazon brothers when the telephone rang. Picking it up, he said, "This is Dr. Bronson."

"Thank God I found you, Ted." It was Maria Corazon and she sounded very much disturbed.

"What's wrong, Maria?"

"I'm worried about Arturo. As soon as he finished his breakfast this morning, he went to his studio and locked the door. He's had the record player going all morning."

"I can hear it in the telephone. Manuel and Pedro told me Arturo was very much upset and didn't want to come to the hospital."

"He's never been like this before. I don't know how he can stand the noise with that thing blaring."

"People with Arturo's mental condition often play very loud music. It seems to calm them when they're under tension and disturbed."

"I didn't worry about him until I remembered that he keeps a .22-caliber rifle in the closet. He uses it every now and then to kill the moccasins that swim down the canal from the Glades and get in his flower beds. Can you possibly come out here, Ted? Arturo admires you almost as much as he loves Michael. Maybe he'll listen to you."

"There may not be time, if he's closeted in that room with a weapon. Is there a telephone extension in his studio?"

"Yes. Why?"

"Bang on the door and tell him I want to speak to him. Maybe he'll answer and I can talk him out of doing something to hurt himself."

"I'll try to call him. Hang on."

A burst of loud music against Ted's eardrums told him Arturo had picked up the telephone extension in his own room.

"Don't try to stop me." The voice was barely discernible through the torrent of noise pouring out of the telephone receiver. "I'm going to help Michael the only way anybody can now."

"Wait, Arturo! A donor is bound to turn up over the weekend."

"Michael can't wait." The halting voice at the end of the connection broke down in a sob and for a moment there was only the blaring music, then it continued, "He'll die if I don't save him. I have my rifle."

"Don't do it, Arturo," Ted begged. "There's bound to be another way."

"Tell Mama and my brothers good-bye for me." The crack of a rifle shot was audible even through the music, then a loud crash as of a body falling to the floor, followed by silence except for the music, telling Ted that the receiver had almost certainly dropped from a suddenly nerveless hand.

"Oh, my God!" Maria Corazon's scream from the other phone drowned out the music. "My baby! My baby!"

"Maria!" Ted found that he was shouting into the telephone and forced himself to be calm. "Stay on the phone a minute, Maria! It's important!"

"He shot himself, Ted." Maria was sobbing. "I can't even go to him. The door's locked."

"Listen carefully and do exactly as I say. Arturo shot himself because he thought there was no other way to save Michael, so we must move fast. I'm going to send a Rescue Squad ambulance to bring him to the hospital—"

"But if he's dead—"

"He may not have succeeded in killing himself. I'll meet the ambulance at the Emergency Room and do everything I can to save him, of course. But if I can't I'll need your permission to transplant Arturo's liver into Michael's body. That's what Arturo wants. It's the reason he tried to take his life just now."

And may have succeeded, he told himself but did not speak the words aloud.

"You have permission to do everything necessary." He could sense the agony in her voice as she realized the choice she was having to make. For, in either event, she was almost certain to lose one son.

"I'll save Arturo if I can, but if I can't, Michael will have his liver, you can depend on that," Ted assured her. "Now get some help and break down the door to Arturo's room so the Rescue Squad won't be delayed when they bring him out."

The telephone clicked off in his ear as the connection was broken. Putting down the phone cradle for a moment, he dialed 911, the Medical Emergency number.

"Rescue Squad, Sergeant Jones," a voice answered.

"Sergeant, this is Dr. Bronson at Biscayne General. Mr.

Arturo Corazon has just shot himself at the Corazon home in Coconut Grove. You can look up the address—"

"I know where it is, Doctor. Go on, please."

"Send a Rescue Squad team there at once and bring him to the hospital Emergency Room. I'll meet them there."

"Right away, Doctor."

"Tell the technicians to use the respirator and also the external pacemaker, even though Mr. Corazon may appear to be dead, and not to waste time trying to resuscitate him. I want him breathing and his heart beating, even if it has to be done artificially. If he's beyond help, I'm going to transplant his liver into his brother, Michael."

"I understand, Doctor. Our best team from Coral Gables will be on the way in a moment. They'll have Mr. Corazon in the Emergency Room in less than thirty minutes."

"Arturo tried to kill himself so Michael could have his liver," Ted explained to the brothers as he headed for the door. "I'm meeting the Rescue Squad in the Emergency Room."

"Will you save Arturo if you can?" Pedro asked.

"Of course. But if I can't, I'm going to take his liver and transplant it into Michael's body. Transplants between siblings usually take well so Arturo's liver is the best one Michael could possibly get. Meanwhile, one of you can go for Maria."

The brothers looked bewildered by the rapid turn of events, but Pedro managed to say, "I'll go for Mama, Manuel can stay here. He's the oldest and can sign any papers you might need to have signed, Dr. Ted."

Picking up the telephone again, Ted dialed the supervisor of the operating-room floor. "This is Dr. Bronson," he said when she answered. "Is the emergency OR set up?"

"All we have to do is uncover the trays, Doctor. What kind of operation should we set up for?"

"In that room, removal of a liver for transplant. If it gets that far, we'll use the main operating theater for the actual transplant but you'll have plenty of time to set it up. Just removing the liver takes three or four hours."

"Then you found a donor for Mr. Michael Corazon?"

"Yes. His brother, Arturo, just shot himself. I won't know his condition until the Rescue Squad ambulance gets here, but when I do, I'll alert you so the nurses can start scrubbing. Call the chief surgical resident and tell him I'll need him to assist me. And tell Dr. Young I might want him to remove Arturo Corazon's kidneys for transplant later, as well as some other organs not damaged by the gunshot."

"Will do, Doctor," said the supervisor.

As Ted left the room on the run for the express elevator, he heard the whine of an ambulance in the distance. The Emergency Room was mercifully not jammed with accident cases when he reached it.

"The Rescue Squad is bringing in a head wound," Ted told the Trauma Center resident who was watching an afternoon soap opera on a TV in the residents' quarters adjoining. "Better warm up the EEG machine."

"To determine brain death?"

"Yes. If the waves are flat on the EEG, we have the liver donor we've been looking for."

"Any idea who the gunshot wound is, Dr. Bronson?" the resident asked.

"His brother, Arturo."

"Good God! Talk about coincidences—"

"Not this time. Arturo shot himself just so his brother can live. Let's all make sure his sacrifice isn't in vain."

Chapter Eighteen

As soon as Liz MacGowan hung up the telephone after talking with Robert Nathan, it rang again, startling her. "Miss Boardman wants to speak to you, Doctor," said her secretary.

"Put her on the phone." Miss Boardman was the special nurse on duty with Princess Zorah on the afternoon shift. When the click in the phone told Liz the connection had been made, she asked, "Is anything wrong, Miss Boardman?"

"Not with the Princess or the fetus, Dr. MacGowan. But I thought you'd like to know Ambassador Almani came in a few minutes ago."

"Did he ask for me?"

"No, but I thought you would want to talk to him, so I'm calling while I'm getting him a cup of coffee he asked for. I've been trying to reach you for four or five minutes but your line was busy."

"Get back to the room but don't tell Sheik Almani I'm coming," Liz directed. "I'll be there right away."

"Yes, Doc—" The nurse's voice suddenly broke off, then came back on, tense now with excitement and alarm. "The power just went off on the floor, Doctor. We have no electricity."

"Get back to the room and make certain the emergency

battery in the advanced life-support system has taken over. Where's Dr. Rubin?"

"On a break."

"Tell the nurse at the station to page him and tell him to get up there stat. If that battery isn't working, we've got real trouble."

Without waiting for the nurse to answer, Liz hung up and started for the door leading to the central corridor that traversed each floor. At the elevator bank, she saw that all of them were at different floors and, without hesitation, jerked open a door marked STAIRWAY and ran up the three flights to the tenth floor. Panting, she opened the door from the emergency stairway. And seeing that the lights were still off on the entire floor, found herself wondering how a power failure could happen on only one floor before heading for Princess Zorah's room.

When she pulled open the door and stepped inside, Liz saw that Miss Boardman had switched on a heavy-duty flashlight and was examining the monitors in its beam. Liz looked first at the monitor that had been recording the fetal heartbeat and her pulse took a sudden jump from fear when she saw that it was dark, as were those recording the patient's pulse and respiration.

"Nobody knows what happened, Doctor." Miss Boardman was near hysteria. "I hadn't been out of the room but a few minutes when the power went off. The emergency battery didn't take over either but Dr. Rubin kept this flashlight here, so I got it out of the closet."

"Had the electric plug been pulled?" Liz demanded, fumbling in the pocket of her long white coat for her stethoscope.

"It's still in place! The first thing I did when I got here was check it."

Placing the tips of the stethoscope in her ears, Liz pulled down the sheet covering the body of Princess Zorah and placed the round flat diaphragm of the instrument over the mound of the patient's abdomen about halfway from the navel to the pubis. She couldn't help noticing, as she listened for the fetal heartbeat, that Princess Zorah's skin was already taking on the dusky hue of oxygen lack, a sure indication, she knew, that the fetus imprisoned in what until moments ago had been the safe haven of its mother's uterus would soon be suffering the same potentially fatal lack unless a vital oxygen supply could be achieved in a matter of minutes.

The sound of the fetal heartbeat in Liz's ears told her it was still strong, but she didn't need her watch to count the rate and realize that it had increased sharply, a sure sign that trouble was not far away. Jerry Rubin arrived while she was listening and, producing his own stethoscope, placed the diaphragm over Princess Zorah's heart area.

"It's still beating by itself," he reported, "but the emergency power system from the battery should already have taken over."

"The first thing I did was call for the emergency power system," said Miss Boardman. "They said only this floor is involved and something—maybe a short circuit—must have knocked off the circuit breaker up here."

"The battery should still have taken over," Jerry Rubin repeated.

"It hasn't so there's no time to waste." Pulling the stethoscope from her ears, Liz dropped it on the bed and started to remove the long white coat she was wearing. "I'm going to do a Caesarean section and get that baby out of there."

"I'll bring up a portable ventilator from the Neonatal ICU," Jerry Rubin said as he started for the door.

"Where's the emergency surgical tray I ordered kept here?" Liz asked the nurse, speaking sharply in the hope of shocking the distraught young woman into moving quickly.

"On the top shelf in the closet, Doctor."

"Clear the table and put it across the bed so I can open the tray on it." Liz moved quickly to the closet as she spoke.

The large cloth-wrapped tray occupied most of the upper shelf. Pulling it down, she placed it on the table the nurse had moved into position across the patient's bed and began to unfasten the sterile wrappings to expose the instruments, dressings and a pair of sterile gloves. Pulling on the gloves, she reached for the scalpel with her right hand and picked up a package of gauze sponges with her left.

"Hold the flashlight so I can see the abdomen, Miss Boardman," she directed. "There'll be some bleeding and a lot of amniotic fluid when I open the uterus but we can clean that up later."

A skilled slash with the scalpel in Liz's right hand opened the Princess' abdomen from navel to pubis, exposing the muscle layer beneath. A second stroke slit the muscles, allowing the peritoneum, the thin fragile lining of the abdominal cavity, to bulge through. This Liz quickly opened, exposing the surface of the uterus underneath, now almost black from oxygen lack.

Moving more carefully so as not to risk wounding the fetus, she cut through the muscular wall at the top of the uterus, above the thick placenta—revealed days before by ultrasound —that would have slowed her reaching the fetus if she'd placed the incision in the normal area for a Caesarean at the front of the uterus. A flood of amniotic fluid burst from the membrane envelope surrounding the fetus. Dropping the scalpel, Liz took a pair of scissors from the tray.

Inserting two fingers of her left hand to push the baby away so it would not be injured, she used the scissors to enlarge the uterine incision to where she could reach in and catch a tiny foot in her fingers. Circling around inside the uterus with questing fingers, she found the second foot and, grasping both, gently extracted the fetus from the haven where it had been the first seven months of its life. With a quick movement, she placed two clamps across the gelatinlike umbilical cord and cut between it with the scissors, removing the baby from any connection with its mother's body.

Holding the now quite blue baby by its feet, she let its head drop to drain out any amniotic fluid that might be in the respiratory tract, upon which it must now depend for the vital supply of oxygen that had formerly been supplied by its mother's own blood. She was hoping for a sudden gasp of breath, perhaps even a cry, but heard none, so, putting her hand behind the baby's upper chest, she jackknifed the small body gently to compress the lungs and achieve artificial respiration.

After a brief moment, Liz released the pressure by straightening the baby out once again but heard no answering rush of air into its lungs as she had hoped would occur. Without waiting, she repeated the movement but that, too, was not successful. Realizing now that this somewhat primitive method of artificial respiration was not going to succeed, she knew she must resort to a more desperate measure in order to expand the tiny lungs.

"Take the surgical tray away," Liz told the nurse, who promptly obeyed. Stretching the baby out on the table, she carefully placed her own mouth over its mouth and nose, then with a gentle force breathed into the tiny body. She felt a surge of thanks when the small chest expanded beneath her hand and, as gently as she had inflated the tiny lungs, she now squeezed the baby's chest to expel the air she had forced into it. When she released the pressure, however, no spontaneous intake of air occurred so she repeated the mouth-to-mouth resuscitation once again. On her third try, Jerry Rubin opened the door to the room and pushed through it one of the portable emergency resuscitators used in the Neonatal ICU.

"I can't get it to breathe spontaneously so I've been giving it mouth-to-mouth resuscitation," Liz told him.

"Judging by the color of its skin, you probably saved its life," Jerry assured her. "I'll take over now."

As she placed the baby on the sterile blanket Jerry held out to her, Liz was suddenly conscious that the room was crowded with people. She recognized the members of the Code Five team, called in for cases of cardiac arrest and similar desperate emergencies. But when the anesthesia resident who headed the team started to initiate the classical routine of CPR—cardio pulmonary resuscitation—upon Princess Zorah, Liz shook her head.

"The patient underwent brain death several days ago, Joe," she told the resident. "We've been keeping her heart and lungs functioning on advanced life support for the protection of the baby. Now that it's out of the uterus and on its own, I hardly think there's much point in starting her heart again."

The resident put his own stethoscope over the heart area of Princess Zorah for a moment, then raised his head and nodded. "You're right, Dr. MacGowan. Somatic death occurred when the power went off to the ventilator pump, but I still can't figure out why the current was interrupted only on this one floor. Or why the emergency battery didn't take over when it happened."

"Maybe we'll never know." Liz turned to Jerry Rubin, who was now expertly sliding a tiny rubber tube into the baby's windpipe and connecting it to the ventilator of the isolette he'd brought from Neonatal ICU. "Any idea what could have happened, Jerry?"

"I checked the battery this morning like Dr. Craig and I do every time we come on duty," he assured her. "It was fully charged."

"How about the baby?" Liz asked. "Do you think it has a chance?"

"Better than that I'd say. For one thing, my guess would be that it must be around twenty-six weeks, which is a little more than you thought before. The temporary ventilator is helping raise the oxygen blood level but as soon as I get this little emir-to-be down to the ICU, I'm going to put him on a high-frequency ventilator."

"What's that?" a first-year resident from the Code Five team asked.

"A marvelous gadget that provides plenty of oxygen by way of puffs of gas perhaps as often as a thousand times a minute."

As Jerry was pushing the isolette with its precious occupant inside toward the door leading to the corridor, the nursing supervisor for the VIP floor came in.

"An electrician from Maintenance is trying to get the circuit breakers for the floor back on," she said. "But every time he turns them on, they trip off again."

Moving to the side of the room, where the power cord for the advanced life-support system was attached to a wall socket, Jerry pulled out the plug.

"Run back to the electrician and tell him to try it again," he said.

The nurse left and moments later the lights in the room came on again. When Jerry opened the door to push the isolette through into the corridor on the way down to Neonatal ICU, the lights on the whole floor were all shining brightly once more.

"Don't let anybody move the advanced life-support apparatus from that room before I get a chance to get back up here and examine it," Jerry Rubin told the nursing supervisor as she helped him push the isolette toward the elevator.

"What do you think went wrong?" she asked.

"My guess would be sabotage," he told her crisply as he pushed the isolette into the open elevator and touched the CLOSE DOOR button.

Chapter Nineteen

At almost the same moment the circuit breakers on the tenth floor snapped off, a Rescue Squad ambulance whined to a stop at the Emergency Room loading platform. Moving swiftly, the technicians expertly removed the wheeled litter on which Arturo Corazon lay, pushing it up the loading platform and into the Emergency Room on the run.

"Your hunch about our needing the respirator was correct, Dr. Bronson," said the sergeant who headed the emergency team. "His breathing had stopped before we got there but his heart was still going. And as soon as we started pumping oxygen into his lungs with the respirator, his color came right back."

Looking down at the pale, still body of Arturo Corazon on the ambulance stretcher, Ted could see no immediate wound where the rifle bullet had entered his body. Before he could ask, however, the sergeant gave him the answer.

"It's hard to put a bullet into your head with a rifle but he knew the most successful way. By putting the end of the gun barrel into his mouth, he was able to reach the trigger. The wound of entry through his palate is so small you'd hardly even notice it, but the back of his head where the bullet came out is a mass of blood, brain and skull fragments. The best neurosurgeon in the world wouldn't be able to save him after that sort of wound."

The technician hadn't exaggerated, Ted saw when he examined the wound of exit. Arturo couldn't have known the anatomy involved but some instinct must have told him how to make sure his liver would be available to save his brother's life. By putting a single bullet through the medulla at the bottom of the brain, where control of vital functions of respiration and heartbeat were located, he had made sure that his sacrifice couldn't possibly be in vain.

"Get him on a gurney and put an intratracheal tube in so we can inflate and deflate the lungs," Ted told the Trauma Center resident. "Meanwhile, I'll slip a catheter-electrode into the subclavian vein and down into the right side of the heart. The odds on a successful transplant will be considerably better if the liver is perfused while I'm removing it with the best perfusate possible—his own blood. Somebody else take a pair of clippers and get rid of his hair so the EEG technician can attach the needle electrodes as soon as she gets here."

"Think it's worth the trouble, Dr. Bronson?" one of the assistant residents asked.

"Probably not, but I can't ask the family to let me remove his liver, and perhaps some other organs for transplant, until brain death has been legally established by an EEG. Is that catheter-electrode tray ready?"

"Right here, sir." The ER supervisor had opened a tray on which was a long catheter through which ran a wire electrode for carrying the electrical current from a pacemaker. On the tray there was also a large needle, with a syringe attached, plus a scalpel possessing a sharp-pointed blade.

With quick skilled movements, Ted cut open the thin Cuban-style shirt worn by many Miamians in warm weather. Slashing away the undershirt beneath it, he exposed the slight hollow just below Arturo Corazon's right collarbone and with the sharp-pointed scalpel made a puncture wound in the skin large enough to allow the large needle to penetrate the skin easily. Picking up the syringe attached to the large needle, he used it to force the point into the puncture wound he had made with the scalpel and on through the muscles beneath until perhaps an inch and a half of the needle had disappeared through the small skin wound.

Moving more slowly now, he felt rather than heard a slight click when the point of the needle went through the wall of the large vein called the subclavian that collected blood from the arm and carried it to still larger veins connecting with the right side of the heart. When he drew back upon the syringe, blood spurted into the barrel, telling him he had entered the thin-walled vein.

Disconnecting the syringe, Ted picked up the catheter-electrode and slid it through the needle into the subclavian vein. Pushing steadily, he felt another sense of resistance when the end of the catheter touched the tricuspid valve between the upper and lower chambers on the right side of the heart. Following the next contraction of the muscle in a normal heartbeat with the resultant opening of its valve, however, he was able to slide the catheter-electrode through for perhaps two inches until he felt it bump against a solid barrier. This, he knew, was the inner lining of the heart on the right side of the ventricle, the muscular portion that sent a surge of blood to the lungs with every beat.

"You can take your pacemaker away, Sergeant," Ted told the Rescue Squad technician. "We'll connect our own to this electrode."

The shift was made quickly, but in the brief period between stimulation by the Rescue Squad pacemaker and connection to the larger hospital machine, Ted could detect no sign of any spontaneous heartbeat without the electrical stimulation.

The EEG technician arrived just then and began inserting tiny needle electrodes into Arturo Corazon's freshly clipped scalp. "A half-dozen electrodes should do it," Ted told her. "You won't need to put in the usual twenty-four."

"I've known Arturo since he was a baby," Mrs. Burke, the ER nursing supervisor said, almost in a tone of awe. "Did you notice what a peaceful look he has on his face? It's almost as if he welcomed death."

"He shot himself for a purpose so I guess you could say he knew his own mind, even with the handicap of a lower than normal intelligence," Ted agreed. "I'm trying to recall something I read in the New Testament a long time ago covering what Arturo did tonight but I can't seem to remember it."

The EEG technician switched on her machine and the paper tape normally recording the electrical waves of the brain started rolling. None of the delicately balanced needles that recorded those waves showed any sign of movement, however, and after a minute or two she said, "There's no electrical activity in the brain, Dr. Bronson."

"Let the record show that Mr. Arturo Corazon was found to have suffered brain death at"—Ted paused and looked up at the clock over the door leading to the Critical Care ward and the main part of the hospital "—1:15 P.M. Be sure to include that time on your EEG record even though it's flat and record the name of everyone here who witnessed brain death, too," he told the technician. "We can all sign it later. I'm going to start removing the liver as soon as we can get him to the OR floor and we may take some other organs for transplant, too, after I talk to the family and have them sign the necessary forms."

"I'll take care of it, Doctor," said the technician.

"Please call the transplant team and tell them I want everybody in the OR immediately ready to scrub," he directed the nursing supervisor of the Emergency Room. "As soon as I can talk to the Corazon family, I'll be ready to start the first-stage procedure, to remove the liver we're going to use in the transplant."

"By the way, Dr. Bronson, I remembered that biblical quotation you were looking for just now," said Mrs. Burke. "It goes like this—*'Greater love hath no man than this, that a man lay down his life for his friends.'* "

II

Ted found the Corazons in the corner of the hospital lobby. Maria was weeping softly and Estrellita Mendoza was sitting close beside her with a comforting arm across the older woman's shoulders.

"Arturo is dead," he told them simply. "It's the way he wanted it to be."

"Do you think he experienced any pain?" Maria asked.

"None, I'm sure," Ted told her. "Arturo knew where to aim to ensure what we call 'brain death.' "

"Are you going to do the transplant right away?" the older brother asked.

"Yes. The sooner I can get it finished, the greater the chance that it will take."

"What is that chance now?" Manuel asked.

"Almost a hundred percent."

"Almost?" Estrellita Mendoza asked. "After what Arturo did, is there any chance of a failure?"

"The only way I could be more certain of success is if Mike and Arturo had been identical twins," Ted explained. "As it is, they have the same blood grouping and with siblings the chances of success are practically a hundred percent. We'll need your signatures on the routine permission forms but there's one other thing I think Arturo would want."

"What do you mean?" Manuel asked.

"The most important gift Arturo gave through sacrificing his own life is the liver that will save Michael. But I also have other patients waiting for kidney transplants and a number of other organs can be transplanted when patients needing them can be contacted. I would like your permission to remove, or let the hospital have removed, any transplantable organ from his body."

"Arturo would have wanted that, too," Estrellita assured him and the others gave their agreement.

"The necessary forms will be prepared in the office of the Department of Surgery and somebody will give them to you for you all to sign," Ted told the grieving family. "We're taking Arturo's body to the operating floor now. I want to get started removing his liver as soon as I can."

"Do you have any idea how long the transplant operation will take?" Estrellita asked.

"Possibly eight hours, but we have one advantage in the fact that I can remove Arturo's liver in one room and, by using the heart-lung pump, keep blood flowing through it until just a few minutes before I have to put a temporary clamp on the main arterial supply. Ordinarily we have to remove the donor liver, pack it in ice and sometimes fly several hundred miles to the recipient. Thanks to Arturo's sacrifice, everything is in Mike's favor."

III

When the body of Princess Zorah had been sent down to the morgue, Liz took the elevator to her office on the seventh floor and dialed the Washington number Undersecretary Longaker had given her.

"Secretary Longaker's office," a feminine voice answered. "Can I help you?"

"This is Dr. Elizabeth MacGowan at Biscayne General Hospital in Miami. May I speak to Mr. Longaker?"

"He's been at the Embassy of Telfa all afternoon, Doctor," the secretary told her. "Can I take a message?"

"If you will be certain he receives it," said Liz. "It's very important."

"I will put it on his desk marked 'URGENT,' Doctor. Because of the situation in Telfa, he expects to remain here all night so he will certainly see it."

"Please tell him that I delivered Baby Elzama by Caesarean section about one-thirty this afternoon. And that he appears to be in excellent condition."

"That is good news indeed, Doctor! I'll send that information over to the Embassy of Telfa immediately."

"Thank you," said Liz. "Mr. Longaker can reach me at the hospital until about ten tonight and at my apartment after that."

Blood and amniotic fluid had stained the summer dress Liz had been wearing under her academic white coat when she operated on Princess Zorah, so she decided to run across to her apartment and change before seeing the afternoon patients. When she crossed the foyer on the way to Biscayne Terrace, however, she saw the Corazon family huddled in one corner, as if for comfort, and realized that something must have happened to Mike. Something of which, being busy because of the tenth-floor power failure and its dramatic series of events, she had not yet heard.

Coming over to where the group was sitting, she put her hand on Maria's shoulder and asked, "Is there anything I can do? I've been operating until just a few minutes ago."

"It's Arturo," Estrellita explained. "He shot himself less than a half hour ago, so he could be a liver donor for Michael."

"Good God!" Liz exclaimed. "Is he . . ."

"Dr. Ted just took Arturo's body to the operating room," Estrellita answered. "He's going to do a transplant. It's what Arturo wanted."

"Imagine the courage it took," said Liz.

"Courage—and love." Maria's voice contained a strong note of pride. "More love than anyone could have asked of him."

"What does Ted say about the likelihood of success for the transplant?" Liz asked.

"Almost a hundred percent," Manuel volunteered. "What do you think?"

"That should be about right. Transplants between siblings take almost as often as between identical twins."

"Your dress is all splattered with blood. What happened?" Estrellita asked.

"There was a power failure on the tenth floor. I had to do an emergency Caesarean section in Princess Zorah's room to save the baby."

"I wonder if Ambassador Almani knew of it?" said Estrellita. "I saw him go through the lobby maybe a half hour ago. I recognized him from the picture that accompanied the story Robert Nathan wrote about him in the Miami *Herald*."

"Did he seem to be in a hurry?" Liz asked quickly.

"More than that. He was almost running. I wonder why?"

"I think I know why," said Liz crisply. "I've got to go across the street to my apartment and change. Be sure and call me if I can do anything for you."

"We can do nothing except wait," Maria told her. "Wait and pray that God will guide Ted's hands."

"You can be sure of that," Liz said without hesitation. "I'd put my life in those hands anytime."

IV

Returning to Biscayne General after showering and changing clothes, Liz telephoned the Neonatal ICU.

"How is His Royal Highness doing, Jerry?" Liz asked.

"When I got him down to the ICU the oxygen in his bloodstream was too low to read on instruments, but the high-frequency ventilator brought it up rapidly. The only thing we've got to worry about now is the possibility of giving him too much."

"How about the APGAR score?" A numerical expression used to evaluate the physical condition of newborn infants, the APGAR score was routinely determined sixty seconds after birth and at regular intervals afterward, until it was determined to be within normal limits. The score itself was calculated from the sum of points gained by an assessment of the heart rate, the respiratory effort, muscle tone, reflex irritability and color and gave a valuable estimate of the condition and prospects of any newborn.

"If I had tried to assess the APGAR the way we're supposed to do, within sixty seconds after you lifted him out of the uterus, it would have been useless," said Jerry. "Now I would say it's practically okay for his fetal age."

"What's your estimate of that figure?"

"From my measurements, I'd guess twenty-six weeks, maybe even twenty-eight. He's a well-developed little fellow, particularly judging from the way he came back after almost complete anoxia for several minutes while you were getting him out of the uterus after the power failure."

"Do you believe he will survive?"

"I'd give you odds on that," said Jerry cheerfully. "He was having a little difficulty in getting enough oxygen, even with the high-frequency ventilator, so I put some surfactant into it. That cleared out what hyaline membrane he may have had in his lung sacs and oxygen is crossing the lung-sac barrier freely now."

"I heard you tell the VIP-floor nursing supervisor you wanted to examine the life-support apparatus before it was sent back to the supply room," said Liz. "Did you find any-thing?"

"I haven't had time to do it, but I'm going up there now. I'll keep you posted on what I discover."

As soon as Liz cradled the telephone, it rang again. The caller was Robert Nathan of the Miami *Herald.*

"I'm calling about the hospital blackout that caused the deaths of Princess Zorah and the Elzama baby a few minutes ago," he said.

"What are you talking about?" Liz demanded.

"One of the *Herald* reporters doubles as a stringer for United Press International. He just had a telephone call say-ing a power failure at Biscayne General had put your life-support system out of operation, resulting in the deaths of both the princess and the baby."

"Who made the call?"

"Our man didn't get any name. As soon as he identified himself as the UPI stringer on the *Herald* staff, the caller gave the information I've just given you and hung up. *Was* there a power failure at Biscayne General early this afternoon, Dr. MacGowan?"

"There was but Princess Zorah was already dead, as you know, Mr. Nathan. Baby Elzama is doing fine in our Neonatal ICU; I happened to be on the floor when the current went off and operated immediately in the Princess' room."

"Then the baby is alive?"

"I just finished telling you that," Liz said a bit tartly. "He was a little anoxic when I delivered him by section but I gave him mouth-to-mouth resuscitation until Dr. Rubin could start giving him oxygen. Now would you mind telling me what the hell this is all about?"

"I guess I owe you an apology, Doctor, but I was a little miffed at the fact that, knowing my interest in the case, you didn't call me."

"It was a simple Caesarean, Mr. Nathan—"

"Hardly simple, Dr. MacGowan," said Nathan. "I'm familiar with several similar cases and I know that, once the electricity failed, you had to get that little fellow out of his mother's uterus in next-to-nothing flat."

"About three minutes for the actual operation," Liz admitted. "I've already notified the State Department that Baby Elzama is alive and well, but I'm very curious about that telephone call."

"All I can tell you is that the caller was a man and asked specifically for the UPI stringer before he gave the message and hung up."

"Why would he specify your UPI representative?"

"He probably knew UPI was following the situation in Telfa very closely and wanted the information to get there quickly, for reasons of his own—which I can guess."

"Can you guess who called?"

"The same person who pulled the plug, Doctor. When did Sheik Almani return to Miami?"

"Actually it wasn't pulled, but you're right about Almani. The nurse on duty reported that he appeared just a few moments before the blackout. He asked her to get him a cup of coffee from the floor diet kitchen, but she took time to notify me he was there so he was alone in the room with the Princess for from five to ten minutes."

"Long enough to sabotage the life-support machine?"

"Probably, especially since the nurse was out of the room calling me when the power went off on the tenth floor."

"Almani was there, so he had to be responsible for the attempt to destroy the heir to the throne of Telfa by cutting off the oxygen the fetus was getting through its mother's circulation."

"But why? And how? The plug was still in place, remember? And the whole tenth floor was blacked out, not just Princess Zorah's room or the life-support system."

"I'd still bet it was Almani," said Nathan. "Was he seen by anyone besides the nurse during or since the blackout?"

"Estrellita Mendoza recognized him moments after the blackout as he crossed the hospital lobby walking very fast. He disappeared through the front entrance and I haven't heard from him since."

"That clinches it," said Nathan. "Have you called the police?"

"What could I charge an internationally known man like Sheik Almani with? False arrest is a serious matter."

"I guess you're right, Doctor," said Nathan. "It looks like you've got a real mystery going out there. Good luck in solving it."

v

While Liz was pondering what, if anything, she should do to make certain that Sheik Almani was punished for the attempted murder of an unborn child, the phone rang again. This time it was Jerry Rubin and he sounded excited.

"I'm in Princess Zorah's old room, Dr. MacGowan," he said. "Can you come up here? I've found the answer."

"I'll be there in a minute," Liz told him. "If your answer is convincing enough, we may have time to catch a would-be murderer."

In the room where she had performed a dramatic surgical operation only a little over an hour ago, Liz found Jerry Rubin sitting on a sheet spread out on the floor, with the parts of the life-support system he had meticulously disassembled lying around him.

"Want to take a guess at how it was done?" he asked Liz with a mischievous grin.

"Don't waste time, Jerry," said Liz on a grim note. "What

we need is evidence. Evidence that would convict a man of murder."

"Here it is." Jerry picked up the heavy electrical cord that had carried the vital current from the wall plug to the motors driving the pumps that had kept blood coursing through the circulation of a dead woman; inflated and deflated her lungs with vital oxygen—delivered secondarily to the fetus through her circulation; sent the nutrient solutions of intravenous alimentation to her body cells—except the already dead ones of her brain; and even delivered rhythmic stimuli to her heart muscle, causing it to contract and pump blood through her arteries and veins.

Bending the cord over his finger, he stretched the heavy insulation that covered the copper wires beneath it to reveal a neat cut through the rubber, exposing the shiny yellow surface of the copper along which the electrical current itself traveled.

"*Voilà!*" he exclaimed in triumph. "The short circuit."

"I see it but I can't exactly comprehend it," Liz admitted. "Perhaps you had better explain, Jerry."

"Remember when I pulled the plug from the life-support system and the electrician working at the circuit-breaker panel for this floor was able to turn the electricity on again?"

"Yes."

"At that moment I knew for certain that a short circuit somewhere inside all these wires, motors and pumps on the floor around me had let enough current through to trip the circuit breakers for the entire floor."

"What of it?" Liz demanded, somewhat impatiently.

"Want me to reenact the crime by tripping the circuit breakers again and causing another blackout—on this floor alone?"

"Please don't," said Liz. "One shock like that a day is more than enough. Please go on with your scenario."

"Imagine you want to stop a life-support system—for reasons of your own—from functioning and, at the same time, create enough confusion for you to get away before anybody suspected what you'd done."

"I can do that. Go on."

"And also imagine you came prepared with a sharp, heavy knife that had the kind of insulated handle electricians use to cut power wires. To accomplish your purpose of shutting down the life support machine, you simply pick up the cord and cut—"

"Through it—"

"Not quite," said Jerry on a note of triumph. "You simply lay the power cord on the floor and cut directly down on it deep enough to penetrate the insulation covering each of the copper strands inside that actually carry the current."

"What does that do?"

"When your knife blade touches the copper, all the current is short-circuited through the blade in a sudden surge of power—"

"Knocking off the circuit breakers on the floor?"

"Exactly. You see, they're placed there to protect everything using electricity from just such a sudden surge of power as you've produced with the short circuit. Yet you haven't actually cut through the life support power cable, and a casual examination would fail to show the insulation cuts."

"Ingenious!" said Liz. "But where's the proof?"

"I found the cuts I just showed you—and also this." Jerry Rubin picked up a small piece of sponge rubber, perhaps two inches wide and four inches long.

"This piece of rubber, plus the insulation built into the handle of the knife the would-be assassin was using, was enough to keep him from receiving a shock, one strong enough to immediately trip the circuit breakers for the floor."

"You've done it, Jerry! You've delivered Sheik Almani's death warrant!"

"What I don't understand is why he would go to all this

trouble when, as Regent for the future ruler of Telfa, Almani had every reason to want the baby kept alive."

"Not any longer," Liz explained. "Instead of appointing Sheik Almani Regent for an heir who wasn't even born yet, when Emir Hassim learned that he had a son, he appointed three members of his own family as a Governing Council, in case he died before the lawful heir was actually born. His brother, Prince Khalil, was named Regent but the whole group—all members of the Elzama family—will no doubt function as Regents until your little charge is old enough to become the monarch."

The younger doctor's lips pursed in an almost soundless whistle. "This is beginning to sound more and more like a Middle East spy drama. Since he wasn't appointed Regent, Almani's next best bet was to destroy the rightful heir to the Emirate of Telfa, creating a vacuum, so to speak, in the government there—"

"A vacuum he was planning all along to fill," said Liz. "Actually, I'm beginning to wonder now whether Sheik Almani didn't persuade Emir Hassim to send Princess Zorah to me for amniocentesis and determination of the sex of the fetus she was carrying just so he could destroy the fetus if it turned out to be a male and the legal heir to the throne of Telfa."

"It all fits," Jerry agreed.

"You've already discovered enough evidence of sabotage to the life-support system and an attempt to murder an unborn child to justify a charge of deliberate murder against Sheik Almani," Liz assured him. "But if the police are to catch him, we've got to move fast."

"Doesn't Almani have some sort of diplomatic immunity?"

"He doesn't hold that office any more. But even if he did that wouldn't give him the right to assassinate an unborn child," Liz said indignantly. Then her face brightened.

"Didn't I see Nick Patterson in the corridor outside Michael Corazon's room when I came on the floor?"

"Mr. Corazon hasn't come back from surgery yet," the nurse who was helping Jerry Rubin volunteered, "but I saw Mr. Patterson using the telephone at the nursing station a few minutes ago."

"A high-ranking FBI agent should know what to do in a situation like this, Jerry," said Liz. "Let's talk to him. And bring along that cut power cord, it's enough evidence of an attempted murder to send Almani to the electric chair."

VI

In the small doctors' office, the FBI chief listened carefully to the stories told by both Liz and Jerry Rubin.

"Have you called the Metro Police yet, Dr. MacGowan?" he asked.

"Jerry just reported his finding of sabotage to me a few minutes ago," said Liz. "But I'm ready to do anything I can to see that Almani is caught and punished. Do you think I should contact the police?"

"Not right away," said Patterson.

"But Sheik Almani may get away," Liz protested angrily.

"Dealing with foreign diplomats, even ex-diplomats, can create some pretty sticky situations—"

"Enough to justify letting a would-be murderer go free?"

"Nobody's advocating that, and least of all myself, Doctor. Sheik Almani's crime is against the government of Telfa and, in the long run, it may be best for them to punish him."

"Is there a government in Telfa with the authority to demand the extradition of Sheik Almani, if he is arrested for murder in Miami?" Liz demanded. "The last I heard, Almani might wind up *being* the government of Telfa—with the blessing of the State Department."

"Did you notify the State Department that an heir to the throne of Telfa is in existence?" Patterson asked.

"Yes. Mr. Longaker was out—I believe his secretary said he was in conference at the Telfa Embassy—but she promised to notify him immediately."

"Then I think you should get in touch with Longaker and tell him of this new development. Do you want me to put the call through? The FBI can often contact people in the government that a citizen might have trouble reaching."

"By all means do," Liz told him.

"I'd better get back to the Neonatal ICU," Jerry Rubin said while Patterson was dialing. "If Sheik Almani stayed in Miami and learns that Baby Elzama is still alive, there's always the possibility that he might make another attempt to assassinate the future ruler of Telfa."

VII

Nick Patterson handed Liz the phone a few minutes later. "Steve Longaker is on the phone, Dr. MacGowan. He just got back to his office after spending the afternoon at the Telfa Embassy."

"It looks like you've had a very busy afternoon, Dr. Mac-Gowan," said Longaker after Liz had given him a brief running account of the day's climactic events. "The government of Telfa is very much in your debt for producing the heir to the throne in time to ward off an attempt by Sheik Yossuf Almani and a radical group of revolutionaries to take over the government."

"Then they didn't succeed."

"No. Thanks to you. When my secretary telephoned me at

the embassy with the good news that Hassim Elzama III was alive and well, General Armin Elzama, who heads the Governing Council appointed by Emir Hassim before his death—"

"Did you say the Emir is dead, Mr. Longaker?" Liz inquired.

"Emir Hassim died about three o'clock, Eastern Daylight Time, Dr. MacGowan. About an hour and a half after, from what my secretary told me in a telephone call to the Embassy of Telfa where I was in conference, you did an emergency Caesarean section and produced a living heir to the throne."

"Then there was no vacuum in the government?"

"No vacuum and very little political disturbance in Telfa, according to the reports received at the embassy. General Armin and the army were able to put it down without any real difficulty. Most of the terrorists Sheik Almani was able to enlist in an attempted revolution—sponsored by the Soviet KGB incidentally—were either killed or captured."

"I'm thankful for that," said Liz. "But what are you going to do about Sheik Almani?"

"Our feeling in the State Department is that we should do nothing, Doctor—at least for the moment."

"Do nothing!" Liz exclaimed. "Are you going to let him go free, when he's guilty of attempted murder of a *fetus in utero?*"

"The fetus in question is no longer *in utero*, to use your own medical description of it, Doctor. And to punish Sheik Almani would involve quite a lot of diplomatic maneuvering on an international scale. A trial, even in Telfa, could reveal a lot of details about international relations that might just as well not be brought out."

"You're not snowing me with your phony logic, Mr. Longaker," said Liz. "But I will listen to reason."

"That's all we ask, Doctor," said Longaker. "You have done your country a great favor by handling a very ticklish situation in a very intelligent and ethical manner. You see, when Sheik Almani realized that you were adamant about using Princess Zorah's body, even after brain death, to make sure the fetus would be viable when you finally decided to deliver it, he no doubt faced the fact that, with a legal heir in existence and protected by a strong Governing Council, the chances of his being able to seize control of the government of Telfa were nil. The logical thing then, was to see that the Emir's son did not live, giving Almani a chance to disrupt the government and perhaps still gain control. For that reason he flew back to Miami, without stopping in Washington or New York, where we had agents at the airports waiting to seize him. He might have succeeded, too, if you hadn't been at the hospital when he stopped the power to the life-support system by creating a short circuit. Fortunately you operated immediately to remove Hassim Alzama III from his mother's body. And in the process accomplished what must have been something of an obstetrical miracle."

"You can cut the flattery, Mr. Longaker," said Liz, but without rancor. "Are you still going to let Almani go unpunished?"

"Personal failure in a major undertaking of any kind is the worst punishment that can be meted out to an ambitious man like Sheik Yossuf Almani, Dr. MacGowan. From what you say, he left the hospital so quickly, after sabotaging the life-support system, that he could have had no way of knowing he had failed."

"His attempt to have United Press International notify the government in Telfa that Hassim Alzama III—as you call him —was dead would prove that, Mr. Longaker."

"I agree," said the State Department man.

"So what do we do now?"

"Exactly what you would ordinarily do in dealing with any somewhat premature infant, Dr. MacGowan. See that Hassim

III receives the same care that I'm sure any other infant in your Neonatal ICU would receive."

"I'll go farther than that," said Liz. "I'll ask Nick Patterson to put an FBI agent on guard by Baby Elzama's cubicle until we learn just where Sheik Almani is and whether he may still try to destroy the child."

"An excellent precaution, Doctor," said Longaker. "Meanwhile, if we here in Washington can take care of the diplomatic situation in Telfa with half the efficiency you have shown in handling a very sensitive situation down there, I'm sure everything is going to turn out fine."

"What about Prince Khalil Elzama, who is now the Regent? In that capacity he's supposed to be looking after Baby Elzama, but I've neither seen nor heard from him."

"You will shortly, Dr. MacGowan," said Longaker. "As soon as we learned that Prince Khalil was a member of the Governing Council, we sent Secret Service operatives to Boston to guard him and escort him to Washington. He's been here since yesterday and will fly to Miami tomorrow morning. You'll find him charming and very cognizant of the significance of what is going on now. After all, he does possess a degree from the Massachusetts Institute of Technology."

Chapter Twenty

The sun was just rising over Biscayne Bay and its rays were beginning to explore the almost empty lobby of the main hospital when Ted Bronson crossed it shortly after six the next morning. He'd seen Michael Corazon safely back to his room on the VIP section after completing the surgery, which had lasted for about six hours.

Removing Arturo's liver for transplant had not been difficult but the actual job of putting it into Michael's body and making all the necessary connections between blood vessels and the bile-duct system had been tedious, largely because the patient had suffered a mild chemical peritonitis from the punctures of his small intestine by at least one of the bullets that had entered his body.

Since the first hours of recovery from an operation as extensive as a transplant of the liver were the most critical period in the postoperative phase, Ted had spent the night in the adjoining room to Michael's on the VIP floor, where the family had kept a weary vigil. Entering Biscayne Terrace, he found an elevator open and stepped inside, but as he reached for the button to his floor pulled his finger back. Obeying a sudden impulse, he pushed the button to the floor on which Liz Mac-Gowan's apartment was located. He had seen her with the Corazon family when he returned to the room with Michael after the surgery but had remained beside the bed for several hours. And when he'd finally gone into the other room, where the family was gathered, he was told that Liz had gone to her apartment.

He had to ring her doorbell three times before she answered. And when she opened the door he saw that she must have been in bed because she had obviously pulled a robe hurriedly over her nightdress and he could see the frothy material of it around her ankles.

"I'm sorry," he apologized. "I didn't mean to wake you."

"That's all right. I'm glad you stopped by. Is Mike all right?"

"He's doing fine. When I connected the gall bladder up to the jejunum at the end of the transplant, fresh bile was already coming from the new liver."

"That's wonderful. Come on in and I'll make us some coffee and toast."

"I'll probably fall asleep with my head on your kitchen table," he told her.

"That's all right, too." Taking his arm, she guided him through the living room to the kitchen. "Have a seat and tell me about the operation while I put on the coffeepot and make the toast."

"It went like a textbook demonstration. Arturo and Mike are fortunately about the same size so I was able to make the connections without having to allow for any difference."

"Did Michael tolerate the anesthetic well?"

"The coma he was in was almost deep enough for me to work without it, but it still took time to make all those vital connections."

"The superior and inferior vena cava, the portal vein, the hepatic artery and the bile ducts—right?" she asked as she bustled about in the small kitchen, starting the percolator and dropping bread into the toaster.

"Give yourself a capital A in anatomy," he told her. "Except that instead of trying to connect up the bile ducts, I tied off the common duct below the gall bladder and then made a connection between it and the small bowel. That way, there's a much better chance of healing."

"Is he in as good condition as you would expect?"

"Better, really. I couldn't rouse him before the operation to tell him what I was going to do."

"It's probably just as well." She dropped two pieces of toast on his plate and, picking up a knife, buttered them for him. "He would have wanted to know who the donor was and that would have upset him very much."

"I'm going to hold off telling him as long as I can."

"Did you get the kidneys you wanted, too?"

"Don Taylor took those out after I finished removing Arturo's liver. While he was in the abdomen, he took the pancreas, too, and afterward, one of the cardiac surgeons removed the heart. It's in Atlanta by now, going into the chest of a young mother who was dying of rheumatic heart disease. The Department of Ophthalmology took both eyes for corneal transplant and the otologists were happy to get out two sets of ossicles."

"Then by sacrificing his life, Arturo gave the certainty of life to two kidney patients—"

"Yes, I'm going to transplant those tomorrow."

"Plus saving a heart patient and maybe a severe diabetic—four people in all."

"To say nothing of giving sight to two people blinded by scarred corneas and to two more who can't hear because their ossicles are frozen in the middle ear."

"It's fantastic!" she said, pouring coffee for them and taking a chair across the small table from him. "As much as Arturo loved his fellow man, I'm sure I know where he is now. And I know, too, that he's happy to have saved so many lives and given new life to so many other people."

"You and I seem to be in the same business these days,"

Ted told her as she was pouring a second cup of coffee for him. "You gave Baby Elzama life by allowing him to develop long enough *in utero* to be safe from the complications of premature birth when you finally delivered him."

"That was nothing to what you accomplished tonight," she demurred.

"I would have been powerless without the sacrifice Arturo made to save Mike," he reminded her.

"And Michael Corazon would have died in hepatic coma within a matter of days if your skill in connecting up the arteries, veins and ducts that enabled the liver Arturo gave Mike to function hadn't been there at the right moment."

Ted managed to smile, though weariness was enveloping him like a mantle. "Like I said, we're in the same business. So why don't we negotiate a merger?"

"Negotiate?" She raised her eyebrows and smiled in the way he had long ago come to love. "What's to negotiate?"

"Nothing except the marriage license that will let you stop taking that damn pill—"

"I stopped it last night, when I saw what Arturo had done in spite of handicaps. Come to think about it, though, they weren't really handicaps to him in doing more than anyone without the love for humanity that was in him could have done—even though he was a victim of what we call handicaps."

"There are ways of turning handicaps into assets. I guess Arturo managed that better than anyone I have ever known."

"When I left the Corazons in the hospital last night, I went down to see about Baby Elzama in the Neonatal ICU," said Liz. "He was connected up to all the things we doctors know how to use to preserve life—an intratracheal tube attached to the ventilator to handle his breathing; a pacemaker to stimulate his heart if it needed it—which it didn't, thank the Lord. The loving care that's such a valuable part of the Neonatal ICU was wrapped around him like a blanket, and I decided that I want one or more of my own as soon as I can have them."

"Just give me two or three hours sleep on your couch—"

"Why not my bed? You've been in there enough times. Besides, the way it looks now, you'll soon become a permanent resident."

11

Arturo Corazon's funeral was held on Friday morning at eleven o'clock. Liz MacGowan pulled her Mercedes to a stop in front of the hospital entrance about ten-thirty and slid over on the seat before Ted could open the door.

"I hope you know where the cemetery is," she told him.

"It's a small, private one in South Miami," he said as he slid under the wheel.

"Any news from the garage about your Porsche?"

"They're still cleaning it up, after the wrecker pulled it out of the Tamiami Canal and hauled it to Miami on a flatbed truck. Black mud from the bottom of the canal had worked its way even into the seats. The garage people said it was going to take several more days at least to get it cleaned up, and even then it would have to dry out."

"Was there much damage?"

"Only a few nicks in the paint where some of the bullets glanced off before that last burst from the rifle flattened the right front tire, plus a scraped fender. Nick Patterson's crew found the bullet they were looking for, too. The rubber wall of the tire stopped the force before it could flatten itself against the steel mesh in the tire itself. The ballistics department of the Sheriff's Office was able to compare it with the bullet I took out of Mike's flank at the original operation."

"Are they the same?"

"When I saw him at the hospital last night, Nick Patterson told me the rifling marks matched to a tee, establishing without question that the man who tried to kill Mike was also the one who tried to kill us that night when we were on our way to Everglades City. They've got him dead to rights and he's singing like a canary."

At Biscayne Boulevard, Ted made a left turn and entered the busy traffic flowing southward toward Dixie Highway, Coconut Grove and South Miami.

"I brought the morning paper," Liz told him. "In case you haven't seen it, you're not only the man of the hour but there's talk of awarding you the Congressional Medal of Honor."

"I only had time to look at the headlines before I made rounds this morning, but I don't think I would relish being a national hero."

"How are the two kidney patients doing that you operated on after you did the transplant on Michael?"

"Fine—and so is Mike. I've never had a liver transplant do as well in such a short time, but that's to be expected. I had the laboratory do a match between him and Arturo before Arturo's body went to the mortuary. The match couldn't have been any better if they'd been twins, so I don't expect Mike to have any difficulty at all."

"What about the pancreas?"

"I put that into a woman whose diabetes has been out of control for a week. When I saw her very briefly this morning, her blood sugar was remaining steady at a normal level."

"Arturo would certainly be happy about that."

"And about what you've been doing the past day or two," he assured her. "Hold the paper up so I can see those headlines again."

The type was black and big:

DRUG KINGS NABBED BEFORE FLIGHT, it read. Beneath it was an account of the dramatic arrest of Sam Gianno and the presidents of two large Miami banks, who had been under close investigation by the FBI, as they were getting ready to board a luxurious private jet at the relatively isolated Opa-Locka Airport near the western edge of Miami.

"Nick told me last night that your testimony before the grand jury yesterday morning was what finally drove the nail into Sam Gianno's coffin," Ted said.

"The idea was to smoke him out," she said. "I'm not sure, but I believe Nick saw that my testimony was leaked to Gianno and the bankers the drug task force was trying to nail so they'd try to run and be nabbed."

"I still don't like Nick's putting you at risk like that," Ted said somewhat heatedly. "If Gianno hadn't decided to run, he could very well have tried to kill you, the way he tried to get Mike at home that morning and you and me by driving us into the canal."

"I was under heavy guard both before and after the grand jury session," Liz assured him. "The whole idea was to flush out Sam Gianno and make him try something that would ensure the FBI being able to arrest him and the bankers in a situation so no federal judge would let them go free on bail to skip the country the way they were trying to do when they were nabbed."

"Did Nick tell you that himself?"

"Yes."

"Why didn't you tell me you were going to risk your neck?" he demanded angrily.

"Because you would have insisted that I not do it."

"You can bet I would have done just that."

"The assistant federal prosecutor would have issued a subpoena and I would have had to testify anyway. But Gianno would have known about that the moment it was issued."

"I guess you're right," Ted admitted somewhat reluctantly. "But I still don't like the idea of using you to smoke out Sam Gianno."

"It worked, darling. My testimony that he was driving the Jaguar that forced us off the Trail and into the canal will help convict him and maybe dry up some of the drug trade."

South of Coconut Grove, Ted turned off the Dixie Highway and took a less-frequented street southwestward.

"Is this a private cemetery?" Liz asked.

"Yes. Years ago the Corazon family bought a parcel of land that was then pretty much outside Metropolitan Miami. Over the years, most of the descendants of the group of Cubans who fled from the Batista regime have been buried here, including Papa Juan Corazon. Arturo had a lot to do with the plantings and he loved to come out here and work, so it's fitting that he should be buried here."

A few minutes more and they turned into the gate. The cemetery itself was small, located on the shore of Biscayne Bay in a beautiful, tropical setting. "How lovely," Liz exclaimed. "I see now why Arturo would want to be buried here. It's almost as if he were among his own flowers at home."

"That's what Maria said when she told me Arturo will be buried in one of the flower beds he loved so much. The family asked me to be one of the pall bearers, but I'll see you after the service is over."

III

"Mr. Longaker phoned me yesterday to tell me Sheik Almani is in Rio," Liz told Ted as they crossed from the parking space to the open grave close beside the small, rustic chapel. "He apparently flew there the same afternoon that he tried to kill the baby."

"Is there any chance of his being prosecuted?" Ted asked.

"Not according to the State Department. The Governing Council in Telfa doesn't want him back there because, if they had to put him on trial, it might stir up his political following and cause real trouble once again. The United States has no desire to prosecute him either. And since neither Telfa nor the United States has a treaty of extradition with Brazil, he'll probably live there."

"I suppose it's enough punishment for Almani that his desire to rule in Telfa was frustrated."

"Did I tell you Jerry and Cheryl Rubin are going to Telfa with the baby when Prince Khalil takes it home in a few weeks?"

"Not to stay, I hope."

"They had the opportunity. Prince Khalil offered to put Jerry in charge of pediatrics at their new hospital and Cheryl could have had the position of chief nurse for the asking, but they'd rather stay here at Biscayne General and I didn't argue with them. Did Erasmus Brown tell you Prince Khalil assured him that the hospital's Research Foundation will be given at least a half million by the government of Telfa in return for saving the next ruler?"

"I still think that money should be for use in your department," Ted told her. "After all, you were solely responsible for saving the baby's life."

"I have no use for it; research was never my forte," said Liz. "Besides, I plan to be pretty busy over the next several years. The best place the money could possibly go is in expanding your organ bank, now that the transplant business is booming once again."

I V

The brief graveside ceremony began with a reading from the New Testament by Father Mulcahy, the young Catholic priest who had been a friend of the Corazon family and particularly of Arturo since he had come to Miami.

"This is my commandment, that ye love one another as I have loved you," he read. *"Greater love hath no man than this, that a man lay down his life for his friends."*

Closing the Bible from which he had been reading, the young priest continued:

"We are met here to commit to the ground the earthly body of a person we all loved and who loved us. Today we may have some difficulty in understanding a love so strong that it would lead the bearer to give his life to preserve the life of his brother. And, perhaps equally important, to preserve the lives of people he did not know, people whose own lives will be saved by organs for which he no longer had a use.

"The two people who have already received his kidneys did not know from whom they had come. Now, thanks to the techniques of modern medical science, they will hopefully be able to live without the fear of having any longer to be dependent upon dialysis to continue their lives. Nor could our friend, Arturo, possibly have foreseen that his own body would provide the corneas with which two people he did not know would be freed from the dark curtain of blindness. Or very important for those who suffer from the inability to hear the lovely sounds that characterize the world around them, someone would once again enjoy the beauty of those sounds because of him.

"Greater love, indeed, hath no man than that he give his life for his friends. The body we are consigning to the earth today no longer contains the true soul and spirit of him whose name we revere: from the very moment when he made the extreme sacrifice, be assured that the soul of Arturo Corazon is among the blessed."

V

Walking back to Liz's Mercedes, after the brief but moving service, she fumbled for Ted's hand. Finding it, she gripped it tightly.

"I'm sure Arturo must be happy that his body now rests in one of the places he loved best of all," she said. "But I know how much Mama Maria misses him, and I don't want to risk any longer being forced to risk missing you, without at least having a small replica of you to comfort me."

"Now that Mike Corazon is out of danger and Baby Elzama will soon be going to claim his birthright, there's no reason to put it off any longer," he told her.

"I quite agree," she said. "Besides, if I don't marry you soon I might be tempted by the opportunity Prince Khalil made me last night to head the new hospital they're building in Telfa—at a hundred thousand a year."

"Over my dead body," he told her. "Just set the day."

"I think it had better be soon. While you were in Pittsburgh, I didn't take the pill and I forgot to take it the night before you got back. So if you don't marry me soon, there's going to be a scandal at Biscayne General."

"You mean . . . ?"

"Unless the symptoms of normal pregnancy Paul Fraser listed in his textbook on obstetrics are wrong, I think you'd better hurry up and make an honest woman of me."

"We'll do it tomorrow," he shouted so exuberantly, leaning over to kiss her, that the driver of an approaching car took to the shoulder when the Mercedes swerved sharply.

"You just made me the happiest man in the world," he said jubilantly. "Where do you want to be married? At home in Virginia?".

"I'd like a small wedding in the little chapel back there in the cemetery."

"It's a lovely spot and it's all right with me. But you aren't even a Catholic and neither am I."

"That doesn't make any difference. You see, I promised Arturo he could be a part of my wedding as an usher, and this way I won't be breaking my promise for he won't be far away. In fact, wherever he is—and I'm satisfied there's no doubt about where that is—I know watching us being married will make him very, very happy."